"*No one's* like me. There aren't any others. I'm *different*. And they're so busy not noticing it they shout it. Why, Duun?" Thorn's muscles began to shake; he clenched his arms about his knees the harder and tried not to show the shivering, but Duun would see. Duun missed nothing. "What's wrong with me? How did I turn out this way?"

Duun's ears went back. "We'll talk about it later."

"You'll never give me my answer. Will you?"

A long silence. Yes and no trembled on a knife's edge. For the first time Thorn felt Dunn was close to answering him and a breath might tip the balance. He held that breath till his sides ached.

"No," Dunn said then. "Not yet."

CUCKOO'S EGG

C.J. CHERRYH

DAW BOOKS, INC.
DONALD A. WOLLHEIM, PUBLISHER
1633 Broadway, New York, NY 10019

DAW Book Collectors Number 646.

First DAW Printing, October 1985

1 2 3 4 5 6 7 8 9

PRINTED IN U.S.A.

I He sat in a room, the sand of which was synthetic and shining with opal tints, fine and light beneath his bare feet. The windows held no cityview, but a continuously rotating panorama of the Khogghut plain: a lie. Traffic noise came through.

His name was Duun. It was Dana Duun Shtoni no Lughn. But Duun was enough for day-to-day. They called him other things. Sey:general. Mingi: lord. Or something very like. Hatani: that was another thing. But Duun was enough now. There was only one. Shonunin the world over knew that, and knew him; and when the door chimed and they came to bring the alien to him, whose who carried it would not look him in the eyes, not alone for the scars that a shonun could see, the pale smooth marks traced through the fur of half his face like the limbs of a lightning-blasted tree, the marks that twisted his right ear and left his mouth quirked in permanent irony and one eye staring out of ruin.

He was Duun, of *Shanoen*. He reached out hands one of which was marred, like his face, and took the closed carrier that they gave him, marking how their ears slanted back and how they turned their heads from his for horror— not of what they saw: they were meds, and had seen deformity. It was the force in him: like a great wind, like a great heat in their faces.

But his hands were gentle when he took the carrier from them.

They went away, appalled and forgetting courtesies.

He waved the door shut and set the carrier on the table-rise, opened it and gathered the small bundled thing from it.

Shonunin were naked when they were born, but downed in silver that quickly went to dapples and last of all to gray body coat and black on limbs and ears and crest. Duun held the creature on its discarded wrapping, on his knees; and its downless skin was naked and

6

pink as something lately skinned, except for a thatch of nondescript hair atop its skull. It waved soft limbs in helpless twitches. Its eyes were shut, in a face flat and not unlike a shonun; between its legs an outsized organ of curious form and various (they said) function. Its mouth worked restlessly, distorting the small face. And Duun touched it with the sensitive pads of his fingers, with the four fingers of his left hand and the two of his maimed right, exploring the hot, smooth feel of the bandage-patched belly, the chest, the limbs. With the merest tip of a claw he drew down its soft lip to inspect its mouth—nothing but toothless gums, for it was mammalian. With the claw he lifted the lid of a sleeping eye; he saw it white and milky, centered with blue, restless in natural shiftings. He touched the convolutions of the stiff, small ears; explored the visible organ and discovered reaction: so it was sensitive. That was of interest. He examined the fat, clawless feet, all one pad as far as the toes. Unfurled a five-fingered hand with the careful touch of a single clawed finger, and the tiny fist clenched again, stubbornly. It waved its limbs. Fluid shot from the organ and fouled Duun's clothes.

Any shonun would have flinched seeing that. But Duun gathered up the wrap about the infant and mopped at himself patiently, with infinite patience. So. Likewise shonun infants

7

performed such obscenities, if more discreetly. It let out cries, soft and weak and meaningless as all infant cries. It struggled with less strength than his own infants had shown.

He knew what it would be, grown. He knew its face. He knew every aspect of its body. He gathered it against his breast in the stinking blanket and rose, went to the package they had brought him that morning and left on the riser by the bed. He held the softly crying creature in the crook of his left arm. for he was still more able with the right hand, two-fingered as it was. He managed to open the case and to warm the milk—not milk of shonunin; by synthesis the meds provided, of their own ingenuity.

There was data, which had come days ago; he had memorized it. The creature wailed; so shonunin wailed, exercising infant lungs. And it breathed the air shonunin breathed: and perhaps its gut would take the meat shonunin ate one day. The meds thought that this was the case. The teeth that would grow would, some of them, be pointed like the major teeth of a shonun. "Hush, hush," he told it, joggling it against his chest. He drew the warmed bottle from the case and thrust the nipple into the soft mouth that quested among the blankets. It suckled noisily and quieted, and he crossed the sand to the riser he had left, sat down cross-legged, rocking it, whispering to it.

"Be still, be still."

Its eyes closed in contentment; it slept again, fed and held. It could not, like a shonun, be taken for granted. He was delicate with it. He laid it finally in the bowl of his own bed and sat beside it, watching its small movements, the regular heaving of its tiny round belly; and when the view in the windows changed and became the nightbound sea, he still watched.

He would not soon tire of watching. He did not bathe. He was fastidious, but he inhaled the smell of it and the soiled blanket, the smells of its food and its person, and did not flinch, having schooled himself against disgust.

They were dismayed when they came, the meds—to deal with him, to examine the infant and to take it back to the facility down the hall to weigh it and monitor its condition. He stalked after them as they carried it in its closed case; he offended their nostrils with his stink.

And never once in all this dealing would they meet his eyes, preferring even the face of the alien to the chance of looking up into the stark cold stare he gave to them and all their business.

They weighed the infant, they listened to its breathing and its heart, they asked quietly (never glancing quite at him) whether there had been difficulty.

"Duun-hatani, you might rest," the chief of medicine said the second day that they came for the infant. "This is all routine. There's no need. You might take the chance to—"

"No," Duun said.

"There—"

"No."

There was uncomfortable silence. For days Duun had looked at them without answer; now the chief cast a searching, worried glance full into his eyes, and immediately afterward found something else to occupy herself.

Duun smiled for the first time in those days, and it was a smile to match the stare.

"You dismay them, Duun," the division chief said.

Duun walked away from the desk on which Ellud sat, gazed at the false windows, which showed snowfall. Ice formed on the branches of a tree above a hot spring. The sun danced in jeweled branches and the steam rose and curled. Duun looked back again, the thumb of his maimed hand hooked behind him to that of the whole one, and discovered another man who preferred to study something just a little behind his shoulder. The false sunlight, it might be. Anything would have served. "It's in very good health," Duun said.

"Duun, the staff—"

"The staff does its job." Never once had the eyes focused on him, quite. Duun drew a deep breath. "I want Sheon."

"Duun—"

"Sheon belongs to Duun, doesn't it? I tell you that it does."

"Security at Sheon—"

"I stink. I smell. Notice it, Ellud?"

Long pause. "The estate—"

"You offered me anything. Wasn't that what you said? Any cooperation? Would any shonun in the world prevent me anything—if I want a woman; if I want a man; if I want money or your next of kin, Ellud—if I want the president turned out naked and the treasury to walk in—"

"You're hatani. You wouldn't."

Duun looked again at the false spring bubbling up in its wintry vapors. "Gods! but you do trust me."

"You're hatani."

He looked back with the first clear-eyed stare he had used in years. But not even that could hold Ellud's gaze to his. "I'm begging you, Ellud. Do I have to beg? Give me Sheon."

"Settlers have moved there. Their title's valid by now."

"Move them out. I want the house. The hills. Privacy. Come on, Ellud ... you want me to camp in your office?

Ellud did not. They had been friends. Once.

Now Duun saw the guarded lowering of the ears. Like shame. Like a man taking a chance he wanted. Badly. At any cost.

"You'll get it," Ellud said. Never looking at him. Ellud's claws extended slightly, raked papers aside as he looked distractedly at the desk about him. "I'll do something. I'll see to it."

"Thanks."

That got the eyes up. A wounded look. Appalled like the rest. The agony of friendship.

Of wounded loyalties.

"Give it up," Ellud asked, against self-interest; against all interests. The loyalty jolted, belated as it was.

"No." For a moment then, eye to eye, no flinching from either side. He remembered Ellud under fire. A calm, cool man. But the gaze finally shifted and something broke.

The last thing.

Duun walked out, freer, because there was nothing left. Not even Ellud. Just pain. And he wrapped that solitude about him, finding it appropriate.

He came to Sheon's hills in the morning, in a true morning with the sun coming up rose and gold over the ridge; and the wind that blew at him on this grassy-flat was the wind of his childhood, whipping at his cloak, at the gray cloak of the hatani, which he wrapped about him and the infant. Ellud's aide showed distress, there on the dusty road that led toward the hills, in the momentary stillness of the craft which had brought them there, over in the meadow. The aide's ears lay flat in the wind, which blew his neatly trimmed crest and disarranged the careful folds of his kilt. The wind was cold for a citydweller, for a softhands like him. "It's all right," Duun said. "I told you. There's no way up but this. You don't have to wait here."

The aide turned his face slightly toward the countryfolk who gathered out of the range of hearing, who gathered in knots, families together, uncaring of the cold. The aide looked back again, walked toward the gathered crowd waving his arms. "Go away, go away, the mingi has no need of you. Fools," he said then, turning back, for they gave only a little ground. He stooped and gathered up from the roadside the little baggage there was, slung the sack from his shoulder. His ears still lay back in distress. "Hatani, I will walk up with you myself."

It was a wonder. The aide met his eyes with staunch frankness. Ellud chose such young folk, still knowing the best, the most honest. Duun felt for a moment as if the sun had shone on him full; or perhaps it was the smell of true wind, with the grass-scent and the cleanness.

He felt a motion of his heart toward this young man and it ached.

But he grinned, old soldier that he was, and glanced at the uphill road, for this time he was the one to flinch, from the youth's innocence and worship. "Give me the sack," he said, and stripped the carry-strap from the young man's shoulder and took it to his own, his right. The infant occupied his left arm, warm and moving there, nuzzling wormlike among its swaddlings beneath his cloak.

"But, hatani—"

"You're not going. I don't need you."

He walked away.

"Hatani—"

He did not look back. Did not look at the mountainfolk who lined the road near the copter. Some of them were the displaced, he was sure. Some of them had held Sheon, having gotten it since he was renunciate. Now they were abruptly dispossessed. He felt their eyes, heard their whispers, nothing definite.

"Hatani," he heard. And: "Alien." Whisper they need not. He felt their eyes trying to penetrate his cloak. They came to wonder what he was as much as they wondered about what he brought. "Hatani." There was respect in that. "What happened to his face?" a child asked.

"Hush," an adult said. And there was a sudden, embarrassed hush. It was a child. It had not learned what scars were. It was only honesty.

Duun did not look at them. Did not care. He was hatani, renunciate. His weapons were at his side beneath the cloak. He asked one thing of the world. These hills. This place.

A little peace.

That a hatani dispossessed them— The countryfolk living at Sheon had surely thought their title secure. The land was fallow; the house vacant; ten years renunciate and it was theirs by law.

But it was what he had told Ellud: there was nothing he could not ask and obtain, nothing in all the world

He felt their eyes. Perhaps they expected him to speak. Perhaps they expected him to care, to offer words to reassure them.

But he only walked past them up the road, the dusty road to the heights and the house made of native stone, deep within the hills.

He heard the copter lift. It beat away with small thumps like heartbeats echoing off the mountainside. It had come and gone often here yestereve and three days before, with other craft, seeing to provisions, to special equipment, to all such things as satisfied Ellud and Ellud's ilk.

Nuisance, all of it.

*   *   *

He prepared himself. He knew that Sheon would have changed. He gathered up his resolve in this as in other things. He needed virtue. He sought it in abnegation. He sought it in lack of caring, when he came, in full noon, to the mountain heights, and discovered the things countryfolk had done to Sheon, which he expected: a sprawl of new rubble-stone building, which destroyed the beauty Sheon had once been, a creation of smooth artistry indistinguishable from the living rock of the mountain wall that flanked it. The house sprawled now, artless and utilitarian, the yard about it cleared and dusty. He was not dismayed.

Only when he came inside and discovered what Ellud and his crews had done—that, that afflicted him. Instead of the country untidiness he had expected (different from the time of his childhood, of stones carefully polished, of spacious halls and a sand-garden where the wind made patterns), the government had worked sterility, lacquered the stone walls, sanded the floors in white, not red, installed a new kitchen, new furnishings, all at great expense; and the smell of it was new and pungent with fixatives and paint and new-baked sand.

He stood there, in this clean, sterile, unremembered place, with its abundant stores, its furniture new from the city—

For the infant. Of course, for the infant.

The meds feared for its health. They wanted sanitation.

And destroyed—destroyed—

He stood there a long, long time, in pain. The infant squirmed and began to cry. And he was very careful with it in his anger, as careful as he had ever been. He searched the cabinets for new cloths; fround the cradle prepared—

The infant soiled itself. He knew the cry, smelled the stink, which had surrounded him, stronger than the lacquer and dry-dust smell of sand.

He laid it down on the sand; he put off his cloak and laid his weapons down on a riser near the fireplace. He listened to it scream. It had grown. The voice was louder, hoarser, the face screwed up in rage.

He took cloths and wet them and knelt and cleaned its filth in starkest patience; he heated the formula and fed it till it slept. He walked aimless in the halls afterward, smelling the stink it had left on him, and the stink of new plaster, new lacquer, new furniture.

He had run barefoot in these halls, laughed, played pranks with a dozen sibs and cousins, rolled on the floor-sand, till exasperated elders flung them out into a yard well shaded with old trees.

The trees were gone. The new wing stood

where the oldest tree had been. So much for homecomings.

He made a fire. There was that one thing left untouched, the old stones of the hearth he had sat by as a child, and there were scraps of demolished outbuildings and fences, in a towering pile near the rocks. He made a fire of them, burning others' memories of home.

He took the infant outside with him, well wrapped against the cold; he took it about the house with him, in the kitchen, at last before the fire itself; he sat on the clean deep sand before the hearthstones and held the infant in his lap.

He had grown accustomed to it. The flat, round face no longer disturbed him. The smell was his smell, compounded of its sweat and his. Demon eyes looked up at him. The face made grimaces meaningless to both of them in the wavering firelight, the leaping flames.

He took its skull between his hands, the whole and the maimed one, and he was careful as if the skull had been eggshell instead of bone. He smiled, drawing back his lips from his teeth, and gazed into eyes which perhaps saw him, perhaps not.

"Wei-na-ya," he sang to it, "wei-na-mei,"—in a hoarse male voice unapt for lullabies; *little bird, little fish*—the house had heard that song before. "Hei sa si-lan-nei . . . ." *Do not go. The wind is cold, the water dark, but here is warm.* "Wei-na-ya, wei-na-mei."

And "Sha-khe'a," he sang, but softly, like the lullaby, which was a hatani song.

It was the deathsong. He sang it like the lullaby. He smiled, grinned into its face.

"Thou art *Haras*," he said to the awful, demon face, to the slittted eyes with their centers like stormcloud. It was the sadoth he spoke, the language of his hill-dwelling ancestors. "Thou art *Haras. Thorn* is your name."

It gazed solemnly up at him.

Unafraid.

It waved its hands. *He*, Duun reminded himself. He. Haras. Thorn. The wind howled about the house, skirled in the chimney and set the flames to flickering in the hearth.

He grinned and rocked the child and did a thing which would have chilled the blood of any of the countryfolk who doubtless huddled together in their dispossession; or the meds; or Ellud in his fine city apartment.

He held it as if it were a shonun child and washed its eyes with his tongue (they tasted salt and musty). There was nothing he spared himself, no last repugnance he did not overcome. Such was his patience.

II They came from the capital. Copters landed, and meds made the long trek uphill carrying their instruments; and downhill going away. They were not pleased. Perhaps the countryfolk frightened them, gathering in their sullen watchfulness at the foot of the road, where the aircraft landed.

They came and went away again.

Duun held the infant, talked to it as he watched them go, mindless talk, as one did with children.

It. Haras. Thorn.

20

"Duun," Thorn said, infant babble. "Duun, Duun, Duun."

Thorn made busy chaos on the sand before the hearth. His cries were loud, ear-splitting; shonunin were more reserved. He still soiled himself. When this would cease Duun did not know. How to teach him otherwise he did not know. Thorn's appetite had changed; his sleep was longer, to Duun's relief.

"Duun, Duun, Duun," the infant sang, on his back before the fire. And grinned and laughed when Duun poked him in the belly, squealed, when Duun used a clawtip. Laughed again. Enjoyed his belly rubbed, fat round belly which began to hollow now, the limbs to lengthen. "Duun." Duun leaned forward, nipped at Thorn's neck. Thorn grabbed his ears, and Duun sat back, escaping the infant grip, disheveled. He had let his crest grow; it sheeted raggedly down his back and strayed now in front of his ears.

He went for the throat again on hands and knees and Thorn squealed and kicked. Clawed with small fat hands, with nails which were all the defense he had.

Duun laughed aloud, well-pleased.

Thorn ran, ran, ran on tottering legs, out of doors, on the dusty earth where outbuildings had been; naked in the warmth of spring.

Duun knelt. No one nowadays saw Duun's

body, the lightning-blasted scars of his right arm, the scars that skeined across his side and leg. But here he wore no more than the small-kilt, in the warmth, with the hiyi flowering by the back door and drifting blossoms down pink as Thorn's smooth skin. Infant hair had gone, come in gold, darkened again in winter metamorphosis. Perhaps it was seasonal; perhaps a phase of Thorn's life. Duun held out his arms to Thorn and Thorn laughed as he plunged into Duun's arms, all dusty-smelling.

"Again," Duun said, and set him upright, crouching again a little distance off to make Thorn run. Infant legs tried and failed, exhausted. Duun caught him, hugged him, licked his mouth and eyes, which Thorn did to him when Thorn had stopped laughing and gasping, clenching small five-fingered fists into Duun's trailing crest and the shorter hair of his forelock, and digging his face for a sly nip into the hollow of Duun's neck when he got the chance, but Duun ducked his head aside and got in a nip first. Small unclawed feet drove at his lap, the small body strained and Thorn ducked down to bite him ungently in the chest.

"Ah!" Duun cried, seizing him in both hands, kneeling, lifting him kicking and squealing aloft at arm's length. "Ah! Devious!"

He hugged him again and Thorn bit again. He had gained teeth, and strength, but they

CUCKOO'S EGG

were not teeth like Duun's. Duun bit at fingers and Thorn caught Duun's mouth and pushed back his lip to try his fingers on Duun's larger, sharper teeth. Duun nipped and Thorn rescued his hand and squealed.

There were more visits. "Bye, bye, bye," Thorn bade the meds sullenly from the porch. He squatted down naked as he was and grimaced then. He had bit the chief med, and the med had come within a little of flicking an impudent youngster hard on the nose.

But the med had stopped himself. Duun was standing there, hatani-cloaked in gray, arms folded.

The meds went away. Thorn made a rude sound and urinated on the step.

Duun went and snapped him soundly on the ear with thumb and forefinger. Thorn wailed.

"Bad," said Duun. The wail went on. Duun went into the house, into the kitchen and got his hand wet in the sink. Thorn followed, naked, holding hands out, wailing all the way and dancing in his distress.

"Shut up," Duun said. And flicked cold water in Thorn's face. Thorn blinked and howled and clawed frantically at Duun's legs, not in rage. Pick me up, that meant.

Duun picked him up, armful that he had become, rocked him with a swinging of his body in that way he had learned the infant liked. A small face nuzzled its way to his neck; this did not always mean biting. This time it did not. Thorn clung to him and snuffled, soiling his cloak with running eyes and nose.

"You were bad," Duun said. To such simplicities the philosophy of hatani bent nowadays. He swung from side to side and the sobs stopped. The thumb went in Thorn's mouth, irrepressible, though Thorn ate meat now, which Duun chewed for him and spat into his mouth. ("Not advisable," the meds said, obsessed with disease. But he did it, which was an old way, a hill way, and easier than urging a spoon past Thorn's dodging mouth, or cleaning up when Thorn fed himself and smeared it everywhere. Duun's mother and father had done this for him. He took perverse pleasure in performing this dutiful service. It shocked the meds. That gave him perverse pleasure too. He smiled at the meds. It was strange. They had become familiar with him. They looked him in the eyes, at least more than once in the visit. "Elludmingi sends regards," they said. "I sent mine," he said in return. And perversely added: "So does my son." *That* sent them on their way in haste. Doubtless to take notes.)

He rocked Thorn and sang to him, absently: "Wei-na-mei, wei-na-mei." And Thorn grew quiet in his arms. "You're getting too big to hold," Duun said. "Too big to make puddles on the step."

That night, when they sat before the fire (the spring nights were cold) Thorn crawled into his lap and sat there a while; and got up on his feet in the triangle between Duun's crossed legs and touched Duun's face, the scarred side. Duun caught the hand with his maimed one. And let it go.

"It's a scar," Duun said.

He did not prevent the exploration. He made himself patient. He shut his eyes and let Thorn do what he liked, until Thorn pulled savagely on both his ears, which was challenge. Duun's eyes flashed open.

"*Ah!*" Duun cried, drawing back his lips in a grimace. Thorn recoiled and stumbled on Duun's legs; Duun caught him in mid-fall and rolled with him, rolled holding him in his arms, never coming on him with his weight. Thorn screamed, and gasped, and when Duun bit, bit back, and screamed and squealed till Duun clamped a hand over his mouth and held it there.

Thorn grew still. The eyes stayed wide with shock. So. So. Fright, not fight.

Duun gathered him to his breast and licked his eyes till Thorn had begun to pant, recovering his lost breath. For a moment Duun was worried. Small hands clutched at him.

He gripped Thorn by both arms and held him up. Grinned. Thorn refused to be appeased.

That night Thorn waked howling at Duun's side, short sharp yelps, gasps for breath. "Thorn!" Duun cried, and turned on lights and snatched him up, thinking he had rolled on the infant and hurt him in some way; but it was nightmare.

Thorn held to him. It was Duun Thorn feared. That was the nightmare.

"Ah," Duun cried, falling back, dragging Thorn atop him. "Ah! you hurt me! You hurt me—" To give him the upper hand. He had no pride in this.

"Duun," Thorn cried and snuggled close.

Sometimes genes were truer than teaching. Alien. Thorn clung to what had frightened him.

"Duun, Duun, Duun—"

Duun held him. It was all Thorn understood.

There was a day, in the morning bath, that Thorn noticed his own naked skin. Thorn scrubbed at Duun's belly and at his own with a rough-textured sponge. Dropped the sponge and put both hands on his own belly, rubbed it thoughtfully. When he looked up thoughts passed in his milk-and-storm eyes, with a little knitting of his brow. "Slick," he said of himself. His speech did not go as fast as a shonun child. But there was a difference of mouths and tongues. "Slick."

Perhaps Thorn wanted to ask, if his young mind had thought of it, when his own pelt would begin to grow. The hair on his head was abundant, tousled curls, which had finally settled on a faded, earthy brown. The eyes had never changed. It was a dangerous time.

Duun took Thorn from the bath and held him in his left arm, hugged him close in front of the mirror. Thorn had seen mirrors. He had one for a toy. He had seen this one many times.

Today there was distress in young Thorn's eyes, and thoughts were going on. Thorn had never seen a shonun child. He had never seen other shonunin, except the meds. Perhaps some terrible thing was dawning on his mind, put together of little wordless pieces, images in mirrors, smooth bellies, a facility for making water in a long, long arc, which was for a time his nuisancefully chiefest talent. He spread his five-fingered hand at Thorn-in-the-mirror, in a way that should bring claws and did not; he grimaced at this Thorn as if to frighten him to flight. (Go away, ugly Thorn.) He flexed the fingers yet again. Made faces.

Duun turned them both away. Bounced him to distract him.

After that Thorn did not mention the difference of their skins. Only from time to time there were small moments which Duun caught: a moment of rest when Thorn, lying beside

Duun, reached and stroked his arm, turning the fur this way and that. Another when Thorn, finding Duun's hand conveniently palm up, dragged it closer to him across Duun's lap and played with it, fingering the dissimilar geometries of the palm, working doggedly at the fingers to make the claws come out. Duun cooperated. It was his right hand. It was not the deformity Thorn explored, but an ability which surely Thorn envied; and Duun was suddenly aware of a silence within the child, a secrecy which had grown all unawares, that small walled-off place which was an independent mind. Thorn had arrived at selfhood, a self which came out to explore the world and retreated with scraps of things which had to be examined with care, compared (sign of a complex mind) against other truths: Thorn had arrived at self-defense, disappointed in his body, it seemed. Aware of his own deformity. And not, truly, aware of Duun's. Duun was Duun. Duun had always had scars; they were part of Duun as the sun was part of the world. There was no past. Thorn had not been in it: therefore Thorn could not imagine it.

But Thorn's hands were not like Duun's. His skin was not. And Thorn had begun to take alarm, suspecting imbalance in the world.

Duun gathered him close, as he had done when Thorn was smaller, rolled him into his lap and poked him in the belly, which Thorn resisted for a moment, and writhed, and finally gave way to, in squeals and laughter and abortive attempts to retaliate in kind. Duun let him have that victory, sprawled backward on the sand before the fire, belly heaving under Thorn's slight weight, in laughter which was not reflexive, like Thorn's. To be touched on throat or belly went against instinct. There was a sense of peril in that abandonment.

But a child had to win. Sometimes. And lose sometimes. There was strength in both.

"Follow, follow," he urged the child, looking downhill. The rocky incline was a great trial for small legs, and Duun's stride was long. Thorn stood with legs apart, arms hanging, and staggered a few more knock-kneed steps. "Keep climbing," Duun said. "You can."

A few more steps. Thorn fell and cried, a weak, breathless sobbing. "I can't."

"You have breath left to cry, you have breath to get up. Come on. *Up!* Shall I be ashamed?"

"I hurt my knee!" Thorn sat up, clutching it and rocking.

"I hurt my hand once. Get up and come on. Someone is chasing us."

Thorn caught his breath and looked downtrail, still hiccuping.

"Perhaps it will eat us," Duun said. "Get up. Come on."

Thorn let go his reddened knee. Limbs struggled. Thorn got to his feet, wobbled, and came on desperately.

"I lied," said Duun. "But so did you. You could get up. Come on."

Sobs and snuffles. Wails of rage. Thorn kept walking. Duun walked with shorter strides, as if the way had gotten steeper for him as well.

"Again." Duun gave Thorn another small stone. Thorn threw. It hit a rock not so high up the cliffs as before. "Not so good. Again."

"You do it."

Duun threw. It sailed up and up and struck near the top of the sheer face. The child's mouth stayed open in dismay.

"That is what I *can* do," Duun said. "Match that."

"I can't."

"My ears are bad. Something said can't."

Thorn took the rock. Tears welled up in his eyes. He threw. The stone fell ignominiously awry and lost itself among the rocks at the bottom of the cliff.

"Ah. I have frightened you. Thorn is scared. I hear *can't* again."

"I hate you!"

"Throw at *me*, then. I'm closer. Perhaps you can hit *me*." Duun gave Thorn another stone.

Thorn's face was red. His eyes watered and his lips trembled. He whirled and threw it at the cliff instead.

So.

"That was your highest yet," Duun said.

III The meds came back. Ellud was with them. "Ellud," Duun said.

"You look well," Ellud said, with one long searching look. With a furtive sliding of the eyes toward Thorn, who stood his ground in the main hall of the house, where the hated meds prepared their discomforts. Thorn scowled. The sun had turned his naked skin a golden brown. His hair, which Duun cut to a length that did not catch twigs or blind him when he worked, was a clean and shining earth color. His eyes were as much white as blue. His nose had gotten more prominent, his teeth were strong, if blunt. He stood

still. His poor ears could not move. Only the
regular flaring of his nostrils betrayed his dislike.

"Thorn," Duun said. "Come here. This is
Ellud. Be polite, Thorn."

"Is he a med?" Thorn asked suspiciously.

Ellud's ears sank. A rock might have spoken
to him in plain accents and shocked him no
less. He looked at Duun. Said nothing.

"No." said Duun. "A friend. Many years ago."

Thorn looked up and blinked. A med came
and got him and prepared to take his pulse.

"Come back to town," Ellud said. "Duun,
come back."

"Is that a request or an order?"

"Duun—"

"I'd remind you that you promised me anything. Not yet, Ellud."

That evening Thorn was silent, gloomy,
thoughtful. He did not ask about Ellud. Did not
discuss the meds.

Thorn slept apart now. There were changes
in his body which made this advisable. He
went to his room of the many rooms in the
house and curled up into his privacy. Duun
came to check on him.

"Are my ears going to grow?" Thorn asked,
looking at him from the pillow as he stood in
the doorway.

Ears. Maybe that was the easiest, least painful thing to ask. Duun stood silent. He had

planned how he would answer about claws
and hair and the shape of their faces and the
difference of their loins. He had planned everything but ears.

"I don't think so," Duun said. "I don't care,
do you?"

Silence, from the small shadow in the bedbowl.

"You're unusual," Duun said.

A snuffle.

"I like you that way," Duun said.

"I like you," came the small, disembodied
voice. Another snuffle. "I like you, Duun." *Love*
was, Duun recalled, not a word he had ever
used in Thorn's hearing. Like you. As one liked
a warm fire. The sun on one's back.

"I like you too, Thorn."

"I don't want any more meds."

"I'll talk to them about that. Do you want to
go hunting tomorrow? I'll give you a knife of
your own. I'll show you how to keep the blade."

"Hunting what?" Snuffle. Shadow-child wiped
his eyes with a swipe of an arm; nose with
another. There was interest in the voice.

"I'm hatani, Thorn. That's something hard to
be. That's why I push you hard."

"What's hatani?"

"I'll show you. Tomorrow. I'll teach you.
You'll learn to do what I can do. It's going to be
hard, Thorn."

Another wipe of the eyes.

"Tomorrow, Thorn?"

"Yes."

"Get to sleep, then."

Duun went back to the fire. Wind howled outside, in cold. The fire leapt. The last of the old countryfolk lumber was gone. They began to use an old log from downslope. He cut it with the power saw he had ordered with supplies and brought it up, bit by bit. None of the countryfolk from the valley would bother the pile he had made on the roadside below. They kept out of his sight and left no sign near the house. But he knew that they were there.

They would know hatani patience. Countryfolk had patience of their own. Perhaps things would change. Perhaps the hatani would die. Perhaps the alien would meet with accident. Perhaps their title would become valid again.

Perhaps they had bad dreams, down in the valley, on the other side of the mountain, out of his sight and mind. Perhaps they dreamed nightmares, imagining that their woods were no longer their own.

Or that the woods might not be theirs again, forever.

He had asked for the house and lands of Sheon. He had not used the lands, till now.

He took his weapons from the top shelf of the locked cabinet where they had remained out of the way of curious young fingers. He had taken them out many times to care for them, and never let Thorn touch them, to Thorn's great frustration. A child should have unfulfilled ambitions; should know some things forbidden. Doubtless Thorn had tried. Children were not always virtuous. That was to be expected. And dealt with.

"Have you ever tried these?" Duun asked, when Thorn sat opposite him, across the blanket from the small array of knives, cord, wire, the two guns, one projectile-firing and one not. "Have you ever handled them?"

"No," Thorn said.

"Will you ever, if I tell you no?"

Alien eyes lifted to him, in startlement that at once dilated and contracted the irises: swift, furtive decision to agree, the easy course, swiftly to be violated—perhaps. If a child wished. There would be a quick flick of a reproving finger against an ear. Perhaps a cuff to make the eyes water. Thorn could endure that. There was no permanency. Nothing was forever. As he lacked a past, he lacked a true future, and believed nothing could thwart him forever.

There was no *can't* for Thorn. Duun had taught him so.

"I am not asking you," Duun said, holding up the solitary finger of his right hand. "I am telling you a thing. I want you to believe this. Will you ever pick these up if I tell you no?'

From childish excitement, from game to perplexity. Thorn's brow contracted in a spasm of anxiety. Perhaps Duun would break his promise? Perhaps he was being teased?

Duun took off the cloak and dropped it behind him. He picked up the wer, a middling blade. He stretched out his bare left arm, fist clenched, and set the knife against his forearm.

"No!" Thorn cried suddenly. A game? A threat? Something he had done wrong? Duun was teasing him?

Duun slowly brought the blade down and down, deeply. Blood sprang out and rained in steady, heavy drops on the weapons and the blanket. He kept his fist clenched and held the arm steady, resting the knife butt on his knee. Thorn's eyes were wide, his mouth open with nothing coming out.

"That's what weapons are for," Duun said. The blood poured, soaked the blanket. "Each time you take them up, remember what they're for."

"Stop it," Thorn cried. "Duun, stop it bleeding!"

Duun held out the knife, the wounded arm still spurting. He turned it in his maimed hand and offered it hilt first to Thorn. "Can you do it?"

Thorn took the bloodied knife. His eyes still

were wide. His lips set themselves, drawn in. He held out his own clenched fist and set the knife to his skin. He drew the blade down the same way, and his face was red and his eyes poured tears; his nostrils and his lips went pale. He drew the knife down. Blood began to drip. The small hand drew away, the knife wobbling in tremors that convulsed the knife-arm and began to involve the other. As Duun had done, he set the knife hand on his knee, and his face was all white and beaded with moisture, while the blood ran down and made another darkening of the blanket.

So. So. Duun had expected last-moment flinching. His own head grew light. His cut was deeper and bled abundantly. He held out his hand and took the knife back. He saw the terror in the child. (What more, Duun? What else? What worse? I'm scared, Duun!)

"It is not a game," Duun said. He put down the knife and pressed his right hand to his wound. "You can hold it. Hold it tight." He got up from his cross-legged posture without using either hand. He went and opened the med kit and pressed a sealing film on the wound. He came back to Thorn with another square of the gel, and pressed the film to Thorn's arm and held it, warming it with his hand until it took and stayed, soft and blood-reddened, over a wound that would scar. Duun held the arm.

Alien eyes looked up at him, white all round. He was tender in his grip. "You won't forget," Duun said. "You won't forget what weapons are. You will never pick them up when I tell you not."

"No." A small weak voice.

"You will use them when I say. And you'll set them down when I say."

"Yes."

"Good." He slid a bloodstained hand past Thorn's head and rubbed Thorn's nape in the vise of his maimed hand till the tension left and Thorn's body gave to and fro with that motion, his eyes still fixed on Duun. "Believe me, Thorn. Believe me in this. You hurt now. But you did what I asked. That was brave."

Muscles in Thorn's face shook, as in some dire chill. His limbs convulsed. Stopped. Duun kept on his massage until the shiver passed. Thorn's eyes lost their wild look. They were wide and moiled with forethought and calculations. (What else does he want? What did I win? What did I do? What next?)

Duun let go. Motioned at the bloodstained weapons. "Clean them. I'll show you how."

Thorn stirred, edged closer to the array of weapons on the blanket. "You said—" he began.

"I said?"

"We'd go hunting. You said—we'd go hunting today."

"That we will. We won't eat tonight if we don't take something."

Thorn's eyes flicked up a second time; Thorn could do that, without turning his head. The look hoped for a joke and Duun made his face implacable.

There was no question, of course. The place was full of unwary game. No one hunted it much. Yet. And a hatani could, in the most desolate place, find some sustenance.

But Thorn would discover this when he was hungry. When he had tried for himself and understood that he was too loud and too awkward.

When he had seen what was in the land, and what the wild things knew.

"I promised you a knife."

A glance upward, wary interest. A stare of white wide eyes.

"The wer-knife. The one you used. That would be a good one for you. You can have it if you like. It's a very good blade. You have to keep it spotless. Even fingers stain it. I'll show you how to keep it."

Thorn picked it up again, by the hilt. Held it.

The gangling boy came up the trail, thinking he was alert: Duun knew. Thorn looked this way and that: his callused feet made very little noise on the dusty track among the rocks.

"*Up,*" Duun hissed. "Look *up.*"

Thorn's head came up. Duun had already moved, lost in the brush.

The boy was still looking up when Duun hit him in the back with a thrown stone. Thorn spun about and threw. Thorn's stone rattled away down among brush and rock. Duun had evaded it with a fluid shift of his hip, and stood untouched.

"Too late," Duun said. "You're dead. I'm not."

Thorn's shoulders slumped. He bent his head in shame.

Whirled and sped another rock underhand.

Duun evaded that one too without more than shifting stance. Thorn did not look surprised, only exhausted. Beaten at last.

Duun grinned. "Better. That did surprise me." The grin faded. "But your choosing this track up didn't. *That* was your first mistake. How did I know? Can you figure that?"

Thorn gasped for breath. Hunkered down on the path, arms on scabbed knees. "Because I was tired. The climb's easier."

"Better still. You're right. Think ahead next time. And think in *all* directions. You know this path. You should have seen these rocks in your head before you came to them."

No answer. Thorn knew. Duun knew that he knew. Thorn wiped his forearm across his face

41

and smeared dust across the sweat. Even at this range he stank of heat.

"Also," Duun reminded him with delicacy, "when you came round the mountain the wind was coming at your shoulder, at an angle to the rocks. Do you see why that should have warned you?"

Thorn blinked sweat and wiped again. He had grown rangier, longer of limb. The belly had gone hollow beneath the ribs, ridged with muscle above the wrap about his loins. Brush-scars showed white on his skin. "Scent," he said. He gasped for breath. There was chagrin in his half-drowned face. "Sorry. I'm sorry, Duun."

"Sorry won't save you. Scent-deaf doesn't mean the world is. You're dead, Thorn."

"Yes, Duun." A faint, hoarse voice. Shoulders slumped again. "You won't catch me again."

"Won't I?"

"Duun—*I'm hungry, Duun!*"

Duun spun around the other side of the tree, leaned there looking at him and scowling. "Hunt, then. Fool. Don't tell me what your needs are. I'll know where to find you. Don't trust me, Thorn."

"I'm not playing, Duun!"

"Then neither will I be." Duun spun round

again. Headed downslope. "I'll hurt you this time, Thorn!"

"Duun!"

Fire crackled, there in the clearing. They made peace. Thorn nursed bruises. It was Duun's catch Duun divided with him, meat which Thorn took gingerly, dancing it from one hand to the next while it cooled down.

"You do well," Duun said.

"For someone who can't smell," Thorn said hoarsely. "Who falls into traps."

Duun flicked his ears. "Good, you worry about your lacks. You'll think of them. You won't forget again."

"Duun, what's wrong with me?"

The question stopped him. The meat burned Duun's fingers and he shifted it in haste, back and forth again, and laid it on a rock. "Wrong. Who said wrong?"

Silence from the other side of the fire. Grievous silence.

"You're different," Duun said. "Or maybe I am. Does that occur to you?"

It had not. Thorn blinked in shock. Then disbelief crept in. There were the meds. There was Ellud. Thorn was not diverted. Duun was pleased with that, too.

"You're smart," Duun said. "You're quick, you're clever. Brave. All those things. You're

Thorn. What if you were the only one? What if? What if I were the only Duun? Would that make a difference? You're all you can be. You don't need anything else. I don't."

"Make sense, Duun!"

"The world's wide, boy. Wide. There's nine seas. There's cities. There's roads and highways. People in a hurry. Cities are full of noise. Sheon's best. That's this place, Sheon. The gods made this whole world and they made Sheon first. You talk to the winds, Thorn. You hear the gods talk back? Do you?"

"I don't know."

"You can't hear that in a city. Cityfolk are scent-deaf. Too many smells. Gives you a headache." Duun tore off a bit of meat and swallowed. "The gods made the world and they made shonunin last, out of the leftovers; and they were missing some. And they were sorry, so one of them gave up a bit and another gave another bit and they filled up the gaps till there were parts enough. That's what we are, all scraps and a bit of the gods' own selves. All patchwork. With good parts and bad. So you can't smell. I've got just six fingers. And you've got five on just one hand."

"How did you—?"

Ah. The fish bit. Duun had thought that bait would lead him astray. Duun shrugged. "I made a mistake. See? Even I make mistakes. And I'm

44

good, Thorn, I'm very good. You don't know how good."

Thorn choked down a bite. He had to chew more than Duun did. Sometimes in his haste he forgot this. He struggled. Stayed silent after. "What happened?" Thorn asked finally. "Duun—what did happen to your—?"

"Ah. Well. I hunted something that bit back, you see?" He held up the maimed hand. "You put your hand into things, young Thorn, you may not get back what you want."

"What was it?"

Duun took another bite. Swallowed. "Eat. It's getting cold."

"Duun."

"Maybe I'll tell you. When you can beat me, fair or foul."

"I never will!"

"Ah. Maybe you won't. But you're several fingers ahead of me. You're younger than I am. My knee aches when it rains."

"Couldn't the meds—?"

"Maybe I didn't want them to."

Thorn's mouth was open. He closed it and stopped asking. His eyes were muddled with unasked questions and too many answers. He had become too wary a hunter to go down a trail that likely to have snares. Thorn took another bite and ate in silence.

"I'll teach you to shoot," Duun said. "You almost hit me with that stone."

Thorn looked up. Distracted again, lured on and promised. (O young fool. Fool who loves me. Thorn.)

"Another sequence," Duun said. "Base ten this time. The numbers are sixteen, forty-nine, fifty-two, ninety-seven, eight and two."

Thorn sat on the back porch of the house. The hiyi flowers bloomed. The insects hummed and made pink petals fall in delirium. Thorn shut his eyes. His brow knit. "Two hundred twenty four."

"Divide by the third in sequence."

Thorn put his hands against his eyes. Pressed hard. "Four point three." He looked up. "Can't we go hunting, Duun? I'm tired of—"

"More decimals."

Another shutting of the eyes. Hands pressed to shut out the light. "Point three zero eight."

"Add nine. Subtract four, eighty-two. Six."

The hands came down. Eyes blinked. "I'm sorry, Duun, I lost it, I forgot—"

"No. You didn't remember. Think. Name me the numbers."

"I—"

"Am I about to hear can't?"

"Didn't"

"Didn't. Didn't. There was a nest of maganin;

46

here and here and here! How many were they? Which groups? Where? *They've eaten you, fool!*"

"Maganin don't come in fifties!"

"I am ashamed." Duun thrust his hands into the waist of his kilt and walked away.

"Duun—"

Duun turned, ears pricked. "You've remembered."

"No! No, I haven't remembered! I can't remember! I don't remember!"

"Then I'm still ashamed." Duun laid his ears back, turned and walked on.

"Duun—"

Duun did not look back. There were tears back there. Rage. It was Thorn's nature.

So was it Thorn's nature to come trailing back into the house, finally, when it was dark, when Duun had made a fire and sat on the sand before the hearth. Duun had cooked food. He had eaten. He had brought Thorn's supper outside and set it wordlessly on the step. Thorn was not to be seen. But it was in Thorn's nature to admit defeat when night came.

Thorn came and stood on the sand beside him. "Two hundred twenty-four," Thorn said.

Duun's ears pricked. "Plus nine. Minus four. Eighty-two. Six."

"One forty-one."

"Ah. You can."

47

Thorn knelt. Leaned on his hands. "What in the world comes in two hundred twenty-fours?"

"Stars. Trees. Kinds of grass. The ways of a river. The stubbornness of a child. The world is wide, young Thorn. I can reckon the speed of the wind, name the stars, the cities of the world. I can read a man's intent in the pupils of his eyes."

Duun swung around and struck, open palmed. Thorn's open palm was there to meet it, stopped it, held and trembled.

"Ah. You are hatani, are you? Back away, little fish. You're not ready to take me. Drop the hand."

It was a trap. Thorn refused it. Thorn held still, eyes wide and white-rimmed, palm trembling against his palm, and Duun lowered his ears.

"Now what will you do?" Duun asked.

"Let me go." The tremor grew. "Let me go, Duun."

Duun reached out his maimed right hand and encircled Thorn's wrist gently with the span of his two fingers. Pulled. The hand refused to leave contact with his palm. The arm shook. Thorn's eyes were dilated, watched his feverishly.

"What are you going to do now, little fish? You have a problem now, don't you? You've let me get two hands into it."

Thorn lifted his other hand. It froze in that lifting, trembling.

"Not wise. Not wise at all," Duun said. "You're overmatched. You'd better stop. Don't you think?"

"Let go,."

"Relax. Relax and trust me."

"No!"

"There was a time I told you, do you remember?—when you took up the knife, I said that you would take it up when I told you; and when I told you, you would lay it down. This is the time, Thorn. Now I tell you to let go. Do you hear me? I tell you to lay it down, Thorn."

The tremor grew. The palm slowly left his palm. Duun clenched his hand on Thorn's wrist and jerked him against his chest. Thorn, utterly off his balance, collapsed against him. Duun grinned, grasped him by both arms, claws out, shook him back in that grip and stared into eyes face to face. "I would have torn your throat out just then. Do you believe it?"

"No."

"Why would I not?"

"I don't know, Duun!"

Duun let him go. Thorn collapsed onto his rump and sat up and rubbed his arms. There would be bruises and clawmarks. Duun knew.

"Are you a fool, then?" Duun asked. "Why did you do that?"

"You would have hit me," Thorn said, perfect logic.

"Yes," Duun said.

Another change. Thorn sat with his jaw loose, stunned silence in his watering eyes. The boy discovered chaos in the world, sums that had no right answer. "The world's full of two-way bad choices," Duun said. "Numbers always work out. You can trust them. That's why we learn numbers. To set some order in the world. There's no other part of life where things work out. Do you see that?"

"Yes." Thorn's teeth chattered. "I see."

"You are hatani. Wei-na-hatani, little fish. A small one. A hatani is not the weapons. Is not the knife, the gun. A hatani is not these things. I told you that the time would come to lay these things down. Now you have no need of them. You can pick up the knife and lay it down again. A hatani is not the knife. Do you understand? Not the skin or the claws or the eyes. Do you understand? I teach you. You become hatani. Inside."

Thorn blinked rapidly. Gasped for breath. "Duun, where did you get me?"

"Where do you think?"

"I don't know."

"But you trust me. Don't go to every morsel, little fish. Some are traps. Don't I teach you? Use your wits. Add only what can be added.

Remember all the figures, even so. Never lose
one. That one will surely come from behind
and kill you. There are no second tries in the
world. Nothing is twice."

"How can you know anything?"

"Remember all the numbers. Even the long-
ago ones. Never drop any. You don't know
when they'll be needed. Reject nothing. You
don't know what you might need. I give you
these things."

"Where did you get me?"

"I pulled you from the river, little fish. You
were drowning and I saved you."

"Is that truth, Duun?"

"I lied." Duun reached out the finger of his
hand and brushed Thorn's cheek, where a light
down had grown. Hair began to grow and darken
elsewhere on Thorn's body. Thorn's hope and
his despair. (It's worse than nothing, Thorn
cried, before the mirror in the bath. I'm all in
patches, Duun!) Other signs were on him. "I
tell you, I think you should cut this, little fish;
you're right: it's here and there—I'd make it
even."

"Stop it. Don't distract me! I want an answer, Duun."

"Ah. You uncover my tricks, do you?"

"I want an answer, Duun."

"The minnow has hatani tricks."

"I want an answer, Duun."

Duun pursed his lips. Laid his ears back. "Put that answer with my hand. Beat me and I'll answer you."

Thorn's shoulders slumped. His head bowed. True defeat. Then he glanced up with a piercing, anxious look.

"Duun—Duun, tell me the truth. One truth. Be fair to me. Do you know?"

"Yes," Duun said, and gazed at him steadily until Thorn turned his face away.

Faith am I when all you trust has died;
Truth am I when all you know has lied.

Choice I bring when the choice you had is sped;
Promise am I when all other faith has fled.

Vengeance am I but I come to you at cost;
One gain am I when all else you want is lost.

Thorn sang. It was a hatani song. Duun listened, as to the other lessons, listened half-dreaming as he played. There was a sweetness in Thorn's voice, all unsuspected, a skill in his hands which ran upon the strings. Perhaps it was a native fierceness that made the boy love this song; perhaps it was the innocence of that downlands child who questioned a hatani's scars, happy in ignorance. Perhaps Thorn only loved the tune. He sang it well.

Duun took over the dkin and strummed out a new rhythm with his two-fingered right hand. Rapped the beat on the sounding-board, and Thorn with native skill took the beat on the small drum.

The young head bent to the music, young eyes looked up slyly from beneath a fall of dark hair, lately shaven lips widened in a grin. Thorn had given up on the hair of his face. That on his body he still cultivated. Besides, the razor burned. (You look better, Duun had told him, when Thorn had done the deed and crept out for approval. And Thorn looked profoundly relieved.) Vulnerable. Oh, vulnerable, young Thorn.

> *Green beneath the summer sun,*
> *White beneath the snow,*
> *All fair my land,*
> *And fair the one I know*
> *Whose paths run down*
> *To mine in evenglow.*

Love and women and things of the world. "A hatani has no kin," Duun said while his hands played on. "When you are hatani to the heart you will not have me."

The drum stopped. But there was no question. Thorn had betrayed himself and Duun had gone no further; Thorn kept his own counsel, grown wary in his years. And having done that much, Duun kept the melody going, gentle harmony. "When I lost the most of my hand, I thought I would never play. I recovered that. Other things I lost. You gain no virtue from loss you never know. There will never be love, Thorn. Never. Do you know that word? —Take up the beat."

Thorn picked it up, bowed his head till his eyes were hid.

"I tell you," Duun said in the low beat of the strings, the counterpoint of the drum. "There's always something left to lose. When you think there's nothing more you're a fool, Thorn; there's something till you're dead. And after that—gods know. Do you know how old you are?"

Thorn looked up. The beat skewed. recovered itself.

"They know in the city. I know. The meds don't come. Half a year and they don't come. You know why, Thorn?"

A move of the head. No. There was dread in Thorn's eyes.

"Well," Duun said, "they don't. Maybe they know what you are."

The beat kept up, regular as heartbeat and as painful.

"What am I?"

Duun looked at him sidelong. "Hatani. Like me. Self-sufficient."

Thorn only stared at him, knowing his tricks. (Foul, Duun-hatani. Wicked and foul.)

"You have a wound, little fish. You bleed into the water. Don't you know this?"

Thorn's jaw set. His eyes were alive with thoughts. "I didn't feel the wind, Duun-hatani. You caught me."

"—again."

"Meds."

Duun looked up.

"You talked about meds, Duun, and cities. What about them?"

"Oho. The minnow takes to deeper water."

"You mean to say something, Duun-hatani. You never say anything you don't want to say."

"Deeper still."

"You called them. Did you?"

"No." The music grew under Duun's fingers, shifted and changed.

"They called you."

"Ellud called."

"Why?"

"To ask how you are. I told them. Improving, I said. Growing. They were satisfied."

"What's Ellud? Why does he want to know?

Why do the meds care? Why do they look at me and never at you?"

"Ssss. There's time. There's a little time, isn't there?"

"Time for what?"

"Tksss. Fool. Walk and breathe at once, can you?"

The beat picked up again, changed, became another thing, strong and temperful.

"Defy me, do you?" Duun launched into a thing more complex.

The beat followed. "Time for what?" Thorn asked. Duun shrugged.

"For Sheon."

"The city? The meds?" Thorn's eyes grew wild, dilate. "Gods—go there?"

"Did I teach you profanity? No. I taught you respect. You're still a child. What a leap of reason. Did I say go to the city?"

"What do you mean—time?"

"That." And Duun launched out on another tune. "Time was, I thought you might beat me, little fish. I thought you might come at me in my sleep. Fair or foul, I said. You ever think of that?"

"I thought of it."

"Why didn't you?"

A long hesitation. "I like my own sleep, Duun-hatani."

"Ah."

Thorn gave him a wary look. Duun grinned at him in no merry way. So Thorn got the joke as well. Jaw set. Eyes flickered in alarm.

(Guard your sleep, little fish. The rules just changed.)

Thorn smiled suddenly, darkly, without humor, and complicated the drum-pulse, making irreverent changes in hatani songs.

(What is a hatani? Duun. Duun is Duun. Like the sun. You become Duun, little fish, and never ask what Duun might be. Duun is the trees and the mountain, environment. Duun is faith kept. You sing the song. Hear the words, Thorn, wei-na-mei, minnow in my brook.)

Thorn poured the tea, sitting cross-legged on the riser in the room before the fire. His hand trembled and there was a shadow about his eyes, a bruising where no one had struck. "Eat," Duun said, on its other side. "You'll climb the mountain today."

Shadowed eyes lifted to him. Shoulders were already slumped. Perhaps Thorn thought of protest. If so he gave it up. Thorn knew the game.

"The black thread," Duun said, sipping at the tea. "Across the door last night. It's a very old trick. Did you know that?"

"No."

Duun grinned and swallowed down a mouthful. "Eat. Eat. You'll break your neck on the rocks."

Thorn filled his mouth and choked it down. He had shaved. He had washed himself. He had waked last night with a knife being laid at his pillow. "You're dead," Duun had whispered, ever so softly, the fifth night, the fifth night of Thorn's sleeplessness.

Thorn had started up, grasped Duun's wrist and lost that battle too, in the pitch black, in the haze of sleep caught for night upon night in fitful snatches.

"You'll try to sleep today," Duun said quietly, over tea. "It might be wise."

Thorn looked at him in bleak dismay.

Duun grinned. "On the other hand, it might not be. Want to sleep, minnow? You might take me now, face to face."

"No. There's a pebble in the pot, Duun-hatani."

Duun stopped in mid-sip. Looked at the haggard face.

"I've drunk no tea," Thorn said.

Duun set the cup down on the riser, in front of his crossed ankles.

"I won't ask my question," Thorn said hoarsely. "That was foul. I'll take you fair. With warning."

Duun drew in a long breath. Thorn had braced himself. Centered himself against the chance of a blow. And Thorn trembled.

For a long moment Duun did not move. Then he held up his left hand in a slight gesture that meant no attack forthcoming, and reached to his belt with the two fingers of this right.

He laid the pebble on the smooth surface.

Thorn glanced at it. There was only that. His eyes lifted, strangely clear.

"I would have given it to you before you left," Duun said. "I would have given it to you when you told me. But, minnow, you offered me quarter. To offer that to me—"

"I'm sorry, Duun."

"The thread was clever. To change the rules was cleverer. Then pride blinded you. Minnow, you've changed the rules. Do you understand?"

A hoarse whisper. "Yes, Duun-hatani."

"Be wary of everything, minnow. And never grant quarter to a hatani. *Fair* is a teaching-game. *Fair* is a box I drew. Should I have used all I had and discouraged you? Now the walls are down, minnow. What will you do?"

"I'd be a fool to tell you, Duun-hatani."

Duun nodded slowly. Thorn picked up his bowl to eat. Set it back then, with a soft click of the spoon against the bowl and looked up at him.

"Yes," Duun said. "It would be good to wonder what's in the food. Wouldn't it? Eat, minnow. I give you that grace. It's quite safe."

Thorn edged back on the riser, set his leg

over the edge. "You said no quarter. I believe you."

"And not my telling you it's safe?"

"No." Thorn got to his feet and walked across the sand, gathered up his weapons from the shelf, his cloak from beside the door. He stopped there and looked back.

Turned and left then. Running, feet thumping down porch steps.

Duun sipped at his tea and set it down at his knee. Thorn expected a little start. Such things he took for granted.

Duun got up, gathered up his own weapons, and his cloak.

No quarter then.

Thorn ran, ran, knowing that there was no time. There was no time to rue the attack, no time for any regret, only the running and the land—

("Wind and land, wei-na-ya: wind and land.")

("Scent-blind: but my knee aches when it rains—")

Turn and turn and turn: a fool's need rules his wit; a wise man's wit governs need.

("A hatani dictates what another's need will be.")

Fool, to do what a hatani said to do!

Thorn caught his breath and sprang for the rocks, bare feet doing what claws might do, shaping themselves to stone as Duun's could not, clinging with their softness: bare hands clinging where Duun's hands might not—swinging on a branch that gave a shortcut round the cliffside, dropping to a slant where Duun's feet would skid, where Duun's leg might fail—

The wind, O fool, the wind is at your face; Duun had checked the wind this morning. There was no corner Duun-hatani did not see around before his quarry even saw the turn—

The pebble in the tea—

Upland or downland? Do what Duun said and surprise him with obedience? Or do the opposite?

Run and run: he was quicker than Duun, that was all he was. He had grown up in these hills; and so had Duun. Thorn was more agile. He could take the high slope on his bare feet at greater speed than Duun—

—but Duun knew that.

Wild choice, then. Logic-less. He darted downslope.

Wind in his face, wind carrying his scent; and he had to get around that bend first, around the mountain shoulder.

Duun was at his back. It was not the pain Thorn dreaded, though pain there would be. It was Duun. Duun himself.

*   *   *

The wind carried scent and Duun breathed it—*fool*, Duun thought, at the edge of the rocks; *but twice a fool is a hunter too secure.* There was the easy temptation—to win at once, to take the rash chance, the wide chance.

But it was hatani he hunted. No more minnow, but fish in dark water.

He smelled the wind and knew Thorn's direction and his distance; he knew the branch of the trail that gave access to the cliff and knew the way Thorn could take that he could not—he knew every track in the hills.

Thorn knew he knew. That was the conundrum: how well he had taught the fish.

And what kind it was, how native-adept, what skill was bred into its bone and blood . . . what intelligence, what instincts.

Five-fingered hands; a surer grip; a talent at climbing: these it had. It had youth: strong legs, that felt no pain.

It knew—if it used its wits—how a once-maimed shonun had to compensate for these things.

And it would, being hatani, try to predict; try then to seize events and turn them.

It smelled of fear and sweat, even when the wind had cleaned the scent. It stank of something else, a bitter, acrid taint.

*   *   *

Run and run: it was speed Thorn had first for advantage. It was agility—Duun's was greatest, hand to hand. But Thorn's was more in distance, in the rocks, in the quick scaling of a tilted tree across a crack—

(Fool! he'll know—)

(But it will cost him time.)

And Thorn had gotten the mountain between him and Duun, gotten stone between them, to confuse the scent.

But Duun could smell where a hand had been, if he got his nose down to it. So Duun claimed.

(Run, minnow. I'm coming, little fish . . . .)

Downland. The opposite of what Duun had said he ought to do: should he confound the choice? What was there to do that he had never done?

(Gods, his gut, his bowels ached. Fear? The chase? The jolts from rock to rock?)

(Something in the food?)

Duun tripped the support. The log rolled down the gravel slope. Hastily done. Rife with scent. He spotted the second trap too, the limb drawn back, and drew back his hand in time.

Double-snared.

(Good, fish. Well done, that. But not good enough.)

*   *   *

Thorn knelt on hands and knees. He had reached the road and crossed it, leaving tracks; he paused to set a rock up on a twig, on a slope where haste might set a foot, then hurled himself downslope, leaving further tracks, leaving a bit of skin on the stones below.

He miscalculated further, sprawled. His face stung with shame. He gathered himself up again, doubled over a little farther on sweating and resisting the easy support of a tree.

(Touch nothing, leave no trace—)

Duun would hurt him. That was nothing. It was the look in Duun's gray eyes. The stare. The scorn.

Thorn bent and caught his breath; and wits began to work. He looked up at the slope he had left.

(Take me now, face to face.)

(The walls are down, minnow. What will you do?)

(Did Duun sleep? Could Duun sleep more than he did these last nights in the house?)

Was Duun-hatani lying awake each night—thinking a minnow might try him? Expecting it?

Was Duun as tired as he?

(Fix the breakfast, minnow. Hear?)

Hatani tricks. A hatani decides what his enemy will do.

A pebble in the tea. (Fix the breakfast, minnow.)

And what his enemy believes.
Anger came into him. He purged it.
(Wield anger; it has no place, else.)
(Is there a use for fear?)

Duun stopped, not yet in the open. There
was the land below. There were the treetops
black and green downslope. There was, beyond
the trees, the great flat plain, the river-plain,
the valley of the Oun, which watered it, narrow in its folds.

And a sudden bleak thought came to him.
Predictive. His heart doubled its beats. He
had chosen the hunter's part. It was that part
habitual with him; Thorn seldom turned, only
tried to disarm his attacks, to defend—to set
snares. It was wise in Thorn

(Face to face with me—Thorn challenged,
and: no, said Thorn, when I offered him a fight.)

It was constantly the running tactic. The
evasion.

(Find me, Duun-hatani. Find me if you can.
Find me where I choose.)

In a different place, a change of grounds.

Duun dared not run. That was always the
pursuer's hazard. Thorn's traps were half-
hearted, token; but there was no tokenness in a
downslope fall. Thorn supposed in him a certain degree of care.

And Thorn was quicker. Younger. Sound of wind.

Duun set out quickly. Anger rose in him and died a quick death.

(Well-done, minnow, if this was your plan. I am not ashamed. Not of you.)

Duun saw his hazard. And being hatani-trained, perhaps the young fool knew what he did.

Perhaps.

Thorn ached still. The first cramps had bent him double. (O gods, gods, gods, his guts.) He heaved himself down at a streamside he had never hunted yet, bathed his face. Livhl-root. He knew the herb. He knew others and chewed the leaves, a foul taste, but it stopped the spasms in his bowels. He had left sign. He had made mistakes when the pain drove him. He chewed the sour leaves he found and swallowed, splashed his face with icy water from the spring. His hands were white with the chills that racked him.

Fool, to challenge Duun. To have offered quarter. To have changed the game. Nothing was safe. He flung himself up again and ran down the stream—

—Old trick. Ancient trick, Duun would say. Do something original.

He had no strength left. His knees ached

with the struggle with the water and the rocks, his bones ached with the chill: his joints grew loose and ached and strained with the sudden turn of river stones. The cold got into his bones and set him shivering.

(Can one die of livhl? *Was* it livhl?)

His ankle turned; he saved himself from a plunge in icy water, waded to the shore, his arms and the legs under him jerking with shivers like drugged spasms. (O Duun, unfair.)

No quarter. None.

Downhill again.

The sun went past zenith. The drug had worked. Duun caught the livhl-stink, though Thorn had been wary, and fouled the brook to kill it. It was in his sweat, on the things his hands had touched. He had taken to the stream and followed that—no craft at all to conceal his exit-point. A snare was possible, if Thorn's wits were not addled. Duun went around the place, picked the trail up without difficulty, though water had killed the scent somewhat. (Well-thought, minnow; the brush is thick, the chance for ambush all too great. Am I to follow you into a thrown rock, a deadfall?)

(Where's the breaking-point, Thorn? The killing-point? The point you turn?)

(Or do you fall first? How long, Thorn?)

Duun hastened. His limp betrayed him. There

was a pain within his side. (Old man, old man—they put you back together; you should have let them replace the knee, regrow the hand—now you rue it, late.)

He found another way—he guessed which way Thorn must head and guessed amiss.

(So. He learned that lesson all too well. Does he read me? Does he know? Or is it random choice he tries? Knowledge or fool's choice?)

(How old is he in his own terms? Not man yet. Not grown. But near.)

(Thorn-that-I-carried. *Haras*, Thorn, that wounds the hand that holds it, the foot that treads it, that tangles paths and bears bitter blooms and poisoned fruit.)

The shadows multiplied in the sinking sun. Thorn gasped for air, withheld his hands from their instinctive reach after support on trunk and log and stone as he descended the valley. He sighted on a stone and went to it, for his legs wandered. He sighted on the next and followed that. Such little goals led him now.

(Get beyond the pale, get to paths strange to both of us. Duun knows the mountain too well—far too well.)

(Go where Duun would not have me go—make him angry—anger in my enemy is my friend, my friend—)

He smelled smoke. It was far away in the valley, but he went toward it.

(Let Duun worry now. Let him come here to find me. Here among the countryfolk. Here among others. Other people.)

(Run and run. Stop for wind. Let us play this game in and out of strange places, in among stranger-folk who know nothing of the game.)

—There must be food, food for taking with hatani tricks. ("They're herders," Duun had said. "Herder-folk. No, little fish, not hatani, nothing like. They respect us too much to come here. That's all. They lived here once.")

(Where houses are is food, is shelter: he'll have to search, he won't know if they'd lie, these countryfolk, or hide me—Perhaps they would.)

There was a trail. There was a stink of habit here even his nose could tell, musty, old dung, the frequent passage of animals.

Thorn jogged up it. Stink to hide his stink. To confound Duun's nose. Tracks to hide his tracks. Let Duun guess. Thorn gathered speed and coursed along the trail. There was the taste of blood in his mouth.

("—They never bother anything," Duun said of farmer-folk. "They don't ask to be bothered and we don't go there.")

("Couldn't we see them, Duun-hatani? Couldn't

we go and see?") Thorn wondered if they were like the meds and Ellud; if there were—
(—O gods, if there were some like me.)
In all the wide world Duun spoke of, there must be more like him.

It was what Duun had thought. Fool! he cursed himself. Fool! To maneuver the enemy and not to see it—that was the greatest fool in the world. Scent-blind, sick with livhl, Thorn was seeking a hiding-place, seeking some place rife with scents, with smoke, with tracks and confusion. Cover himself in shonun-scent.
Thorn was going to the one place forbidden him. Change the rules. Upset the game.
Find outsiders and raise it another level still.
(Duun, what's *wrong* with me?)
(*Slick*, the infant said, rubbing at his stomach.)
Faces in the mirror.
(Duun, will my ears grow?)
Duun laid his own ears back and put on speed, risking everything now, risking shame, that a minnow might trap him.
But Thorn already had.

There was a house in the twilight—not a large house like theirs up on the mountain, but a ramshackle thing part metal and part wood. There were fences, put together the same way, of bits and pieces. *Fences*—Thorn guessed that

71

word: *fences*, Duun said, kept countryfolk cattle from the woods: and *cattle* Thorn had seen, from high on the mountaintop, white and brown dots moving across the flat in summer-haze. ("City-meat comes from those," Duun told him. And Thorn: "Can't we hunt them?" "There's no hunting them," Duun had said. "They're tame. They're stupid. They stand there to be killed. Staring at you. They trust shonunin.")

("And they *kill* them, Duun?")

White animals huddled in their pens. Lights burned near the house on a tall pole in the twilight. Thorn saw the power lines, that led from there two ways, the house, and off across the land— (The power unit's far away then. Can there be other houses near?) He skirted brush, came up nearer, where he had a closer view of the house, the dusty yard beyond its fence. Hiyi grew there, along the row, all in leaf in this season, flowerless. He heard high voices, the closing of some door. "I'll get you," someone shrilled, but there was laughter in the voice. "I'll get you, Mon!"

More shrieks. Thorn came closer, taking to the road. Beneath the lights, in front of the porch, two small figures ran and raced and played chase.

"Come in here!" a voice called from the open door. "Come in, it's time to eat."

They were children. They ran and shrieked and yelled—

Duun's kind. Thorn's heart stopped. He stood there in the road and looked beyond the fence and likewise the children stopped their game and stared, they on their side, he on his.

They were like Duun. Like him, in grayer, paler coats. With Duun-like ears, eyes, faces— with all that made up Duun.

"Aiiii!" one screamed. The other yelled. They hugged each other and yelled—to frighten him, he thought; he stood his ground, trembling at the sight. More of Duun's kind came out.

But children were like Duun. Children were not born hairless; he was not a child gone wrong, failed in growing—

—He was—

(Duun!)

He drew back. A man had run out onto the step. "Get in! Get inside!" Thorn thought it meant him, and delayed. "Ili! *Ili!* Get the gun!"

(O gods! Guns! Duun!)

He spun on his heel and ran. He heard doors slam, more than once. Heard running come toward the fence, heard voices at his back. "Gods, it's *him!*" one yelled, and others took it up. "It's that thing—*that thing!*"

It was a trap. Duun had made it. Duun had snared all his paths, all the world: there was no way, nothing, anywhere, that Duun had not seen and set up to trap him—

(Got you, minnow, got you again—)

Thorn snatched breath and left the road, darted into the undergrowth, hearing the howl of animals at his back, hearing shouts raised— "*The thing on the mountain!*— It's him, it's come!"

(O *gods*, Duun—gods—) Breath split his side. Branches tore at him. He ran and something in him had broken, ached, swelled in his throat—

They hunted him. They all did. There was no help.

No quarter.

Leaves burst into flames near him. Beamer. He heard the whine of projectiles.

Splinters burst into his face. He flung his hands up, hit a tree or some such thing: impact numbed his arm and spun him. The ground came up. He felt twigs stab his hand, earth and leaves abrade the heel of it. He scrambled to turn over and get his knees, his legs under him, eyes pouring tears; the numbed arm flopped at his side. He heard more shots whine.

"*There he is!*"

He dived and dodged and stumbled to his knees again, aware of shock. Once he had fallen from the rocks and been like this, numb from head to foot, and scared and breathless—had risen and walked and run again and known only later where he was, to find Duun gazing down at him from the high rocks.

To find Duun coming down to him, game

abandoned, to take his face in his maimed hand, jaw pinched between thumb and forefinger, and look into his eyes—

"You hear me, little fish? You hear me? *Duun!*

Thorn slipped to one knee and got up again, turned, his shoulder to rough bark. There were lights, the howl of beasts, there were shapes behind the lights, people shining lights wildly this way and that into the brush, over him.

"Get it! There it goes!"

He put the tree between them and him and ran again, left arm swinging like a dead thing at his side. (*I was hit. It was a shot that knocked me down. They shot me. Am I allowed to use my knife?*) He ran and ran, sliding on the slopes, tearing himself on brambles. (*Is this real? Is it game? Duun—Did you set this up? Am I supposed to kill? Duun, I'm scared!*)

He came down the slope, skidded at the bottom, spun on one foot and ran left along the streamcourse.

A shadow rose up in his path. He flung himself aside to escape it, but it was *there*, shonunsmelling, blocking the strike of his right arm, and a voice said: "Thorn!" before a two-fingered grip came up at his throat and spun him off-balance and crushed him in a choking hold. Thorn bent, caught one-handed at the arm and tried a throw. Sickness jolted through him to the roots of his teeth. He was pulled back and back stumbling in the leaves, and a grip twisted his wounded arm. "Get out of here!" Duun hissed into his ear. "Thorn, Thorn—it's me! Run for it! Get home!"

Duun's hand let go and shoved hard in the middle of his back. Thorn ran. He ran and slipped on leaves and ran again; his side ached. Fire shot through it. His arm ached and the pain jolted through each step.

(Get home!)

(Do I believe you, Duun—do I do what you say? Is it a trap, Duun?)

A gun cracked. Several. He heard the echo off the hills. There were shouts—there were voices, the howl of beasts.

(But Duun's back there.) Thorn stumbled to a stop, hit a tree in his blindness and leaned his back on it. His sight hazed. The pain was one vast throbbing now, beyond pain, or it had gotten to his heart. He blinked the night as clear as it would come. There were lights. There were more voices raised—shouts and cries and howls; again the discharge of a gun.

(Duun!")

Thorn began to run downslope, holding the loose arm still as he could. Branches jabbed into his face and he ducked his head aside, ran blindly, trusting the slope of the land to tell him downhill from up—fended brush finally with the right hand and let the left drag on the brambles in cold, vast shocks. He heard his breathing, felt the tearing of his chest—there was no more night, no more world: it had shrunk to body-size, all sound diminished to the sound of his breath and his heart.

(They'll kill him like the cattle! Duun!)

A branch thrust into his way, wrapped living round him, locked and held. "Thorn! Dammit— fool!"

Thorn hung there, on Duun's arm. Duun's strong grip spun him, seized him by both arms and shook him, snapping his head back.

"Fool! Where were you going?"

He could not answer. The pain came on in waves. Duun shook at him again. It was Duun. It smelled of Duun. (Scent-blind. Scent-blind fool.)

"I had to hurt someone," Duun said. It was anger. Duun shook at him. "You hear me, fool! I had to hurt someone for your sake."

"I think—I think—" Shock came on him. His jaws passed his control, locked and chattered. And Duun took him to the ground. ("How many times did they get you? Gods. Gods. I see it . . . .") He stretched him out there on the forest slope and probed the arm, while here and else-where came and went for him.

"Why?" he asked Duun. "Why did they do it?" While his jaws spasmed and chattered and the pain came and went. "Duun, were they supposed to do that?"

"Shut up," Duun said. And hurt him, whether by intent or accident. Thorn went out a moment, came back with Duun slapping gently at his face. "Can you move the fingers? I've got a gel on it. Move the fingers. Hear?"

Thorn tried. He thought they moved. He clenched his jaws, because Duun hauled him up against his shoulder and pulled him to his feet. The world went upside down as Duun's shoulder came into his groin and heaved. Pain. The arm swung. Jolting pain as Duun moved. The world went black and red, phosphenes darting in his eyes, in the dark. Branches raked his back. There was instability as Duun climbed, so that he dared not move. But the pain, the pain . . . .

There was a darkness. Duun swung him down and let him to his knees on the slope, holding onto him. Duun's breath was in his face.

"You've got to walk," Duun said. "Hear me? Hear me, Thorn? You've got to walk now." Duun got an arm about him and pulled up on him. "Walk. Hear me?"

Thorn heard. He tried. He heard Duun's gasping breaths, leaned on him, struggling for purchase on stone and earth and mold. "Climb," Duun said. "Dammit, climb!"

Howls rose behind them in the woods. They

lent Thorn strength. Duun's curses did. Duun carried him a time, and flung him down in the leaves with a jolt that knocked the breath from him. And slapped him after. "Breathe, dammit, breathe."

He tried. He gasped. And Duun lay down on him and panted. Their hearts jolted one against the other and the pain kept time with it.

Another climb. Duun had gotten him on his feet again. Thorn had no memory how. "The road's not far," Duun said. "They won't come above it. Come on."

And sitting then, sitting on a flat roadside stone where Duun set him, Duun holding him with one hand about his arms and the other against his chest. There was color in the world. It was dawn.

"Breathe. You've got to walk again."

"Yes," he said. He questioned nothing. Duun was Duun, source and force. Like the sun, the wind. He sat a moment and got up again, his heart hammering, his body swaying in the height of the world, with the treetops like black water whispering below them.

They walked. He and Duun. Duun's hand in his belt; Duun dragged his sound arm about his ribs and held it by the wrist. Going was easier on the road. Thorn's feet discovered pain, lacerations that small stones wore at. His mouth was dry as the silken dust. The wind was cold on his bare skin and Duun was warm.

Another rest. "Sit down," Duun said. "Sit down." And drew him against him and held him in his arms.

"Why did they shoot?" Thorn asked, because that answer eluded him. "Duun, why?"

"You scared them," Duun said. "They thought you'd harm them."

Scared them. Scared them. Thorn recalled the children. He shivered. Duun's arms clenched him hard.

"Fool," Duun said. He deserved it. He was ashamed.

He slept. He opened his eyes on the ceiling of the big room in the house with no memory how he had gotten from the road. He heard Duun coming and going. (Guard your sleep, minnow. Dared he sleep?)

"Drink," Duun ordered him, lifting his head, setting a cup to his lips. He turned his head away, not wanting to be twice victim. (Fool. Won't you learn?) "*Drink*, damn you, Thorn."

He blinked, all hazy. "Livhl—"

"Dammit, no. I'm telling you drink, this time."

He drank. It was sweetened tea. It hit his stomach and lay there inert and he was glad to have his head down at level again before it should come up. "I lost," he said. "You beat me, Duun."

"Be still." Duun's maimed hand brushed at his hair. (Duun holding him, Duun playing games, Duun touching him that way long, long ago.) "Meds are on their way. I called them. Hear?"

"Don't want meds." (Ellud standing in the room. An old friend, Duun said. Be polite.) "Duun, tell them don't."

"Hush. Be still." The touch came at his hair again. At his face. "Rest. Sleep. It's all right. Hear?"

(Duun in the bedroom door at night. Go to sleep, little fish. There were no black threads in the doorway. No games. Go to sleep now, minnow.)

"They'll pay for it," Ellud said. Ellud had come with the meds. The house stank of disinfectants, of bandage and gel and blood. And Thorn's distress. Duun folded his arms and gazed at the hearthstones. At dead ash. "They have to," Ellud said. "Don't they?"

There was criticism implied. Duun looked around at Ellud and stared. Ellud flinched as Ellud had done sixteen years ago. But it took longer. There was wrath in Ellud now. There was offended justice. "Anything," Duun reminded him hoarsely. "But no. Don't charge them."

"You've left me with no choice. They fired on you."

"Did they? I don't remember that."

"They called the magistrate. They confessed. They know what they did."

"So." Duun walked away toward the closed door. The medicinal smells offended his nostrils. His ears lay down. He limped. Every muscle he owned was strained. Ellud wore his city clothes, immaculate. Duun wore nothing but a small-kilt. And let the scars show. He might have worn the hatani cloak. He had left it hanging. "I'll talk to them, Ellud. No charges."

"They can't do a thing like that and get away with it—"

"Because I'm sacrosanct?" Duun turned back to him, ears flat. "You promised me anything, Ellud. I'm asking you. No charges. Deed Sheon back to them."

"They tried to kill you!"

"They damn near did. Good for them. They're not bad, for farmers. Do I have to take this on my shoulders too?"

Ellud was silent a moment. His mouth drew down.

"So you get what ought to make you happy," Duun said. "I'm coming in. I trust you'll find a place."

More long silence. "It's about time. It's about

time, Duun. I'll have a copter up here. Lift you out." ·

"He'll walk down," Duun said. "Day after tomorrow. He'll be fit."

"Past them? Gods, hasn't there been enough trouble?"

"He's hatani, Ellud." Duun met the darkness in Ellud's stare and matched it. "Understand that. He'll walk out on his own."

Thorn gained his feet after the meds left. Duun thought he would. "Sit down," Duun said, sitting himself, on one of the risers that rimmed the room. The floor sand was trampled, dotted with darkness. Thorn had bled on it, amply. Thorn hung now in the doorway with his arm slung in a cord about his neck; his skin had an ugly waxen color, excepting the arm, where blood-reddened gels plastered an incision. There would be a scar. A long one. It had missed a major nerve; so the meds said. The bone was chipped but not broken. "You've got a lot of plasm in you for blood, boy. Left most you owned down in that valley. Come sit down."

Thorn came. Duun was polishing his weapons. Thorn sank down on the riser on his knees and sat down carefully, one leg off. There was sweat on his hairless brow. His hair clung to it.

"We're going," Duun said, "to the city. We'll live there now."

"Leave here—"

Duun looked up at him. Sheon was lost. Twice now. There was darkness in his stare; and Thorn stared back at him with alien, clouded eyes, with thoughts going on, and dread. (Why did they shoot, Duun? Is this revenge? Is this against me? Was I wrong, Duun? What did I do, down there?)

"I don't want to go, Duun."

"They'll come later and gather up the things we'll want. These—" Duun polished the blade. "These we take."

"I don't want to go."

"I know that." Duun looked at him. Tears shimmered in Thorn's eyes. "The countryfolk get the land. It'll belong to them now. It'll pay, maybe, for what I had to do. Do you understand me, Thorn? Haras? Do you hear?"

"Yes, Duun-hatani."

"We'll fly out of here. We'll go to a place where the wind stinks and you won't understand a thing you see. You'll ask me your questions in private. There'll be people around us. Always. No more hunting. No more woods. Just steel. Just thousands and thousands of people. A lot of shonun like that life. You'll learn to."

Thorn bowed his head onto his arm, against

his knee. Duun was aware of him. Duun looked only at the blade, gently polished the razor steel in small strokes of an oiled cloth. Oil-smell and steel. Steel and oil. His half-hand held the cloth, the whole left hand held the blade.

"Give it away, Thorn. You're hatani. Hatani own nothing. Only the weapons, the cloak on your back. This time it's only a place you lose. When you're what you will be, you'll own nothing at all. I only used this place. You and I. It was a stage. It's gone now."

Thorn's face lifted. He had smeared his face with wiping it. His lashes were wet. "I'm sorry, Duun."

Duun's hands stopped in a long silence. Then he took up the motion again. "You lost a year, perhaps. A year here. Maybe two. Then we'd have gone, all the same. It's not much, two years. Your eyes are running. Do that tomorrow and I'll beat you. Do you hear?"

"Yes," Thorn said.

They started in the dawn: they walked slowly on the winding track and there was no anger evident in Duun. "Joiit," Duun said once, naming a birdsong. Thorn thought then that in the people-teeming place Duun described to him there could be no birds; and the sound from the woods made his heart ache. The very wind in the leaves did that. The silken feel of the dust under his sore feet. His arm ached as he walked. His head was light. They had closed up the house and walked out of the yard. And once Duun had looked back and Thorn did, just when the house was going out of view. It looked no different than it ever had when they left it in their hunting. The light was the same on the brown stone walls, with the hiyi growing here and there in lavender-edged green; all of it was from this distance, in the morning, stained and tinted like the earth. It was like every morning. The house appeared to wait for them. Would go on waiting, through the days. Someone would come, Duun said, to strip the rooms. The countryfolk would come and take it back. The children would explore the rooms, play tag in the yard—

—hunt in the woods. They would know the old tree that was good to lie on in the sun; the hollow rock that overlooked the little pond back in the hills; they would know the tracks and trails where Duun had led him—

Thorn shed no tears. When his heart hurt that much he looked away at the sky, the road, he said something, no matter what, he clenched the fingers of his wounded arm, which made it ache and took his mind away.

He did that when the bird sang. And when the wind blew in the leaves that way; and when he realized he could smell things even scent-blind as he was, like dust, and grass, and the rough-raw scent of lugh-flowers, which was strong when one bruised them, when Thorn-the-child pulled off their heads and found his hands all sticky with sap, all one flavor with the sunlight and the giddy golden blooms—

Everything came flooding in. Sights afflicted him with farewells, all along the road. And Duun was silent for the most part. (Duun was young here too. He knew the old tree, the stone—the paths—he showed them to me. I took them from him. Duun!)

The trees spread away from the road in a purpling-green flood of treetops. Beyond them the valley fell away where countryfolk lived, a pale haze of land beyond that, flat as flat: and vast sky, delirious blued violet, and streamers of cloud like pond-ice, high, high above the plain, going off into milky white.

Terror afflicted Thorn. The sky was all too large beyond the mountain. To fly, Duun said. There were machines; Duun had mentioned them. Now and again when the meds came he had seen one far away, before it went out of sight behind the mountain. Sometimes there were white trails in the sky: planes, Duun said. People fly in them.

(Where, Duun? Where do they go? Why do they go? Can they see us?" Thorn-the-child had waved at such planes, standing dizzily atop the tallest rock he could climb: "Here I am, here, here!")

(Notice me. Give me a sign you see. Here I am, are you like me? Do you see other children where you go? Have they skins like mine? And eyes like mine? And have they five fingers too?)

(Thousands and thousands of shonun in the city. Will there be some like me?)

The road wound down and down, among the trees and out of them. Far away was a sound the wind never made, that grew: machine-sound, thumping in ominous accents that always spoke of meds.

"They're coming in," Duun said. "They'll be early. Waiting for us."

The strangers came up the road to meet them. Not the meds, but others, dressed from neck to foot in blue and gray. Wearing weapons. Thorn hesitated when he saw them, but Duun kept walking, so he knew they were acceptable. "You didn't need to," Duun told them when they met. "We have orders," one of them said; that was all. Thorn stood still in the encounter at a turning of the road. They looked at him, these strangers, and they looked away, as if he had no importance, being only an appendage, Duun's. And the blue-clad folk led off, walking down again, with one of them behind them, another by Duun's side.

The mountain stopped being theirs then. Strangers owned it. Strangers came to get in the way of their last moments with it, his and Duun's. He knew why Duun wanted them away. But Duun would not tell them no, and walked without looking at things like trees and stones, as Duun had looked about him before they came. Without talking to him. Duun was bitter. Duun hurt. Thorn knew it. (My fault. My doing. All of it. They should take me and go away and Duun would still have his mountain.) But no one offered Thorn that choice. Perhaps it did not exist.

Down and down, the last little distance to the flat, around the last turning of the road.

A machine sat in the meadow; it had huge blades. It had flattened a circle all around itself in the milky green grass. There were broad dusty roads that met there, and people stood there at that crossing, far removed.

"We've kept them off," said a man who had not spoken before. Only not a man like the Duun, like Ellud, like the meds. This one was broader-hipped, walked differently, had a quiet, smaller voice. *Woman*, Thorn thought, hearing that, and his heart picked up its beats.

("Women are," Duun had told him, when he was small, "us and different.")

("How different?" Thorn asked.)

("Inside. Outside, in some things. They have

a place inside they make babies. Men put them there; women make them.")

("How? child-Thorn asked. "*That* does it," Duun said, and showed him what this was. "I haven't got that," Thorn had said, looking at himself. "Duun, I haven't got that. Mine's all outside.")

("You're different," Duun had said.)

("Am I a woman?")

("No," Duun said. "You're a child. You're going to be a man.")

("How do women make babies?")

Duun had not answered then. Or he had forgotten. Thorn knew the answer later. ("See this," Duun had said. Showed him the young inside a deiggen Thorn had killed. "They're babies. You ought not to kill the does. See the eartips. Don't hunt that kind.")

Thorn remembered that. But he had gotten a deiggen-baby out of its womb and laid it out on a flat rock to see it. It was not the death he remembered strongest, or the blood. It was that it had had no hair, was naked-skinned like him.

(I was born and grew wrong. They got me out too soon.)

He watched the foenin mate. (*That's* how? He was appalled and interested at once in the black bodies one on the other's back, the curi-

91

ous spasms they made as if one of them were sick.)

("Shonun do it face to face, usually," Duun said. Thorn was twice appalled. It was odd enough to do from the rear. Having someone watching back right in one's face—)

This—woman—had a gun on her hip. She swayed when she walked. She had a bright white crest but she had shaved it far back as did all the cityfolk, not like Duun's, which was black and long and swung freely when he walked.

Thorn thought of the foenin. Clenched his hand to drive that thought away. He had made enough difficulty for Duun. It was not spring. It was not appropriate. There was something about smell, but Duun refused to discuss this with him.

They walked out onto the flat toward the machine and foenin blurred in the waft of oil and warm metal. The copter. They would go up in the air in that. It looked too heavy. Thorn forgot about women. His heart began to beat in terror. (Fool, he told himself. Duun had warned him. The thing had gotten here, it would get away again with them inside. He would not be afraid in front of strangers. He would not stink of fear where others not scent-blind could smell it. He would not shame Duun. *I will beat you,* Duun had said, to get his attention; now Thorn

remembered that and knew why Duun had
threatened him. Not to be shamed by him. He
would not flinch when they led him in.)

It was the countryfolk Duun watched, the
spectators the guards had kept far off on the
other road. He kept his ears aslant, shutting out
what words the wind might bring him. He
smelled the scent of them even at this range.
His mind painted him hate; and fear. He was a
fool to shut down his hearing; one of them
might have brought a gun.

But they had called the magistrate and turned
themselves in. In fear, he thought bitterly, of
more general retribution. In responsibility, late-
arrived. Sixteen years they had waited, in the
hope of Sheon's land.

(So it's yours. Enjoy it. And be damned.)

He was ashamed of the thought. He had come
here for virtue and took away—

—took away this shadow at his side. And the
cold stares of those who had seen a hatani
bend his vows. Who had lived for sixteen years
in fear of what happened on the mountain they
coveted.

Well, well. It was not a mistake, perhaps.
Duun looked toward the copter, exchanged
perfunctory courtesy with the guard-captain,
snagged Thorn with a gentle clawtip on his
inner arm. "Come on," Duun said looking at

the captain. (Be done with it. Don't draw it out. Get us out of here.)

Thorn walked by him, lifted his head to wonder at the blades—Duun hit him in the back. "Fool, keep your head low beneath these things!" Thorn ducked and went; but the rotor was only lazily turning now. Not even enough for wind.

Up the steps then, to a metal world, to plastic seats, the smell of oil and fuel. Duun settled Thorn—"There, that's the buckle. Push, that's right. That lets it loose. That tightens it. Keep it on." He looked Thorn in the eyes, which no one else would meet, and saw stark terror there. Duun frowned and worked his way past Thorn to his own seat to buckle in.

The crew took places. The guards climbed aboard aft, making the craft rock on its runners. The pilot brought the engines up—whup, whup, whup! Thorn looked toward the side window, looked ahead, looked his way. Duun reached over the shared armrest and gripped his arm, once, sharply, with the claws all the way out. (Behave!)

Thorn settled then. And the whup-whup-whup grew louder, the aircraft tilting as it lifted, tilted and swung its tail about as the country-folk ran in the dust the blades kicked up.

Wh-wh-wh—! Sky in one view, ground in the other. He gave a look at Thorn, saw the cords in Thorn's neck stand out as he braced himself. Another grip of claws. Thorn visibly relaxed. Turned his face to Duun's with studied serenity.

So. Duun slipped his finger down Thorn's arm, to the place on Thorn's wrist where veins lay next the surface. The pulse throbbed beneath his finger-pad as if the heart that drove it was going to burst.

"Keep your eyes on the horizon," Duun said into Thorn's ear. "Helps your stomach."

"I'm not scared," Thorn shouted back. But the copter turned off for the west then, sharply, and Thorn's fingers clenched on his armrest.

The great flat, more hills, an hour and more of trees and roads and herds that raced beneath them in a brown tide. Suddenly the great sheet of a bay spread itself beyond a brown rim of trees, water shining silver in the sun and going on forever to the south. Thorn forgot his terror and pointed—"What's that?"

"Djohin Bay," Duun shouted back. "That's the sea out there, minnow! That's the great wide sea!"

Land came up eastward beyond that shining surface: outthrusts of the city, a stain against the sky. "What's there?" Thorn yelled into the rotor noise.

"That's Pekenan," Duun said. "That's the port town. The city's coming up. There—that's the shuttle-port, see that gray ribbon there."

"What's a shuttle-port?" Thorn asked. "What's a port town?" His skin was white in the sunlight that streamed through the copter's side windows. He sweated. It was too soon to have traveled. Sights and strangeness multiplied. (Don't faint on me, minnow, not here, not now. There's more.) "Here." Duun fished out an inhaler from the kit at his feet. He had brought it with their gear. "Put that in your mouth— Breathe in hard." He pushed the spray and Thorn choked, coughed. Fell back against the seat with a shocked offended look. But he lost the waxen taint. His pupils dilated. "There. Want more?"

"No, Duun," Thorn said earnestly. He turned and looked out the window.

Duun had little desire to look. He knew what he would see. The capital. Dsonan. The tall buildings where shonunin lived one on top of the other.

"Look at those!" Thorn cried suddenly, pointing at the city-center.

"I've seen them, minnow." Tall buildings failed to interest him. "We're going to land on one. We're going to live there. Inside." To explain more than that took too much shouting. The rotor noise depressed him. He remembered the perspective of the concrete canyons, the buildings passing under them. He took Thorn by the wrist and held his finger on the pulse.

Thorn looked at him, knowing what he was doing, looking as if he were vastly ashamed of a heart he could not control. "Look down," Duun said as they began to fly over the city. "Get used to it."

Thorn did not flinch. The pulse sped as the perspectives shifted beneath them. ("What's that?" Thorn asked, when a train whisked below them.) What's that? Duun had not wanted questions yet. There would have been time. The pulse fluttered beneath his fingertip with unbearable rapidity. "Are we coming down?"

"They never miss," Duun said. "Watch the roof, minnow. See the circle there. That's where we land."

VI

The window gave them a brook, a woodland. Duun cared nothing for it. The wind from the air-conditioning brought wood-scent. It was, like the opal sand on the floor, synthetic and expensive. Thorn marveled at it, touched the window—"Are we turning?"—because the scene moved. "No," Duun said with acerbity. "Have you forgotten? There's city behind that wall. Behave yourself. You don't own this. I don't. It's all here, that's all. Don't be impressed with it.

("Whose is it?")

Duun regretted then bringing up the matter.

And perhaps Thorn suspected then that he had been in the company of more than one illusion maintained for him. Thorn's ebullience ebbed away and left a look of pain, the fine-drawn look of someone scant of resources. The lack of sleep for days, the purgative, the hunt, the wounds; a heart which had worked harder than the engines had in the copter flight—which had had, perhaps, all a heart ought to bear for a while. Duun went into his room, delved into his kit and took out a sedative, went into the kitchen and mixed it in milk.

The apartment was larger than the house had been. There were four bedrooms, the kitchen, a sitting room, dining hall, office, bath, gymnasium, sunroom (a lie); there was a library; a viewing-room; a sauna; a robing-room; a pantry; a laundry; a servant's quarters, but that was vacant. A security post. That was not. But Thorn knew nothing about guards and monitors and the hall outside. There were several rooms that feigned sunlight well enough to have growing plants, if one bothered. The bath and master bedroom had a wraparound tridee screen that doubled as windows—gods knew, it was not all nature scenes the builders meant with that. And a man grew tempted. There were recourses in the city. There were places a man or woman could go, amusements to be had. A hatani would be discreet. But even a hatani might—with a woman of discretion—find some out-of-season comforts. Duun laid his ears back. Hours in this place and it was as if sixteen years had not happened. Except for the presence which turned up at his shoulder.

He turned and handed Thorn the cup. "This is yours. Drink it. Go lie down."

Thorn took it. Perhaps Thorn was not quite that scent-blind. His eyes acquired wariness. And weary puzzlement.

"Sedative," Duun said. "Drink it. Go lie down. You'll sleep."

"Duun." Thorn set the milk on the counter. His face was white again. He leaned against the wall, not so strong as he pretended; he had been limping when he came in. "Have you been here before?"

"I lived here." Duun picked up the milk and picked up Thorn's hand and joined one firmly to the other. "Drink that. Shall I convince you, Thorn?"

Thorn drank it. All. He set the cup down again.

"So you've found out what you don't know," Duun said. "Does the world scare you, Thorn? You have to pick out the illusions here, that's all. You have to know what's real and what's not."

"You'll be with me."

"Haras-hatani. Thorn. What do I hear? Is that

100

need? Is that something I have and you don't? What is that thing?''

"Courage." Thorn's voice was hoarse and hollow.

"Do I hear can't?"

"No, Duun-hatani."

"The meds want you. They want to take you and take that arm apart again; they want to put their machines on you and get pieces of your hide and measure you up and down. I told them to wait a day or so."

Silence. Thorn's eyes were dilated. It was not all the sedative. "Thank you, Duun-hatani."

"Get to bed."

Thorn went. Limping.

So. So. There was no rebellion. Thorn might have. Duun stared out the vacant kitchen door. The place smelled of remodeling, beneath the wood-scent. Beneath the false wind and the false images. And the sand under his stone-callused feet felt too light, like powder.

He walked into the bedroom and found Thorn in bed. It was night. Duun's senses knew that, though the wall-images were out of synch and showed mid-afternoon. Thorn slept, the pale blue sheets clutched in a brown, smooth hand. The face had taken on a hollowed look, the jaw lengthened, the cheekbones more prominent.

Final changes. Almost-manhood.

Duun selected for night-image. The lights went

out and a dust of stars shone on the walls, about the sleeper. The air-conditioning breathed a noncommittal scent, something synthetic and vaguely like the sea.

"Well, Duun?"

Duun tucked up his feet cross-legged on the riser (city manners came hard after sixteen years), rested his arms on his thighs and let his hands fall limp into his lap. (Well?) He looked up at Ellud, who sat on his desk, surrounded by the appurtenances of office, monitor, communications. Worm-in-web. Lines went everywhere from here, all over the world. "He's well," Duun said. "I don't think there was damage. A scar or two—what's that?"

Ellud looked at him; Duun looked back with a forever-twisted smile. It was humor and Ellud seemed finally to decide it was and not to like it. "The deed's been settled. The countryfolk are abjectly grateful. The matter is closed."

"Good."

"I'm fending queries off your neck, Duun. You know that."

"I know. They'll keep their hands off him. Tell them all that. He'd never seen a copter. He can run all the household things, well, the dishwasher he'd not seen. He's what I am. I told you that. The meds will respect him. Or I'll deal with them. No. *He* will. I'll give him leave."

"I wouldn't advise that."

"He's hatani, Ellud."

"A handful of farmers damn near killed him. For the gods' sweet sake, man, they'd have killed him! What were you doing about it?"

"Running. They almost killed me, you know. A half dozen men with guns aren't to disregard. I didn't teach a fool. And they surprised him. Not with the guns. With their reaction. They're lucky he ran. They're very lucky. Even with the guns. You can tell your staff that."

"They won't provoke him."

"They're not to talk to him. That rule still holds. Please, thank you, and sit down. Breathe in, breathe out. No comments. Nothing. And respect. They'll respect him. I do mean that."

Ellud drew a long, long breath and let it go. "How mature is he?"

"Very—in some ways. Not at all in others. I'm telling you: no one talks to him."

"For how long?"

"As long as it takes."

"They want to use the tapes."

Duun frowned. "Give me a little time with that. I'll say when."

"You've had sixteen years!"

"So has he. Who knows what he needs? I want your meds away from me, Ellud. Or I find another place. Somewhere the other side of the world if I have to."

"As long as it takes, is it?"

"That's the way."

"All right. I'll keep them off your neck. I'll talk to staff. Maybe you should get some rest. Have the meds check you too."

"That's not what I need."

"What is?"

"Is Dogossen still around?"

A silence. "She moved to Rogot, a husband. Second, now."

The years caught up to him, all in one dull ache. "Well. Hounai? Same?"

"You want a woman, Duun? I'll ask around on the staff. Maybe—"

"No hatani." He looked down, studied the patterns of his hands, whole and half. "I don't want a hatani. Nothing like. It's been a long time."

"I hope to the gods it has."

Duun looked up. It had been half a joke. Ellud's ears drew back and lay down tighter to his skull under Duun's stare. "Believe me," Duun said. "*Hire* someone. I don't want conversation. By the gods I don't want another wife. Let's keep it business. Not a staffer either. Someone at the port. Let security worry itself."

"I'm not your—"

"Call it friendship." Duun's voice was rough and hoarse. His hands clenched and unclenched when he knew it. And Ellud's ears lay back.

Ellud went on looking at him as if Ellud wished to look away.

"Duun-hatani—" Carefully. With fear and offended sensibilities and prudent questions boiling in him Ellud would never ask. Like harm. And solitude. And sanity. The silence stayed there a long, long time.

"I'll want staffers too," Duun said. (So what have you done, Ellud no Hsoin? What do you dread? Violence? Old friend—what do you expect?) "Good ones. Young ones who know how to take orders."

"That's a contradiction in terms." Ellud's laughter was hasty as if he much wanted to laugh, to turn matters elsewhere. To be light with him. But the laughter died. "How many?"

"Four, five. Male and female. I'll let you do the picking. He's got to learn people. They can be older. Say—twenty, twenty-five. They'd better to the gods be stable. You understand."

A long silence. "I want those tapes started."

"You've forgotten," Duun said softly. "This is your office. But you don't control things. I do. Old friend. I'm not your backwoods employee come to the big city. I'm not one of your staffers."

"They're putting pressure on me, Duun."

"They."

"The council."

Duun drew a deep breath. Shut his eyes and thought again of the woods.

"Duun."

His eyes opened. Ellud sat there as if frozen. "They don't run this either," Duun said. "Sixteen years. Memories are short."

"Two members have died. Rothon and—"

"I know. I read all the news out there. What do you think I was doing? I know who's in and I know what they can do; and that's too bad: they dealt with a hatani. They can't undo that."

"Duun—they might try to kill you. Even that."

Duun laughed.

"Politics," Ellud said. "They'd be fools to try, but politics has made fools before. Don't take it lightly, Duun. That's my guard at your door. You'd better thank the gods it is. And the woman will be from my staff. I'd feel better. Be polite, Duun-hatani. Some of these young fools worship you."

He laid his ears down. "Dammit, Ellud."

"You want to work off something else than that, Duun-hatani?"

"Rescue me from fools."

"I'm trying to. From one I used to love, Duun."

Duun stayed still a long, long time. Grinned finally, and felt the scar pull at his mouth. Laughed once shortly; Ellud looked alarmed. "Gods," Duun said, "I'm drowning, and someone has a rope."

Ellud looked the more disturbed. His eyes showed whites.

"I own the world," Duun said. "Women don't see my scars, my charge adores me, and my last friend calls me a fool." He laughed again, flung his feet down to the sand and stood up. "I cherish that," he said. And left.

Young muscles strained, knotting and stretching under a hairless, sweat-drenched back: the arm held, and Thorn hauled himself upward on the exercise bar, up and down, up and down. Duun walked up on this in the gymnasium, walked up quietly on the well-trampled, sweat-pocked sand and stood there with arms folded a while. Finally Thorn's efforts flagged, became an upward struggle. In perverse humor Duun landed a swat on a vulnerable backside, claws out, and Thorn flinched and made the lift, then dropped, turning in the movement. Gasping then for breath, but bright-eyed with the morning and his health. Duun pursed his mouth. "Not sore, is it?"

"No." And a little wariness crept in. Duun studied him. Thinking. Thorn had gotten easy; and now Duun was thinking, and looking at him that way, and that was cause enough for wariness. There was a great deal in this place where things went on behind the walls, where Thorn waked to find himself adrift in the night sky, and stifled a scream which would have brought Duun's swift disgust. So Thorn turned on the stars each night himself, and walked dizzily to his bed, and flung himself down and made himself look up, about, lying wide-limbed as he had lain on a summer hillside, undefended against the sky that slowly turned. He remembered how it felt to fly. Remembered the land turning giddily under his sight, and the shifts of weight, the falling-feeling amplified by height enough to turn cattle into insects and valleys into folds of cloth. And the dark and the stars took him and whirled him until that flying sensation was back, and he lay there deliberately, overcoming his fear, and going to sleep with it. Some fears Duun set into him for a reason; at this one Duun would laugh, Thorn felt that this was so—and Duun's scorn was worse that the heights, worse than any falling. He hoped now for Duun's approval . . . the quickly hooded glance, the tightening of the mouth—for such small things he worked, but they had meaning. The slap that stung— that was a joke; Duun joked with him, and dared him, and that meant—meant perhaps an end to Duun's restraint with him—Duun's pity. Duun's —(he felt)—disgust with this place and what had brought him to it. (Forgive me, Duun-hatani. Forgive me for all of it. For us being here. For me being helpless and dis-appointing, and, gods—don't be angry, Duun.)

Duun poked him in the belly. Hard. Thorn withstood that. He centered himself, expect-ing—some sudden move. A blow that could take his head off. Because Duun knew he could turn it. Thorn thought of that. Suddenly he was not thinking of the blow; timing-sense deserted him and he shivered, flinched, knowing it. And Duun saw that too.

"Where's the mind, Haras?"

Thorn centered himself again. Duun walked around behind him. Thorn's ears strained. He listened to the soft sound of Duun's tread on sand. His own rapid breathing dimmed his hear-ing and endangered him. He did not move un-til he heard Duun on his left, then turned his head, pursuing the movement which teased the tail of his eye.

Slowly Duun extended his right hand toward Thorn's face—(Attack?) Thorn's heart jumped and in a critical moment the hand had passed his reaction-point and he let it, let Duun touch his jaw. A two-fingered grip settled gently on either side, where no one's hand belonged but his teacher's, but the slow-moving hand too quick for him if he should move. He was vul-nerable to that. He knew it. He cherished it. When Duun discovered weaknesses in him he attacked them, but this was the allowable one, this one was his safety that kept the games all games. Duun never took that away. Duun's dark eyes were on a level with his own, poured force into him, like the dark of night, like the dark and all the stars in which he whirled and perished.

"What is your need, Haras-hatani?"

(O gods, Duun—don't.)

"What is your need, Haras-Thorn? Why did I get through your guard? To what are you vulnerable? Name me that thing."

"You, Duun-hatani. I need you."

The grip hurt. Bruised. "What am I to you, minnow?"

Words failed him. The grip grew harder. Gentler then. The eyes shifted, let him go and he could blink. Duun drew his hand back and Thorn was shaking.

"You understand what I did to you, minnow? You understand how easy it was? Do you think I could do it again?

(Duun holding him by the fire, Duun touching him, all the warmth there was. Not to be touched again. Not ever to allow that to Duun or anyone—) Tears stung Thorn's eyes. (Your eyes are running. Do that tomorrow and I'll beat you.) "Yes," Thorn said. His chest ached. "Yes, Duun-hatani. Right now you could."

Duun's eyes on his. Dark and deep and cold as the artificial night. A second time Duun's hand lifted. (I'll hurt you this time, Thorn.) Thorn lifted his hand ever so slowly and opposed it. Duun seemed satisfied. Walked around him again and the skin of Thorn's back crawled. His buttocks tensed. Once more to the side and in front of him.

Like a lizard-strike this time. Thorn flung up his hand and palm hit palm with a slap that echoed. No force then. No pushing, from either side. Duun signed with his other hand. Thorn accepted it, maintained wariness while Duun disengaged his hand and put it behind him.

Inviting a strike. (Try me, fledgling.)

"I'm not a fool, Duun-hatani."

"You're less one than you were," Meaning the matter of the farmers, Thorn thought. It was all in these days Duun had ever hinted on the matter.

"I'm not ready, Duun-hatani."

"The world doesn't always ask if you're ready, Haras. It's not likely to." Duun set his hands in his belt. "You're going to have other teachers. Oh, I'll be here. For now. But there'll be others. Other young people. They're not hatani. They know you are."

(People like me, Duun? Are any like me?) But the question hung in his throat. ("What do you need, Haras-hatani?") It was deadly. It opened him up in ways he knew better than to confess. "When?" he asked. (Duun, I don't *want* other teachers.)

(*Want,* minnow? Do I hear *want?*)

"Tomorrow. Mind, don't show off. You'll be better in some ways, worse in others. You're good in math; you'll learn to work new ways—not in your head, this time. On machines. They're not hatani. If you hit one of them you'd kill him. Do you understand that? Your reactions are too quick. And they don't know how to stop you. So your reactions have to be quicker. To keep from reacting at all— Do you understand that? Lay down the knife. Lay it down when you're with these people. Let yourself be open. So. Stand still." A third time Duun reached toward his face. Thorn's hand lifted—stopped in indecision. (Trick? Or what he means?) He let Duun touch his jaw, let the touch trail down and beneath it. "That's good," Duun said. And drew the hand back again. "Remember that. They're like that. None of them could stop you. None of them would have a chance. None of them know how to stand, how to move. They won't touch you. That's the one thing they'll understand. Even if they forget that— don't react. Understand, Thorn?"

VII

They were five: Elanhen, a youth whose back had black tipping on the gray, broad of shoulder, with a wary eye turned to the world and a diffident and ready grin; he was first and easiest in his manner (wisest, Thorn thought: the manner is all he gives the world, he keeps all the rest reserved.) There was Cloen, a smallish fellow whose belly-fur had dapples—("Don't remark on it," Duun warned Thorn in advance when Duun described Cloen that way. "His baby-mark's still with him.") And Cloen was least outgoing, and quickest to frown. (He has a wound, Thorn thought; it bleeds into the water. Cloen would be an easy mark. If I were after him.)

And Sphitti, lank, unkempt Sphitti. They called him that, which was a kind of weed (like Thorn). Sphitti would sit and think and think and he hardly talked.

Lastly there was Betan—who was female; who moved with a wide-hipped stride, whose grin was sudden and whose wit was quicker than the rest. Betan *smelled* different. Betan wrinkled her nose at him and grinned in a way no one had ever looked at him, which frightened him. (Confidence. She *knows* things. She knows things I don't and knows she knows and she knows she can take me.) If Duun had looked that way at him and laughed inside like that Thorn would have gone cold to the soles of his feet. He would have eaten nothing and drunk nothing Duun could have dreamed of touching and not dared sleep in his bed. That a stranger looked at him this way was devastating. He stood staring back the first time that they met and put on his most frozen, expressionless face.

(They don't have the moves, Duun had insisted. But Duun had lied before.)

They met, all five of them, in a room Duun took him to, on a floor above the floor where they lived. "Go inside," Duun said, and under the eyes of a watcher at the door, made to leave him, which prospect alone filled Thorn with panic. "Mind your manners." Duun did not say, mind what I told you. It was what Duun did not say that always weighed heaviest. Thorn was expected to remember those things without being told. "Yes, Duun," Thorn had said, and committed himself on his own, as the watcher opened the door to let him in. The touch of Duun's hand in the middle of his back was a dismissal, not a shove.

Four strangers got up off their seats when he passed the foyer, four strangers whose commingled scent was artifice and flowers, in a white-sanded room as large as the gymnasium: it had five desks; and the windows in this white sterility showed a thicket like Sheon's woods, a tangle for eye and mind. He would smell of fear to them. He stopped still. "Hello," said the one he discovered as Elanhen. "Hello," Thorn said, and put the best face on he could, a face he had seen in Duun when he met the meds. "I'm Haras." Haras he was to outsiders, his hatani-name. They told theirs. That was how it started. "We're a study-group," Elanhen said. "They say you're good."

He might have been furred as they were, four-fingered, with ears and eyes like theirs. (I'm different. They shot at me at Sheon. Aren't you shocked, the least bit?) But no one affected to notice.

(Duun, Thorn thought, Duun knows them.

Duun set this up. Duun arranged it, all.) He felt
the walls of a trap about him. He let them
invite him to the desk that was to be his and
show him the computer. "You have to catch up
with us," Elanhen said. "Sit down, Haras-hatani."

He did. He took the keyboard onto his lap
and tried. He had trouble with the keys, but
not with the math. He fouled the machine once
and he was ashamed, looked up at Sphitti,
thinking to meet scorn.

"Try again," Sphitti said. "From the beginning." Without rancor.

The others watched him. Thorn centered his
mind, recalled Sphitti's instructions and got it
right this time.

"That's good," Betan said, and Thorn looked
guardedly her way. *Good* was not that easy a
word to win. He suspected humor at his expense. (What are they up to, when will it come?
What game are they playing?)

He tried not to make mistakes. He listened to
things and remembered them.

Duun did not mention the matter of the school
that day or the next. (When will he move?)
Thorn slept lightly, feared his food and ate with
attention to taste. (He won't warn me the next
time. He won't. He'll move. How? And when?)
A panic had settled on him, a sense of things
slipping away from him, the chance that Duun

himself might go, now that there were so many others to take care of him.

(What is your need, Haras-hatani?)

He might wake one morning and find Duun gone, only because Duun knew how desperately he needed him, and needing him was wrong.

Perhaps Duun was waiting for something. (For me to attack *him*, for me to start it this time . . . .) But Thorn would lose. Events had proved that. And he nursed a more dreadful suspicion: that if he did not he would lose all the same—for Duun would not abide defeat. Duun would go. He would be alone finally, utterly alone, among all the meds and the strangers they foisted off on him. So he wished only to hold his own. Forever. And not to displease Duun, which seemed mutually impossible.

He played the dkin for Duun. He sat on the riser. ("We're in the city now," Duun said, "and cityfolk don't use the floor except to walk on." It seemed unreasonable to Thorn. He liked the warmth of the sand and the ability to shape himself a place in it. But Duun said; and he did as he was told.) He played the songs he knew. Duun played him others. This had not changed, and it soothed him and made Duun smile.

I one day wandered down a road
that I had never known;
I one day came upon a path
that I was never shown.
It wended up and down the hills
And wandered through the dell,
And there I met a clever man
Whose like no song can tell.
I never met a man his like:
I never hope to say
How he was like and unlike me,
This man I met that day.
He had my look, he had my eyes,
He had my ways, for true.
Why, fool, he said, and sang the song
That I've just sung to you.

Thorn laughed when Duun had sung it. Duun smiled and adjusted a string. "Let me have it," Thorn said.

"Ah, there's no revenge. My repertoire is endless." The scarred lip twisted. It did that in such a smile. "Damn." The string had snapped. Thorn winced. "It's old," Duun said. "Quite old. I'll get another tomorrow." Duun gave the dkin to him to put away, and Thorn took the instrument and put it carefully in its case. "Get some sleep," Duun said.

"Yes," he said. And turned, again, on his knees on the riser, for Duun had gotten up and come up behind him, and Thorn was wary of that. He looked up. Duun stared at him a long moment and turned and walked away. The silence left Thorn cold. He snapped the case shut.

(He was thinking something. He was planning something. He meant me to know. Gods, what?)

Duun stopped in the doorway that led back to the other rooms. Looked back again. Walked on.

(Waiting for me to do—what?)

(Does Duun ever do anything without a reason? Does he ever make the least move without a reason?)

(I'm scared of those people. Does he know?)

A confusion of white light and white sand— the gymnasium spun and the sand met Thorn's back: he rolled and came up on his feet with lights exploding in his eyes.

"Again," Duun said.

Thorn's left knee buckled and went out from under him. He landed on his knees in shock, feeling the abrasions. The skid had cost his shoulders too. Sweat stung there. He knelt there and lifted a hand to signal a wait till the daze should pass.

Duun walked over and took his face between

his hands, pulled his eyelids back to face the light, felt over his skull.

"Again," Thorn said. Duun shoved his head free with a force that rocked him, cuffed his ear and backed off.

Thorn got to his feet and stood there wide-legged and wobbling.

"So you haven't learned it all, minnow. Slow, this time. Step by step again."

Thorn came, reached out his hand in the slow dance Duun wanted, turned and turned and ended up again in the way of Duun's slow-moving arm.

"That's how. Do it, minnow."

There was a counter for it. It arrived against Thorn's ribs in slow-motion and he evaded the feigned force of it. Sweat flew from him and spattered the sand, flung from his hair as he snaked his body back. Duun faced him, hands on knees. Duun did not sweat. His tongue lolled at times, his mouth open and showing his sharp teeth. But it flicked and licked the saliva clear. Duun bent now and invited attack. "Keep it slow, Thorn. I've still got tricks."

Thorn had thought he knew them. The light that danced in Duun's eyes alarmed him. He had never seen Duun extend himself against him. Not truly. He understood that now.

Duun's hand flicked out and touched him on

the cheek when he came in. "You're dead. *Dead*, Haras-hatani."

Thorn wiped his face. His centering was gone. He recovered it. (Don't be bluffed. Turn off the fear. Turn it *off*, minnow.)

Duun got a grip on him. Bent him back, holding him from falling. Duun let him go; but Thorn rescued himself from that shame with a tumble up again, sand coating his sweating skin.

Duun turned his back on him and walked off.

"Duun. Duun-hatani." His face burned.

Duun turned. "You don't have to say *can't*. You *are* that thing. The world doesn't wait for your moods, minnow."

"Try me!"

Duun came back and laid him straightway breathless on the sand, then stood looking at him. "Well, it wasn't *can't* that threw you that time. Did I promise you a miracle?"

Thorn rolled over and tried to cut Duun's ankles from under him.

Thorn ended on his belly this time, spitting the sand that glued itself to his face and hands and body; Duun's knee was in his back, his arm twisted painfully. Duun let him up and sat down on the sand.

(Invitation?) But Duun held up his hand. "No." Duun said, "not wise." Thorn knew where that attack would have taken him—into Duun's grip when he refused to go sailing over Duun and halfway to the wall. And Duun's teeth at his throat. Never grapple, Duun had hammered home to him. Nature shorted you, not me. And Duun had grinned at him that day to make the point.

Thorn tucked his knees up and locked his arms about them, panting. Sweat ran into his eyes and he wiped a gritty hand across his brow, flexed the fingers and held them out.

"You're pulling your claws, Duun-hatani." Pain welled up and hurt his chest and it was not all the pain of several meetings with the floor. "You'd have me in tatters. You'd tear my throat out. Anybody normal—would."

"Eyes," Duun reminded him, with a touch at his own brow-shadowed eye. "That's worst. You let me at your face. Never."

"I'm sorry, Duun."

"You wouldn't be sorry. You'd be blind. Damn right I pull it. You do that again I'll scar you. Hear?"

Thorn rocked his body in something like a bow. He hurt. His bones ached as if they had all been reseated.

"Yes, Duun."

"But as for the claws—they might take you if they could touch you. If you were a fool. I'm very good, Thorn. Doesn't that tell you something?"

Thorn paused a long time. The ache got into his throat and stuck there, embarrassing him. "That I might be."

"Did you touch me?"

"No, Duun-hatani."

"Do I hear *can't* now?"

"No, Duun-hatani."

"The outsiders have gotten into your head. Their moves have infected you. Do you let them touch you?"

"They touch each other. Not me."

"They touch you—here." Duun touched his brow. "You lose your focus. Youth, Thorn. Give that up too."

Thorn drew another painful breath. (They're yours. Aren't they? A hatani dictates the moves others make . . . . Duun-hatani.) "What can they teach me you can't?"

"What is ordinary. What the world is."

(The world is wide, minnow.)

"Duun—they act like I was nothing unusual."

Duun shrugged.

"They're lying, aren't they?"

"What does your judgment tell you?"

"They're lying. They're pretending. You sent them. You're in control of all of it."

"Tkkssss. You have a suspicious mind, Haras-hatani."

"You've always been. Is that close enough to beating you? *No one's* like me. There aren't

any. I'm different. And they're so busy not noticing it they shout it. Why, Duun?"

"You build bridges in the sky."

"On rock. On what I see and don't see."
Thorn's muscles began to shake; he clenched
his arms about his knees the harder and tried
not to show the shivering, but Duun would see.
Duun missed nothing. "What's wrong with me?
How did I turn out this way?"

"Doubtless the gods did it."

The blasphemy shocked him, from Duun. He
piled one atop it. "The gods have a sense of
humor?"

Duun's ears went back. "We'll talk about it
later."

"You'll never give me my answer. Will you?"

A long silence. Yes and no trembled on a
knife's edge. For the first time Thorn felt Duun
was close to answering him and a breath might
tip the balance. He held that breath till his
sides ached.

"No," Duun said then. "Not yet."

"He's intelligent," Ellud admitted. Duun
clasped his crossed ankles and returned a stolid
stare. "Did I say not?" Duun asked. "What else
do your young agents say?"

Ellud laid back his ears. "I handed them over
to you."

"Come, Ellud. How many sides do you face at once?"

Ellud shifted uncomfortably on his desk. "I'm fending rocks, Duun; you know that."

"I know that. I want to know who you're talking to."

"The council. The council wants to talk to him."

"No."

"You say no. They get no from you and come to my back door. I'm getting supply shortages; I'm getting delivery delays; I'm getting records lost."

"Not coincidence."

"Not at this rate," Ellud said. Duun drew a deep breath and straightened his back; Ellud held up a hand. "I'll take care of it, Duun. I'd have come to you if I couldn't."

"How does Tshon report me?"

Ellud's mouth dropped. "Duun—"

"I'm not offended. How does she report me?"

"I—told Council you're quite stable. Her report was an advantage. To both of us."

Duun smiled. With all the horror that expression had for the beholder; and he was always, with Ellud, aware of it. "I sent council a letter. If they want a hatani sanction individually and singly—let them forget their contract. The government made it. They've got it to my dying day."

"Or his."

"Are you telling me something, Ellud?"

"I don't remember telling you anything. I'd have to swear I didn't."

Few things disturbed Duun's centering. This was one. Ellud grew very still, hands loose in his lap, for a long while staring at that stare.

"If there were to be an accident," Duun said.

"I don't know how it would come. He's hatani, you said. He wouldn't be easy. Duun—you have to understand. It's not just council; it's public pressure: the matter at Sheon—got out."

Duun said nothing and Ellud lifted a modifying hand, sketched diffident explanation. "They called the magistrates, the magistrates called the province head—back when they thought they'd run afoul of the Guild, when they thought they'd hatani troubles up to their armpits—well, the matter got blown up larger: a few offices got onto it, and a few wealthy landholders at some dinner party— Well, a note went out to political interest here. And Rothen's successor—"

"Shbit."

"Shbit! Exactly. Wants to play politics. On the issue the whole thing's gone sour." Ellud made a helpless motion. "Duun, hard as it is to think anyone could be shortsighted enough—"

"I don't find it hard at all. "I have a very fine appreciation of venality. And stupidity. Tomorrow doesn't come and a stone cast up doesn't come down. For a renunciate, I'm a very practical man, Ellud. You should remember that."

"I remember." In a small, hoarse voice. "Duun, for the gods' own sake—they're trying to get between you and the Guilds. You know that's how they'll work. They're trying to slow my office down with their paper-delays. They want documentation of malfeasance. I'm making duplicates of everything. I've got them in a packet in hands that will get them to the Guild—if—anything should happen."

"Wise."

"People are frightened, Duun."

"Go on guarding the back door. I'll take care of the front. I will."

"For the gods' sakes—"

Duun gave him a cold stare. "Calling on Shbit would solve it."

"You couldn't get to him."

"Couldn't?" Duun pursed his mouth. He drew in air that stank of politics and his blood ran faster. "Watch me."

"Gods. Don't. Don't. Ammunition's all I want. Listen—Duun. Just let me take it awhile. Let me handle it. What happens to me when the pieces start hitting the ground? You've got the Guild. I've got no cover. You thnk I can't manage it? I managed it while you were rusting in the hills for sixteen years. For the gods' sake, leave politics to me and get me what I need.

You've got enough in your lap. Trust me for this."

Duun scowled. "Meaning?"

"Just—let me pile up data. Awhile."

"The Guild's another answer. He might make it."

"Gods. You don't mean that."

"We're very catholic."

Ellud's ears sank in dismay.

"I'm working on it," Duun said. "I tell you that. But he's not ready yet."

"You know what that would cause?"

"And prevent."

There was a long silence. Then: "The tapes, Duun. For the gods' sakes, *start* them. Can you do that?"

Duun stared and thought about it. "Yes."

They sat together, Elanhen and Betan and Sphitti and Cloen: "This is the way it is," Elanhen said. "We get scored together. All of us. You're the one they threw into the group. If you don't learn, we fail together."

"We get thrown out of our jobs," Betan said.

"What's your *job?*" Thorn asked, because everything they said puzzled him.

Their faces went closed to him then, on secrets they would not share.

*   *   *

"You've got a problem," Betan said, leaning over his shoulder while he plied the keyboard in his lap and watched the window across the room become a glowing display. Lines blinked and intersected. "That's the trajectory. With that acceleration where will you intercept?"

Sometimes the problems made vague sense. And sometimes they did not.

(What in the world comes in two hundred twenty-fours?)

(Stars. Trees. Kinds of grass. The ways of a river. The stubbornness of a child.)

(I can reckon the speed of the wind, name the stars, the cities of the world—)

". . . in order, the particles—"

Betan brushed his arm as she bent above him. She smelled of something different. She had no reticence with him. She took no care how she leaned past him. The column of her throat was undefended, her body sleek coated and ripe with musk—

"You got it right," Sphitti said as they clustered about his desk sitting on its edges. "Here's an application now. If you were drifting in midair—no friction and no gravity—"

(They're trying to trip me.) "You can't."

"Say that you could."

Betan flicked an ear at him. Perhaps it was a joke at his expense.

"Write it down," said Cloen.

"I don't have to."

"Let him do it his way," Sphitti said. Then he had to get it right.

"That's right," Elanhen said then, checking what he said.

"Damn hatani arrogance," Cloen said when he was not quite out of earshot, when he and Elanhen were off together at Cloen's desk.

It hurt. Thorn was not immune to that.

(Duun, what do I do when people insult me? When they hate me? How do I answer, Duun?)

But he never asked it aloud. The shame of it distressed him. And he thought that he should come up with that answer on his own.

"Just the sounds," Betan said. "It doesn't matter what it means. It's a test of your recall. Listen to the tape and memorize the sound."

"It's not words at all!"

"Pretend it is. Just try. Record it. Play it back till there's no difference."

Thorn looked at Betan, at Sphitti. At two gray pairs of eyes. He felt indignation at this, as if they had made this one up. But they had never joked with him, not on lessons.

He put the plug into his ear and listened. Tried to pronounce the babble. (They'll be laughing. It sounds like water running.) He looked around at them, but they found other things to do, with the computer and with their own studies. He turned back to his work, put his hands over his eyes to shut out the world.

(Remembering days on Sheon's porch, the hiyi blooms—)

He mouthed the noises. He slowed down the machine and ran it fast and memorized the sequences. It was harder than Sphitti's physics. The plug gave him an earache.

"I've had enough of that," he said after he had gotten the start of it down and they gathered about to hear it. He would never have said that to Duun, but they accepted such things.

"That's all you're supposed to do in the mornings," Elanhen said. "You keep at that."

Thorn sat there amid his desk. He thought that he could beat any of them (even Betan, because Duun had made him believe that he was good).

"Get to work," Cloen said.

"I'm going home," Thorn said.

"You can't. The door's locked. The guard won't let you."

"Shut up, Cloen," Betan said. "Thorn, do the work. Please. I'm asking."

Thorn glared at Cloen. At Betan too. (But it was pleasant that they said please to him. No one did. It occurred to him that they had to worry what they would do if he grew recalcitrant; and that they had to fear him (even Betan)

131

the way he had to fear Duun. And that was a pleasant thought.)

He cut off the tape, found his place in it again as the others drifted back to their places; and he did what Betan had asked until his ear hurt and his head ached.

But when they were leaving he contrived that Cloen should brush against him.

He sent Cloen against the foyer wall with a move of his arm. And stood there, in a shocked tableau of fellow-students and the guard outside the open door.

"I'm hatani. Lay a hand on me again and I'll break it."

Cloen's ears were back. His jaw had dropped. He stood away from the wall and looked at Elanhen. "I never touched him!"

Thorn walked out. An escort always came to bring him home. Duun's idea, Duun's direction. Thorn swept a gesture at the man waiting for him outside and never looked back.

"Go to the gym," Duun said when he came out of his office; and this was not habit, but Thorn went, and stopped and turned. Duun shoved at him.

"I think you hit me," Duun said, with a darkness in his eyes; and sudden fear washed over Thorn like icewater. Thorn backed up. He had not hit Duun; and one thing came to him at once: that someone had been on the phone when he came in. "What should I do about it?" Duun asked. "Well, Haras-hatani?"

"I'm sorry, Duun." Thorn sweated. (Gods, *move on me!* Come *on!*) His concentration shredded. He dared not back out now. And he had never faced Duun in temper; he had never looked to. (O gods, Duun, don't kill me!)

"The knife, minnow. Lay it down. Do you hear me? I'm telling you—lay it down."

Thorn went off-center, shifted his balance back with a lifting of his head. Stood there with his arms loose and a quaking in his knees.

"That's good." Duun patted his cheek. "That's very good."

(O gods, Duun, *don't!*)

The clawtip traced a gentle path down to his jaw. "I want to talk to you." The hand dropped to his arm and took it, hurling him staggering to the center of the floor.

"Duun-hatani, I'm sorry!"

"Sit down."

He sat down on the fresh-raked sand. Duun came and hunkered down in front of him.

"Why are you sorry?" Duun asked. "Because of Cloen or for me?"

"You, Duun-hatani. I shouldn't have done it. I'm sorry. He—"

"What did he do?"

"He hates me. He hates me, that's all, and he's subtle about it."

"More subtle than you? Haras-hatani, I am confounded by his capacity."

Heat rushed to Thorn's face. He looked at the sand. "He tries to be subtle. Anything I do is wasted on him."

"You're different; just like Cloen with his baby-spots. And you suspect everyone's noticing. And you want to make sure they respect you. Am I halfway right?"

"Yes, Duun-hatani."

"You have a need, Haras. Do you know it? Can you say it to me?"

"Not to be different."

"Louder."

"Not to be different, Duun-hatani."

"Was it reasonable, what you did?"

"He won't despise me!"

"Is that so important? What do you own? What does a hatani own?"

"Nothing. Nothing, Duun."

"Yet here we live in a fine place. We have enough to eat. We don't have to hunt—"

"I'd rather hunt."

"So would I. But why are we here? We're here because of what we are. You own nothing. You have no self-interest. If this Cloen should ask you to remove him from a difficulty you would do it. He would have no right to dictate how you did it; or when or where—but Cloen is your charge. The world is your charge, Haras-hatani. Do you know—you can walk the roads and go from house to house and no one will refuse you food or drink or a place to sleep. And when someone comes to you with a thing and says: help me—do you know what to warn him: Do you know, Haras-hatani? Do you know what a hatani will tell him?

"No, Duun-hatani."

"You will say: 'I am hatani; what you loose you cannot recall; what you ask you cannot unask; what I do is my solution.' There was a wicked man once who called a hatani. 'Kill my neighbor,' he said. 'That's not hatani business,' the hatani said and went away. The wicked man found another hatani. 'My life is wretched,' the wicked man said. 'I hate my neighbor. I want to see him die.' 'That is a hatani matter,' the hatani said. 'Do you give it into my hands?' 'Yes,' the wicked man said. And the hatani struck him dead. Do you understand the solution?"

Thorn looked up in horror.

"Do you understand?" Duun asked. "His problem was removed. And the world was eased. That's what you are. A solution. The helper of the world. Do you want my solution for your problem?"

Thorn's heart beat very fast. "What should I do, Duun-hatani?"

"Tell Cloen to hit you once. Tell him to use his judgment in the matter."

He looked at Duun a very long time. His gut ached. "Yes," he said.

"Remember the lesson. Do as you're told. Someday you'll be wise enough to solve problems. Until then, don't create them. Do you hear?" Duun reached out and closed his hand on Thorn's shoulder. "Do you hear?"

"I hear."

Duun let him go.

VIII

"It certainly didn't help matters," Ellud said, with the report aglow in his lap. He flung it aside and the optic draped itself over the stack of real paper and went on glowing with ghostly, damning letters. "I chastised my staffer. I don't know why I picked him. But, dammit, Duun—you passed him."

"For his faults," Duun said. "As well as his virtues. I never expected perfection. I didn't want it. That's why I stayed by your choices."

"Damn hatani tricks," Ellud said after a moment. "I understand what you're doing. But I

137

don't like it with my staff. Cloen could have been killed."

"I didn't judge so. In that, I was right."

"It's in the record what happened. It was too well witnessed. I can't get rid of it. And with all the sniffing about the council's doing, I wish to the gods I could."

"What did happen was my fault. Power without restraint. I counted on two more years at Sheon. Haras *was* restrained. I'll tell you something which should be evident. Hatani solutions are too wide for young minds. His morality is adequate to hold his power back. It isn't adequate to use it."

"To make him hatani—Duun, *that's* what's sent the wind up the council's—"

"I know."

"I took it for a figure of speech. That it was all you could teach. It was what you knew how to teach."

"Come now."

"Well, that it was easier. But you mean to go all the way with this. When they get that rumor—"

"Try to be discreet."

"If the Guild could just devise something— clever, if they could find a halfway status—"

"There's no halfway. To give him what I've given him—with nothing but restraint to manage it? No."

Ellud reached and turned off the recorder. There was dismay on his face. Terror. "For the gods' sake, Duun. Have you lost your senses? What are you after? *What are you after, Duun?*"

"Shbit will have gotten my letter by now. Things should be quieter, from council quarter."

A brief silence, no more comfortable. "What did you tell him?"

"I offered him salutation. I felicitated him on his council appointment. I wished him health. I signed it. It was a simple letter. He hasn't answered. I expect your supply difficulties to clear up slowly, but I do expect them to clear up."

"You're not the man I knew." Ellud fidgeted with the hem of his kilt. "I don't know how to understand you."

"Old friend. You had courage enough to stay in office this long. I trust you'll keep on with it."

"I have to. Without this office I'm a naked target. They'd go for me. Shbit and his crew. Dammit, I've got no choice. They'd eat me alive."

"I'm here. Trust me."

Ellud stared at him.

"Did Cloen hit you?" Duun asked when Thorn got home. Duun leaned easily in the doorway of his office, ears pricked.

"No," Thorn said. There was no satisfaction

in that tone. (How much do you control, Duun? Do you know already? Do you always know?) Duun gave him no clues. " 'Cloen,' I said. 'I was wrong in what I did. I'll let you hit me once.' Cloen stood there with his ears back and he raised his hand no then. And walked off across the room and got busy."

Duun turned and went back into his office.

"Duun?" Thorn pursued him as far as the doorway. Duun sat down and turned on the computer. "Duun, did I do what you wanted?"

"*Did* you do what I wanted?"

Thorn was silent a moment. "I tried, Duun."

"Do I hear can't?"

"No, Duun."

The sounds grew less hard. Thorn worked, his eyes shut, his lips moving in repetition of the tape. When it played back it was the same.

"It sounds identical," Cloen said. "I can't tell a difference."

Cloen was careful, since that day. Cloen's face never betrayed anything but respect. And fear. There was that too.

"I've finished it then."

"That one." Cloen licked his lips and looked diffident. "They sent another one. It's not my doing," Cloen said quickly.

It had to be believed. Cloen did not have the

look of lying. Cloen drew the cassette from his pouch and offered it.

"I like chemistry better," Thorn muttered. He felt easier with them since the day Cloen had not hit him. He could say such things and hint at everyday needs, the way they did. He put that manner on and off at the door. It occurred to him that it made them easier with him. He could laugh with them, sometimes, because he had convinced himself he was not the object of laughter. Or if he had been, it was of little consequence.

(But I hate these sound-lessons. I hate this nonsense. I think they like giving them to me. Like a joke on the hatani they can't beat any other way. I play jokes too. I can make the computer give Sphitti a readout he never expected. He'd think it funny. I wish I *could* do more physics and less of this.)

(I wish Betan would sit here with me instead of Cloen.)

(I daren't think that. Duun would break my arm.)

"Thanks," he said dryly and pushed the new cassette into the machine.

Cloen let him alone. They were growing apart. Thorn's shoulders widened. Poor Cloen's baby-spots persisted.

Betan was absent a time. ("It's spring," Elanhen said, and sent heat to Thorn's face.

"She's been taking a suppressant but she wants to take a holiday. She'll be back.")

"It's spring," Duun said that evening. "I understand Betan's gone on holiday."

"Yes," Thorn said. He had the dkin on his knee, tuning it. He went all cold inside, for reasons he could not plainly define, except the matter of Betan was a place he protected from the others like some galled spot. And Duun knew unerringly how to find these things. "They said she was on suppressants but she wanted to go on holiday. I think she has some friend."

"Probably," Duun said matter-of-factly. "I'll warn you to be polite at school. Men don't have seasons. But their sisters and their mothers and half their friends do. And Elanhen and Cloen and Sphitti do have lives outside of the school, you know. Don't put any pressure on them."

(What about on *me*?) —You're hatani, Duun would say. If Thorn were fool enough to ask. Hatani don't have needs.

(Gods, I don't want to get into *that* with him, not today.)

Betan did come back. She came sailing in one day all smiles and what had been an all-male society of careful courtesies and few pranks became lively again.

(As if the heart came back into the place.)

Thorn felt something expand in his chest, as if some anxiety had let go. Spring was over.

"Have you missed me?" Betan asked.

The others flicked ears and rolled their eyes in a way that they would do when they talked about forbidden things. So it had a ribald flavor.

"Yes," Thorn said simply. Dignity seemed best. (They're joking about her being in season. I'll bet none of them got close to a woman this spring.)

(Neither did I. Neither *will* I. A hatani has nothing. Owns nothing. Betan has property in the city. She doesn't have to marry. She could have all her children to herself.) Between Duun and the ribald jokes Thorn had learned some few things. (But I'll bet someone will make her the best offer he can.)

"When Ghosan-hatani came to Elanten there were two sisters who asked her to judge between them and their husband. They had married the same man for a five-year, each in succession. They all three were potters and he was promised a potter's shop from his mother's heritage, so a marriage seemed profitable. But during the fourth year of the first sister the second sister bore a child which was only hers. The husband refused to consummate the second marriage if the woman did not disinherit this child. And both women would lose all they had invested in this shop. 'This is a small matter,' Ghosan-hatani said when the sisters came to her. 'Judge it yourselves.' Of course the husband was not there. He had no desire to have it judged. And the second sister looked at Ghosan and lost her courage. 'Come away,' she asked her sister. 'We were mad to ask this hatani.' And that sister ran away. But the first sister stayed. 'I want a judgment,' that sister said. So Ghosan-hatani went door-to-door in Elanten and asked everyone in the village what they knew. And she asked the magistrate. And everything confirmed what the sisters had said. 'Give me a pen,' Ghosan said. The magistrate gave the hatani a pen. And Ghosan wrote in the village records that the shop belonged to the child and to his descendants; and if not to them it belonged to the village of Elanten.''

"They would hate the child," Thorn objected.

"Perhaps they would," Duun said. "But when the child was grown and the husband was beyond his prime, what would keep him from turning the husband out? The husband not only consummated the marriage, he wanted to marry the women for good, but they only married him one year at a time for the rest of his life, even through he was very kind to them and to the child. The industry still exists in Elanten, and exports all over the world."

"Do hatani marry?" Thorn asked. He was

thinking about Betan. His heart beat fast. (Ought I to have asked that? It wasn't the point of the story.) But there was a feeling in him that came in the night, when he had a vague and disturbing dreams, when he waked ashamed of himself. But Duun said nothing about these times, Duun only looked at him with that guardedness that did nothing to reassure him. (Does Duun do these things in the night? Something is wrong with me. Why shouldn't it be? Who was my mother and father? Was I like that child?)

(Did some hatani judgment take me away from my mother? Was it Duun's?)

"There are instances," Duun said.

"Were you ever married?"

"Several times."

It shocked Thorn. (He's done—that—with a woman.) Thorn's face went hot. (I might.) He thought of the foenin in the woods. And shifted restlessly, and hugged his knees. (Think of something else. What else has Duun done? What made his scars? Is it all one story?)

"There was a hatani named Ehonin," Duun said. "He had a daughter with a woman not his wife. This daughter when she was grown trekked to another province where Ehonin was by then. She asked him to judge between him and her since her mother had married and disowned her. Ehonin made her hatani. She died in her

145

schooling. This was her patrimony. Ehonin knew she was not able. She was weak. But he gave her what he had. To kill the wife wouldn't have helped."

"He could have made the daughter marry."

"That would have been another solution, but there was no other participant. He could hardly drag someone into the situation who wasn't involved. That's never right. When the hatani himself is involved in the case, the judgments are never what they ought to be: the fewer people the hatani has in the case to judge, the fewer solutions are available."

"He could have made the woman's husband adopt the girl!"

"Indeed he could, and there was a husband. If the girl had asked him to judge between herself and her mother's husband he might have done that. That was also how Ehonin suspected she would not be hatani. She asked in haste even when she'd had ample time to think. Or she didn't want anything to do with the husband. That's also possible. In any case he had nothing to work with: to have gone to the mother and asked her truth would have been pointless. There was no recourse in her. And the daughter had asked none. That left himself and the daughter for principals. He had no other answer."

"If she hadn't asked him a hatani solution he might have helped her."

"Indeed he might."

"She was a fool, Duun-hatani."

"She was also very young and angry. And she hated her father. None of those things helped her."

"Couldn't he warn her?"

"She was old enough to have walked across a province. What point to warn her? But perhaps he did. Anger makes great fools."

"This is the velocity of the system through the galactic arm."

"Is it absolute?" Thorn asked. He had learned to ask; and Elanhen looked pleased. "No," Elanhen said. "But consider it so for this problem . . . ."

They were back to physics. At least two of every five-day set.

There was history. ". . . In 645 Elhoen calculated the world was round. This was his proof. . . ."

". . . in 1439 the hatani took down the shothoen guild and set up the merchant league in its place—"

". . . in 1492 the Mathog railway joined the Bigon line and cities grew along the route—"

". . . in 1503 Aghoit made the first powered flight. By 1530 Tabisit-tanun flew across the Mathog . . . . He crashed in the attempt at a polar crossing. His son and his daughter inherited his interest in the guild and the daughter was lost in a second attempt when ice on the wings forced her landing in Gltonig Bay. That was the last radio message. The plane was found abandoned and no one knew what became of her. The son made the flight successfully in 1541."

". . . Dsonan became capital . . ."

". . . The Dsonan League took the Mathog. Bigon resisted. The hatani refused to involve themselves without an appeal from Bigon and there was bloodshed until both sides appealed for settlement. It was the first use of aircraft—"

". . . Rocket-bombs were first developed—"

A great unease stirred in him. He turned and looked for help . . . not Cloen's. About the room the others were at their desks. He held the keyboard on his lap and put in Betan's name.

"*W-h-a-t?*" the reply appeared white-lettered at the bottom of the screen.

Thorn hesitated. Typed. "*W-h-a-t y-e-a-r a-r-e w-e i-n?*" His face burned. He waited for an answer with his heart pounding. Nothing touched the screen. He looked up and saw Betan leave her desk and walk across the sand to him with a puzzled look on her face.

"I don't need your help," Thorn said. "It's just a question."

Betan looked at the screen and looked at him. Her ears flicked down and up and her fine mouth pursed. Standing this close, she smelled of warmth, of flowers, and he wanted Sheon back, he wanted the world as simple as it had been, and the smells of earth and dust and the answers he used to know. "It's 1759," she said. And gulfs opened up about him. Doubtless Betan thought him a fool. Of course they had all grown up in the world and he had had only Sheon. She laughed at him. "Why?"

"It never came up, that's all." He sent the screen on another scroll. It stopped at 1600. Ended. "I need a new cassette."

Betan sat down on the edge of his desk, rested her hand above his knee. The touch burned him. He looked desperately elsewhere, searching with the tail of his vison for where the others were, but they were all on their desks.

"I'm sorry," Betan said. "I shouldn't have laughed." And she smelled of difference and warmth and his heart pounded against his ribs. She pressed against his ribs. She pressed on his knee and strained his leg and he wished he could get her hand off before something else happened. "Sheon's not quite the world capital, is it? Look, if you need help with that I'd be happy to stay."

"Duun wants me to be in the gym by noon."

"Ah." She gave his leg a pat and got up. "But it's 1759. The 19th of Ptosin. It's summer out."

He was suddenly , overwhelmingly conscious of the blankness of the school's white walls. The falsity of the windows behind which (sometimes) was the noise of machinery. The world closed in on him like the clenching of a fist about his heart.

In Sheon the leaves would be green and the hiyi pods opening; the foen-cubs would come tottering out and hiss at the—

—curious country-folk children. Mon was the name of one. They owned his house now. They lived in its rooms. Sat by the fireplace on the warm sand, all together.

Mon. Mon. Mon. He hated that person.

The city closed about him. Imprisoned him. But it was his fault. All his fault. His difference caused it.

"Haras?"

"I can't."

Betan gave up and wandered off, went back to her desk and sat down cross-legged with her back to him. Thorn picked up the keyboard again and looked at the screen.

A message came to him. *"BETAN: Well, tomorrow, then. I could answer questions, things that bother you."*

He watched it scroll by three times. His heart beat faster and faster. *"B-e-t-a-n,"* he typed, addressing the response. *"Y-e-s."*

*   *   *

Thorn picked himself up and dusted the sand off. He bowed. "Yes. I see."

"Again," Duun said. It was not always that Duun stripped down to the small-kilt for practice. Duun did that today, so that his scars were evident, like lightnings through the gray and black hair of his body and his maimed arm, of one fabric with the scars on his face, so that they acquired a fearsome symmetry which Thorn had sensed in those years before he knew that they were scars, or knew that every man in all the world was not marked as Duun was marked, or had not but half a right hand, or did not smile after that permanent fashion, which Thorn knew now was enough to daunt any opponent Duun ever faced. It daunted him now. (He means to put me to it today. He has something in mind.) And it came leaping into his mind in one fatal rush that it had been a very long time that Duun had left him in peace. (Not to interrupt my studies—surely that was why. Or I've gotten better and he won't try—)

That thought vanished in one missed attempt, in the far too lengthy offbalance moment he had to fall as Duun took his feet from under him.

Duun often grinned at such moments. This time he stood there with a dour face, signed no attack and watched with hands on hips as Thorn recovered himself from his drop-and-rise.

"Again."

"Duun-hatani, show me that move to the side again."

Patiently Duun showed him. Thorn bent himself to it and tried a trick in the midst of it, a joke.

Duun's hands closed on him and dumped him to the ground. (He saw it.) Duun might have laughed, but Duun's face never changed. Thorn hesitated on the safety of the floor a moment, looking up at him. (Gods. He's got something in mind. Something's wrong.) Thorn shook the dazzle and the thoughts and the day from his head and brought himself to his feet again, centered in the tightest possible focus, no thought to anything, no thought, no heartbeat but the beat of the dance, the light and the dust. It was not the city, it was Sheon's noon, and the yard about them, and Duun faced him in purest simplicity.

Pass and evade, strike and recover and pass and turn.

"Better," Duun said, and that one word ran down his nerves like fingers on the dkin. "Better. Take the offensive."

No hesitation. Thorn struck and caught and Duun spun off across the sand, up again in a move that never stopped.

Counter again and attack.

Again.

Again. Thorn floated out of a kick aimed at his hip and struck.

His hands met flesh and he spun again in distress, in time to find Duun coming up again from the sand and a kick coming at him he only scantly evaded.

Time, Thorn called, lifting his hand. Thorn's breath came in great gasps. Duun straightened not quite entirely, breathing no easier, and put his hand to his left side. (Gods, I *hit* him, I hurt him, O gods, his ribs—)

"That was good," Duun said. "You got through my guard."

(He wasn't going to stop. If I hadn't called halt—)

(—he'd have kept coming. He'd have taken me.) Thorn found himself trembling in the knees when he understood that.

(Not another pass, please, Duun, not another—)

The darkness ebbed from Duun's eyes. Reason came back. Duun straightened, pricked his ears up and gave a left-sided smile that with the permanent quirk of the right side, held a deceptive innocence. "Hot bath," Duun said. "Both of us. You're shaking, minnow."

"I didn't pull that. I thought—"

"We'll do simple figures tomorrow. I thought you were getting to that stage. We can hurt each other. No more ungoverned practice. It's gotten too dangerous."

(I didn't win, I didn't beat him, there's no beating him without killing him—)

Duun walked away from him. Duun was limping, but not much. Thorn wiped sweat from his face and found his hand shaking.

(In everything he ever promised me—he always knew that.)

He was abysmal in his lessons. The figures floated past without meaning. He studied his history and the dates settled into his mind but the names eluded him.

"Something's bothering you," Sphitti said. "Do the sound-routines. You can do that."

It insulted him. (I'm hatani, he wished to shout at Sphitti; things don't bother me.) It was the worse because it was patently true. Cloen walked warily around him. Elanhen worked silently at his own console on something abstruse and statistical, while Betan gave Thorn looks over her shoulder and said nothing.

Can I help? the message said in the bottom of his screen.

After, he sent back, and nothing else.

(Duun had cheated him. Duun had maneuvered him all his life. But why did Duun spend his life on one student? Why did Duun have so much wealth and the countryfolk live in a tin-roofed house—but now they had Sheon; and Duun had this place, which was at the top of one of the tallest buildings in Dsonan, in the capital of the world, where power was. Why me? Why Duun? Why all this effort?)

(Why do I know so little about the things I want and so much I never wanted to know, and why do they lock the doors and guards take us where we go in this building? Guards for what? What do they guard? Us? Someone else?)

(I used to live here, Duun had said.)

(Ellud's an old friend.)

(I grew up at Sheon. So did Duun. Where did he know Ellud from?)

The numbers blurred. Thorn keyed in letter function.

Betan Betan Betan, he wrote, and again, *Betan*, and filled the screen with the repeat key.

The hours dragged. The clock came up noon and in silence they shut down terminals and got up off their desks. But Thorn kept his terminal alive. He had told the guard who walked with him that he would have extra work to do. "I have to catch up in my history," he said when Sphitti asked. The others passed him without a word to him, talking to each other—perhaps Betan had changed her mind, perhaps Betan would forget, it had only been a casual thing to her. He heard the door snick shut and turned about on his desk and saw Betan come back in.

Thorn stood up. Betan walked to his desk and they both sat down knee-to-knee on the side of it. She was grave and looked at him in a quiet way no one but Betan used, not even Duun. She sensed something amiss. He knew. His heart sped and his breath grew tight; but she smelled of flowers and herself, she always did, like sun and warmth. "Something's wrong," she said, but it was different the way she said it. Her face was vastly concerned, open in a way no one else was with him. "What is it?"

"I almost beat Duun yesterday." Thorn was dismayed by the way the exaggeration leapt out so easily and then he could not take it back.

"Was he angry?"

"I don't think so." His breath grew tighter. "Betan, I lived at Sheon—" (but she knows that, this is a stupid way to start) "—I don't know the city, I've never been outside, except once, when I flew in— You do, a lot, don't you?"

"Oh, yes. I go to the coast every spring."

(Conjuring ribald jokes and student humor and mystic somethings every male in the world knew but him, more marked than Duun, scent-blind and naked as something newborn.) Betan sat close, knee touching his knee. Her eyes were wide and dark. "I never learned," he said, and lost track of what he was saying, (not hatani,

no: she was not; he did not need to be, for once
he did not have to be complex, only simple,
with Betan, who used to frighten him and now
set her hand on his knee and slid it up.) He put
his on hers, and felt the silkenness of her fur
and felt the muscles slide, alive and taut as she
leaned and stretched and came up against him
with her hand on his body. "I never learned—"

He felt things happening to him all at once,
felt things vastly out of his control and brought
it back again. It was all very clear suddenly
what he wanted and what his body was doing
on its own, and he held her against him and
maintained that good feeling as long as he dared,
until he felt everything slipping again, and he
took her belt and unfastened it quickly. She
unfastened his. Her head burrowed underneath
his chin and she leaned on him, all warm, and
her smell had changed.

It was fear. He flinched, jerked her back by
both arms and she twisted in his grip—"*Betan!*"

The door opened beyond her. A man walked
out into the foyer. Betan jerked out of Thorn's
hands and scrambled off the riser.

Duun.

Betan stopped, of a sudden crouched and
backing away. Thorn got to his feet. "Dammit—
Duun!"

Duun stepped marginally out of the doorway
and waved Betan to it. She hesitated.

"Get out!" Thorn cried. (Gods, he'll kill her—) "*Betan! Get out!*"

She skittered out the foyer doorway and through the outer door like escaping prey. Duun glanced after her and looked back at Thorn.

Thorn shook. He stood with one foot on the sand and one knee on the desk and shook with reaction as he put his clothes together. Duun stood there as if he would wait forever.

"Leave me alone," Thorn said. "Duun, for the gods' sake leave me alone!"

"We'll talk later. Let's go home, Haras."

"I haven't got a home! A hatani doesn't have anywhere! He hasn't got anything—"

"We'll talk later, Thorn."

Thorn shivered convulsively. There was no choice. (There's never been a choice. Come home, Haras. Give up, minnow. Pretend nothing's wrong.)

(But she was scared. She panicked. Scared of me—)

"Come on," Duun said.

"I wish you'd been a little later!"

Duun said nothing. Held out his hand toward the door. Thorn left the desk and the room blurred. (Your eyes are running, Thorn.) He walked out and in a vast blurred haze Duun walked beside him down the hall to the elevator. The silence lasted all the way to their door and past the guard there. That watcher was noncommittal, as if he read them both.

Duun closed the door behind them. Thorn headed for his room.

"There was no choice," Duun said. "You know what you'd have done to her?"

"I wouldn't have hurt her!" He spun about and faced Duun squarely, at the distance of the hall. "Dammit, I wouldn't have—"

"I have to be more plain to you about anatomy."

"*I wouldn't have hurt her!* I'd have—I'd—" (I can't; couldn't; but touching her, but her touching me—)

"I can imagine you'd have tried." Coldly, cooly, from age and superiority. "Common sense was nowhere in it, Thorn. You know it."

"Tell me. Lecture me. Gods, I don't mind what you do to me, but you came in like that on her—What do you think you did to her, Duun-hatani? Is *that* your sublety?"

"I promised you an answer. Years ago you asked a question and I promised you an answer when you could beat me. Well, you came close yesterday. Perhaps that's good enough."

Shock poured over Thorn. Then reason did. He flung up a hand. "Dammit, *dammit*, you're maneuvering me! I know your tricks, you taught them to me, *I know what you're doing, Duun!*"

"I'm offering you your answer. That's all. What you are, where you came from—"

"*O gods, I don't want to hear it!*" Thorn turned. He ran. He shut the door to his room and leaned against it shaking.

The intercom came alive. "When you want, you can come out, Thorn. I don't think badly of you. Not in this. Even a hatani can take wounds. This is a great one. Come out when you can face me. I'll wait for you. I'll be waiting, Thorn."

He was dry-eyed when he came out. He unlocked the door and walked out into the hall, and down the hall into the main room. Duun was there, sitting on the riser that touched the wall. The windows were all stars and dark. Nightview. Perhaps it was. Duun did not look at him at once, not until he had crossed the sand and sat down on the riser in the tail of Duun's view.

Then Duun turned his face to him; and there was no sound except something mechanical behind one window and a whisper of air from the ducts.

"Have you come for your answer?" Duun asked.

"Yes," Thorn said. He sat upright, hands on his thighs, ankles crossed. He looked unflinchingly at Duun.

"You've studied genetics," Duun said. "You know what governs heredity."

(Be quick. Drive the knife in quickly, Duun.

O gods, I don't want to sit through this.) "Yes. I understand."

"You understand that genes make you what you are; that every trait you manifest is no matter of chance. A harmonious whole, Haras."

"Are you my father?"

"No. You had none. Nor mother. You're an experiment. A trial, if you will—"

Thorn was strangely numb. Duun's voice drifted somewhere in the half-dark, in the timelessness of the view. The night went on forever and he went on hearing it.

"I don't believe this," Thorn said finally. Not because he did not believe it was something equally terrible. But that he saw no way to accomplish it. "Duun. The truth. I'm something that went wrong—"

"Not wrong. No one said wrong. There are things right about you. But you're different. An experiment. You know how conception takes place. You know genetic manipulation's done—"

"I don't know how it's done." (Clinically. Precisely, like a lesson. It could not be him they discussed, a thing in a dish, a mote floating in a glass.) "I know that it is done. I know they can put things together and come up with something that didn't exist before."

"You know when someone wants a child and there's a—physical impediment—there's the means to bring the embryo to term. A host.

Sometimes a volunteer. In other cases a mechanical support system. An artificial womb. That was so in your case."

(A machine. O gods, a machine.)

"There's nothing remarkable in that," Duun said. "You have that in common with a thousand, two thousand ordinary people who couldn't be born any other way. Medicine's a marvel."

"They made me up."

"Something like that."

He had struggled not to cry. The tears welled up out of nowhere and ran down his face, endless. "When they were putting me together in this lab—" He could not talk for a long time and Duun waited for him. He began it again. "When they made me did they bother to do it twice? Is there anyone else like me?"

"Not in all the world," Duun said. "No."

"*Why?* For the gods' sake *why?*"

"Call it curiosity. There are undoubtedly reasons adequate for the meds."

"The meds—"

"They're your fathers if you like. After a manner of speaking Ellud is. Or others in the program."

"What are you?"

"A hatani solution."

Small warnings went off. A prickle of alarm. (Self-preservation. Why should I bother? Why should I care?) But there was fear. "Whose?"

162

"I might have done many things. I chose to give you the best chance I could give. The only chance I'm equipped to give. Like Ehonin and his daughter."

"Who asked for it?"

Duun was silent for a long time. "The government."

"Asked a hatani solution?" The enormity of it washed over Thorn like a flood. Duun's stare never gave him up.

"You are one of my principals. I gave you all I could give. I'll go on giving that. It's all that I can do."

The stars glittered on, awash. "I wanted to love her, Duun."

"I know."

"I want to die."

"I taught you to fight. Not to die. I'm teaching you to find solutions."

"Find this one."

"I've already been asked."

Thorn shuddered. All his limbs shook.

"Come here," Duun said. Held out his hands. "Come here, minnow."

Thorn went. It was a pathetic thing Duun offered, shameful for them both. Duun took him in his arms and held tight till the shuddering stopped. After that he lay still against Duun's shoulder for a very long time, and Duun's arms cradled him as they had done before the fire, in Sheon, when he was small.

He slept. When he woke Duun had fallen asleep over him, and his back ached, and it was all still true.

IX "Well," Ellud said, "we're still tracing the files as far as we can. When official channels decide to fake a record they can do it with remarkably few tracks."

"No matter." Duun kept his back straight. The cracked rib and a twisted night put slowness in his movements; and he sat cross-legged on the other riser in Ellud's office with a cup of herbal tea in his hands. He savored the warmth and the quiet. "I congratulate the council. The security service background—true or false— accounted for the way she held herself."

"Young and bright and probably indebted as hell to someone."

"Try Dallen Company. Trace it and make as much noise as you like. It ought to keep Shbit prudent awhile."

"I'm embarrassed about this."

"She cost them. A lot of years forging that identity. What worries me is how she got out of the building untracked. Dammit, how did they foul that up?"

"We're trying to find that out too."

Duun stared at Ellud a moment and poured himself another cup of tea from the vessel which sat at his left knee. He lifted the cup and looked at Ellud again, making his face expressionless, his eyes uninformative as glass. "He's growing to be a man, all fine points aside; the matter was bound to come up. Betan was a solution when I picked her. I sensed she had the nerve to deal with him. That was understatement, at least. Thorn, gods know, could take care of himself—up to a point. But at least she was bent on creating an incident. That's likeliest. And at worst case, she would do that and kill him in the process. If she could. She had nerve for it. Pity the Guild didn't get her."

"Free-hatani?"

"I've thought of that. I don't think so. Free-ghota, maybe."

"Good gods, if you thought that—"

"Hindsight. She might be the same vukun as Shbit's own bodyguards. They're capable.

Maybe even one of Dallen Company's guilded hire-ons. She botched it up if killing was what she intended, but she wasn't bad. And I doubt it was all that simple." Another sip of the tea. "You won't find her, not now, I think. She likely did clear the building. Look for old friends in Security."

"I'm doing that."

"She'll probably suicide after she reports. I embarrassed her, and not in her youthful modesty. Shbit will see the body disappears. I'll be glad to see her go to him, frankly. It'll make solutions a lot neater."

"I don't *like* this kind of thing."

"I don't like it either. I may yet visit Shbit. But this discomfiture ought to slow him down a while. He can't bring his witness to light now. That's all spoiled—the charges of assault and ravishment—" Duun drew a deep breath. Ellud's distress was evident. "Well, it's over. For a while. I put him to work in the gym this morning, refused all further questions, and poured a sedative down him afterward. Right now he's sleeping and Hosi's standing over him. Tomorrow, well, we'll change that school situation. I think it's best. With thanks to your staff. I'd like to pull him out, get him out to the country—"

"Gods, no! We just had one security breach. You want another business like Sheon?"

"—but I know it's not feasible."

"Duun. Duun-hatani." Ellud reached beside him on the desk, picked up the optic sheet and waved it. "I'm getting inquiries. We've got a slow leak that's going to become a panic, for the gods' sake, Duun! We haven't got that much maneuvering room left. I want that program to go on, I want it back on schedule. I'm telling you this. It's not just Shbit now. It's coming from the provinces. We're getting inquiries. Do you understand?"

"I've always understood. There's a limit, Ellud. The mind has limits. I want him tranquil. I want him whole. He's closer now than he ever was. But give him room"

"He doesn't know about Betan, does he?"

"How could I explain that without getting into the whole council business? That's why I couldn't stop her on the spot. What would I say? Some people want you killed? He already avoids mirrors. Let the scars heal over before he gets the rest." It was the two-fingered hand that held the cup. Duun contemplated that, rolled it in his fingers and set it down. "Put Sagot on it."

"She couldn't."

"Ask her. No, I'll explain to her. She's old, she's canny, and she's female, and that's the best combination I can think of to handle this."

* * *

The guard still stood at the door, the same as always, and Thorn turned to look at the guard who escorted him to the upper floor—not a hard look, not vengeful. (He put Duun onto it.) At first Thorn had thought of Cloen. But Thorn had not been devious, had not—truly—thought of covering his tracks, not thought he had to.

Going through that ordinary door this morning was all that he could do. ("Betan's gone," Duun had told him yesterday. "She's been transferred. It was her request.") ("Did you kill her?" Thorn had asked, cold and shivering a second time. It was not a rational question, perhaps; but the very air felt brittle, full of doubts, full of duplicities. And Duun looked him in the eyes when he answered: "No. No such thing—" as soberly as ever Duun had answered him, as ever Duun had told him half-truths, had kept the world from him until Betan let it in.)

(What year are we in?)

(I shouldn't have laughed. Sheon's not quite the world capital, is it?)

Thorn walked in, into the foyer with its stark white walls, its plain white sand, the severely arranged vase-and-branch on its riser. The sand showed the raking it got at night; a solitary line of footprints led around the corner into the large main room in which all the windows were white and blank.

He followed it and stopped in the archway

in front of all the vacant desk-risers. That single track led to the farther desk in the stark white room, the one that had been Elanhen's.

A stranger sat there, legs crossed, hands on thighs. The nose and mouth and eyes were rimmed in white that graduated to a dusting, except the eartips. The crest was stark white. The arms were gaunt. Thorn stared, thinking he saw disease.

"Come closer." It was a thin voice, matching the body. He walked closer and stood staring. "You're Haras. Thorn."

(Gods, doesn't he know?) Laughter welled up like blood in a wound, but he could not laugh in this great sterile quiet. (He?) Thorn suddenly suspected not, for reasons he could not quite define. "Where's Elanhen? Where's Sphitti and Cloen?"

"My name is Sagot. You're staring, boy. Does something about me bother you?"

"I'm sorry. Where are the others?"

"Gone. Sit down. Sit down, Thorn."

He did not know how to refuse a voice so gentle. Duun had not taught him how to say no to authority. He had learned it on his own; and the world was too perilous to go recklessly in it. He sought the nearest riser and sat on the edge of it, feet dangling.

"I'm Sagot. You haven't seen anyone old before, have you?"

"No, Sagot." Saying anything seemed difficult. (Age. Gods, she's so brittle—it *is* she, it has to be. Will I get like that? And she knows me . . . she's a friend of Duun's—)

"I'm going to teach you now."

"Not them?"

"No. Just you. Shall I call you Haras or Thorn? Which do you prefer?"

"Either. Either, Sagot." (What do I call her? Is she hatani? Or one of the meds? Oh, get me out of here, Duun, I want them back! Even Cloen, if not Betan, at least Sphitti! At least Elanhen, at least someone I know!)

"I've had two children. Both boys. They're grown and have children of their own and their children have grown children. It's been a long time since I taught a boy. I always liked it."

(O gods.) The gentleness found quick flesh, slid in like a knife: shocked the tears loose again so quickly there was no retreat, no covering it; Thorn put his face into his hands, disgracing himself and Duun, and his chest ached as if something had broken there. He sobbed. He shook with tears. When he had gotten control again he wiped his face and nose with wet hands and looked up because he had to.

"You're a fine young man," Sagot said. "I like you."

"You're lying, you're lying, Duun put you up to this—"

"Doubtless he did. But you're still a fine young man. I can see that in you. I can see more than you think I see, I've brought up too many boys not to have had a young man wail and pour his troubles into my lap now and again, and young women too—I confess to you, even a few who weren't so young, all wailing and shaking with the troubles that were great to them then. Lamentations like that, they're like great storms. They're good for you. They come sweeping through the woods and break a few limbs. But they herald change. They bring the turn of seasons. They make things new. There, that's good. Your eyes are bright—very handsome eyes, if different. They're blue, aren't they, when they're not running."

"Let me alone!"

"It's amazing how much young men are alike; first the wails, then the shouting. I know it hurts. I've buried two husbands. I know something about pain."

"Are you hatani?"

She smiled. "Gods, no. But I know Duun. You know a hatani can do a lot of things, but when it comes to others, well—reason can't solve everything. 'Take care of him,' he said, 'Sagot, talk to him, teach him—' 'Now why should I do that?' I said. 'I've got my work, I've got things to do, I've got fourteen great-great-grandchildren, I don't need another boy—' But then I got to thinking, it's been so very long. They're all grown. I'm a hundred fifty-nine, young lad, and I've traveled all over the world, I've trekked down rivers, I've been to the two poles, I've written books—some of the books you study, by the by; I've had nine husbands, lovers I've forgotten, a few I haven't, and I've patched young knees, set bones, birthed babies and seen enough in this world not to be shocked at anything, that's the truth."

"Maybe that's why Duun wanted you with me." Bitterly. But somewhere in the chatter the pain in his chest stopped, and Sagot made it stop, and he had no more wish to run away. He sat there with his feet dangling, his five-fingered hands in his lap and the remnant of tears drying on his naked face. (But Betan's furred skin was silk and tasted like she smelled—)

"I don't think you think enough of yourself," Sagot said. "It's very well to be hatani, but you're not *all* that thing, you know, the way you're not just that pair of eyes or that pair of hands or that sex between your legs—" (The heat flew to his face.) "Oh, well, boy, I know, I know, you've only now discovered it and for a while it's the most of you, but that passes, it gets less important, the more of you there gets to be, the more abilities, the more thoughts, everything changes and shifts until the world's so wide and the things you are get so complex there's no containing them. You're not just Thorn who was born in a lab, right down this hall; you're Thorn the hatani, Thorn my student, Thorn who'll go places and do things and be things Thorn hasn't even thought of, and I haven't, and you'll find answers to your questions and questions yet to answer, which makes life, after all. So wail and take on if you have to, and if you want to come here every day and pour it all in my lap, well, that's doing some good, if you need to. But when you're done with that and you're quite ready I've got a lot of things I want to give you—it is giving, you know, a kind of gift. When you've lived as many years as I have you want to leave something in the world, and my teaching's that thing; it's what I do."

Another sob overtook him, unexpected, like a sudden breath. But it hurt less. Thorn wiped his face with a swipe of his hand, quick, distasteful. He slid back on the riser and tucked his feet up. There was no choice. Sagot left him none. "I'm listening, Sagot." (O gods, what has she got to teach?) Sagot teemed with secrets, frightening as Duun. As implacable. As difficult to get around. "Are you sure you're not hatani?"

Sagot laughed and even that was gentle, a fragility about her voice. "I take that for a compliment. What do you like best, what study?"

"Physics."

"Physics, then. Show me what you know. I'll find out where to start."

"If an object were traveling at the speed of light, and a man traveled on it to the nearest star—what is that star?"

"Goth."

"And distant—?"

"5 light-years."

"5.1. Be precise for this. And this man was forty; and he left a sister on earth when he went. . . ."

"There's a kind of parasite infests the brains of cattle on the Sgoht river. I remember once seeing one—"

"You were there?"

"Child, I lived nine months on the Sgoht, and I had a village magistrate for a lover. He had a ring threaded so, right through the side of his lip, and it looked odd, I'll tell you, when he smiled. He had been married six times and he had a great notch in his nose where one of his wives took a stick to him, but she was a crazy woman and her daughter was crazier. She took it into her head to sell her mother's land, that's right, without owning it—she was going to sell her *expectation* of inheriting it to this man she was living with so she could get

the money to go downriver and get a husband
who owned a grocery, don't ask me why, but I
think food was quite all she could think of—
she must have weighed two hundred, all of it.
Well, the magistrate my lover finally gave her
the money to get her out of town, and that fool
man she was living with went after my lover
with an axe—"

"Gods, Sagot!"

"He did. And chased him round and round
the office and out into the street before someone shot this crazy man. Rumor had it the
cattle sickness got him, that that woman fed
him from diseased animals; but my lover the
magistrate said anyone who married that woman
was crazy from the start."

"Watch the monitor. This is a simulation
game. This is an instrument panel—there's your
fuel, do you see, there's your altitude, there's
your compass. . . . You remember your ride to
the city, don't you?"

"Of course I remember."

"Well, this isn't a copter. It's a plane. Use the
toggle and the keys—let me show you. Here's
the runway—this is an old-fashioned plane. But
we'll start with that."

"Can you fly?"

"Oh, well, yes, I used to. My eyesight's against
me now. I stay to the commercial planes."

"Commercial."

"Dear lad, planes go back and forth all over the world all the time, how do you think one would go?"

"Rail."

"Oh, well, it's all mostly freight, nowadays. Let's try taking off again; I'm afraid we've just crashed."

At some time the pain stopped. Thorn woke up one morning and realized he was past the sharpness of it; and that it had gotten to a kind of regret in which he did not have to work so hard at self-control; and finally, at breakfast with Duun on still another day, he hurt with a different pain, that he and Duun had had little to say to each other beyond the necessities of two people living with each other, and Duun's teaching him in the gym. There were no tales in his life but Sagot's; there was no sound in the house, but sometimes in the long evenings he and sometimes Duun played the dkin with indifferent passion—Duun aimlessly or working out long and vexing compositions that frayed Thorn's nerves; Thorn playing gloomy hatani songs or the lightest, most trivial ditties he had known from childhood, like accusations hurled at Duun. And Duun would sit and listen, or retreat to his office for peace and (sometimes, for Duun's side pained him) Duun would take a sedative and close the door of his room.

He was Sagot's ward. Duun only lived with him and went turnabout at fixing meals, and saw to his drill and his practice (but Duun ached when he breathed and even that was indifferent).

(He held me all night, that night. That must have hurt. He could hardly move when he woke up. He never complained.)

(Is it ever going to heal?) In one part of him the sight of Duun reduced to walking into the gym and giving instructions and walking out again gave Thorn satisfaction.

(But he's too quiet. He doesn't talk to me. What's he waiting for?)

(O gods, I wish he'd yell or frown at me or even look me in the eyes. His shoulders stoop. He moves like Sagot does. I'd never have caught him in the first place, but his balance was on his bad side in that pass. If he was younger, if he hadn't ever been hurt, gods, he must have been impossible to beat. I'd hate to have met him then.)

(O Duun, *look* at me!)

(Why should I care that he took Betan, he took Elanhen, Sphitti, even Cloen, he takes everything I care for, he sent Sagot and someday I'll walk in and he'll have sent her away too, everything, everyone.)

(He spied on me. He's probably tied into the computers there at school, I know he could, all you have to do is put the codes in, we're in the same building. He knew everything, he read everything Betan and I passed back and forth, probably the guards reported to him.)

(O Duun, I don't *like* this quiet. I don't like you looking like that, it hurts.)

But one noon he came back from Sagot and Duun was in the gym, was waiting for him when he had shed down to his small-kilt and got out on the sand. Thorn waited for instruction, but Duun walked out, swinging his left arm a bit and working it back and forth.

"Duun, be careful."

"Thorn, I don't need you to tell me careful. Just remember what I told you: no all-out strikes. Let's go a fall or two."

Duun took him. It took a good long while, and it was craft that worked Thorn off his center and brought Duun's foot against his back.

"I'm dead," Thorn said, and sat down on the sand. Duun sat down less quickly, breathing hard, licking at his teeth. Thorn panted for breath and leaned on his knees and stared back at him. Grinned suddenly, because getting beaten by Duun was in the nature of the world and made it feel less lonely.

Duun grinned back. No words. It was better after that. Duun played that night, one old familiar piece after the other, and the music brought them back, dkin and drum, not the sad songs but the songs with tricks, hatani humor, subtle and cruel.

Thorn slept that night, and waked about the middle of the dark with the stars giddy about his bed and the air breathing false chill winds as if they came off winter snow; everything was still, and he had some vague terror that he could put no name to.

(Duun was here. He was here a while ago.) Perhaps it was a subtle scent the air-conditioning had dispersed. But the door was closed.

Thorn's eyes searched the room, the dark, seeking outlines and knowing Duun's skill. (Is he still in the room? Is he waiting till I move?) Thorn's heart raced, the veins pounding in his throat. (This is foolish. How could he pass the door? It's noisy; I couldn't sleep that soundly.)

(Could I?)

His heart hammered wildly. (He wouldn't. He *couldn't*. Not after Betan. He knows I'm mad. I hate him. I hate him that he does this to me.)

He hurled himself out of bed. (Never trust him. Never take Duun for granted—) But there was nothing there, only the false stars in their slow dizzy movement.

Thorn sat down again on the edge of the bed. His heart still slammed against his ribs.

(What's the world like? Full of Sagot's kind? Or Duun's? What's he up to? What was I made for? Why does the government care whether I live or die—enough to call on a hatani to solve my problem? He could kill them. Kill me. He gives me a chance, he says . . . a chance against *what*?)

(A hatani dictates others' moves. A hatani judges. A hatani wanders through the world setting things to rights again. A hatani can leave a pebble in your bed—in your drink—can pass a locked door and track you in the dark. He's a hunter . . . not of game. Of anyone he wants. What else is he?)

(Everything Duun does has a cause. And Sagot's his friend. Maybe—maybe Betan was. No. Yes. O gods, maybe it's *all* set up. Could Betan take a thing like me by *preference*? Was she curious? Curious—about what she'd let do *that* with her?)

(Sphitti laughing and joking with me, Elanhen too, from the time we met. Wouldn't it be natural to flinch? But they were prepared for it. They *knew* what I'd look like. Maybe Cloen was the only honest one—the only one who ever told me the truth.)

(Fool, you knew that, you knew it from the time you walked into that room and you wanted to believe something else. You saw how Betan moved—you thought *hatani* then and put that thought away.)

(She flinched at the last, she flinched and I reacted—I smelled the fear, her nerve broke—I pushed back, it scared me, it was reflex, she was up against me and I smelled the fear—)

(Thorn, where's your mind? Did you leave it at Sheon, on that hill, when you went back for him? Can you forget how Duun works?)

(I love him. Does he love me?)

(Is even Sagot real? All her chatter—from the start—'I like you, boy.' Thorn, you fool.)

(Did Duun tell the truth, what I am and where he got me?)

Thorn sat there with his hands locked between his knees; and at last he got up and turned on the lights, checked the bed, as if there could be a pebble there. There was none.

(I hate him. I hate him for what he's done to me.)

(It was the best thing in the world when he smiled at me today.)

X "Again."

They used the wer-knives this time, the blades cased in clear plastic. Duun bent and took the pass, snaked from Thorn's strike and Thorn evaded his, fell and flipped up on his feet a distance away. "Is that a move you invented?" Duun asked dryly, and Thorn lowered his head and looked under one brow in that way he had when he had done something foolish. "I invented it just then," Thorn said, "when I landed on my heel. I'm sorry, Duun."

It was well-done, nevertheless. Duun laid his ears back. "Again."

Three more times. The wer-knives met in a way they never met when they were naked steel, plastic touching plastic and giving too much resistance. Duun floated back and stripped the cover from his blade. Thorn's eyes betrayed dismay, but Thorn pulled the sheath from his and threw it aside.

Naked steel. Duun gripped the knife in his maimed right hand, held the left close to it, ready to change off on short notice. Thorn did the same, maneuvering and watching nothing but his eyes and that blade.

Duun moved, not the feint that was his habit, but straight attack, aborted at the last instant when he saw Thorn cover; evade; to a feint, double-feint, hand-shift, retreating circle, side-slip, hand-shift.

Blade hissed on blade and slid clear; continuing drive, a floating attack.

Thorn escaped it with a fall and roll, came up again with sand in his hair and a desperate parry, for Duun kept coming and the wall was coming at Thorn's back.

Thorn sensed it and moved, too quickly. Duun shifted hands and blade rang on blade as Thorn backed up in free space again.

Duun called time. "Dammit, that steel's too fine to be treated like that! Keep edge off edge!"

"Yes, Duun." Thorn sucked breath in. Sweat ran in his eyes and he wiped it.

"It's that damned handedness again. You know what you did?"

"Went to the right," Thorn said. His shoulders sank. He wiped sweat again. "I feinted left."

"But you went to the right, fool!"

"Yes, Duun. I thought you'd think I'd go left this time for sure."

"Not when you never do it! Gods, surprise me once!"

Thorn's face was all chagrin.

"Up!" Duun struck, lizard-quick. Thorn escaped, escaped, escaped, attacked and escaped with a ringing of the blades.

Duun hit him then, averted the blade and struck his arm up with his fist. Thorn flung his own arm up to lessen the force, skipped back and covered himself again.

Duun called time again and Thorn looked down at his wrist as if he expected to see blood. "At least," Duun said, "you didn't stop when I hit you."

"No." They had hammered that one out in painful lessons, beginner habits unlearned with bruises. "I'm sorry." Breathless, with another wipe at the sweat. Thorn meant the blade-touch.

"You've developed a whole new form of fence, the artful covering of your mistakes! You're best at your escapes!"

"I'm sorry, Duun-hatani."

"This isn't hand-to-hand. In this, young fool, you've got a damn sharp claw! Rearrange your thinking and use it. Again!"

Thorn came at him. He evaded it, struck, evaded, struck.

"Hold!"

Thorn flinched back. Stood there with the breath rasping through his mouth and sweat running in his eyes. He straightened. "I'm sorry, Duun." It had gotten to be a refrain. There were always mistakes. His look was contrite.

Duun reached a hand toward his face, slowly. Thorn stepped back. There was threat in that stance, wariness. Duun smiled.

Thorn straightened his shoulders back, panting. (Why do you shout at me? Why do you curse me? What's wrong today? I'm trying to listen, Duun, don't make fun of me like that.)

"Let me touch you, minnow. This once."

The knife-hand lowered. Thorn stood still. Duun came close and put his palm in the middle of Thorn's chest, on flesh gone pale without sunlight, on flesh slickly sweating so that hands slipped off it, if one grappled without claws. The heart jumped beneath his hand in steady, labored pulses. There was no flinching. No shivering. Duun moved the hand up to the side of Thorn's neck and felt the same pulse. A slight flinching. Reflex. Or teaching. He looked into alien white eyes: it was curious how little the blue centers had changed from the first time he had looked into them, an infant lying on his lap; a round-bellied child clambering on his crossed ankles and trying to pull his ears; a boy's face gazing up at him in sudden shock at finding him on the trail—

They had never seemed to change size. The bones about them did. The face became hollow-cheeked and the jaw lengthened and its skin roughened in dark hair Thorn kept shaved. . . . (They'll laugh at me, Duun; my body hair just doesn't get thick enough and I'm not going to grow it on my face like that, all patched up and thick here and not there.") Thorn shaved his body here and there too, where the patchiness was worst. Clipped and groomed and gods, *tried*, not to grow a coat any longer, but at least not to let the changes in his body overcome the Thorn they both had gotten used to. Thorn smelled different than he once had. The chest and shoulders were wider and muscled, the belly flat and hard, the loins narrow, the legs long-muscled and agile. Strong, Thorn could lift *him* nowadays, though gods knew Duun had no intention to let him try.

Strange, Thorn was not ugly. Seventeen, nearly eighteen years, and Duun looked at him eye-to-eye, even having to look up a little lately. And there was in Thorn a symmetry that made that face probable on that body and the composite of him fit together in a grace of motion that no aesthete could deny. ("When you got used to him he's beautiful," Sagot said. "Frightening, like some big animal you've gotten closer to than you wanted. But you want to watch him move. There's a fascination to such things, isn't there?)

The pupils dilated and contracted with thought. With anxiety. (Is this a game, Duun? Am I supposed to do something?)

Duun walked away, turning his back on that look. Perhaps Thorn picked up his anxiety. It was acute now.

("We've got to go with it," Ellud said. "Duun, you're put me off; first it was Wait till he's got the first tapes down. Then it was: The Betan business has him upset. Now it's: There's a last few things I have to teach him. Duun, we're out of excuses.")

Duun picked up the cap for the wer-knife. Looked back across the room where Thorn was doing the same thing. Ripple of muscle, the reach of an arm. Thorn was whole this morning. Duun wished to remember this.

"These are the words: I know you can remember them. You won't need much study. *Ship. Sun. Hand. Warning.* They're equivalents to these sound patterns." Sagot played the tape in the recorder wand she held. It was all a complicated thing, and Thorn centered himself, not to diffuse his concentration on his surroundings. The guard had not brought him to the familiar room this morning, but two doors down, into a place with the slick, bare floors that shouted meds, a place that was large enough, but there were two large risers and a clutter of cabinets: the windows showed illusory desert, which only made the place seem starker, less comforting. Sagot was there waiting for him, sitting cross-legged on a desk with a keyboard in her lap; there was a keyboard and monitor at her knee. "Sit down," Sagot had said, and the guard went out and closed the door on them.

"I. He. Go."

Thorn had thought *simulator* when the guard brought him to a strange door. He enjoyed that, the fast interaction with the computer, the imagination of flight, and land skimming beneath illusory wings. Gods, they had a screen in one room that made it all seem real. He sat in a machine in that room that had controls very like the copter controls had looked, and the whole machine could move under him, incline and tilt with the screens so that the first time he had had to clamp his jaws to keep from screaming when he lost control and the room spun. He was better at it now.

("Meds?" he had said at once to Sagot,

alarmed. "Sit down," she said, "it's patterns today.")

"Stop. Man Radio. Stop."

"Is it some kind of language?"

"Do your patterns, boy."

(Something's wrong. Sagot's mouth is hard. Did I ask something wrong? Is she worried about this place?)

"Concentrate."

Thorn worked at it. He put meanings with the patterns. Sagot left him listening to his tapes over and over again and he hated them. He mouthed the sounds, resenting it. It was not a good day. Duun had been surly at breakfast; surly in Duun's way, which meant quiet and thoughtful and not giving him anything from inside him, only the surface, like a puddle frozen over. Sagot gave him stark orders and went off and left him in this room, disappearing through the inner door and coming and going in perfunctory checks on him.

(They've been talking to each other. Duun's mad at me and he's told Sagot. I haven't done anything to make Sagot mad.)

(I was stupid about my moves yesterday, I can't stop going to the right all the time, I'm worse when Duun yells at me, I wish he'd hit me, even, I don't mind his hitting me, I deserve to get hit when I leave my side open like that. It's like I've reached a point I can't improve anymore, and Duun knows it, and I'm not good enough to be hatani, not quite. He's worked so long to teach me, and I go off to the right like a fool and he ought to shout at me, he should have cut me and maybe I'd remember after that.)

There was a scar across his forearm and one on Duun's.

(I always remembered that.)

"Boy."

The machine went off, Sagot's intervention. He blinked at Sagot, who had brought him a pill and a small cup of water. (Gods, it is meds. What's wrong? Do they just want to look at me?) "Sagot, I don't want to swallow that. I'm not sick."

She went on holding it out. There was no choice, then. He picked the pill off her black, wrinkled palm and put it in his mouth. He had no need of the water to swallow it, but it made his stomach feel better; it threatened upset. (Is that what has Sagot acting strange? Is there something really the matter with me? Does Duun think so?)

"I want you to go next door with me," Sagot said. "Yes, it's meds. You're going to lie down a while and I want you to be good about this."

(You smell afraid, Sagot. So do I, I think. Gods, what's this about?)

He got up. He towered over Sagot, but Sagot

reached and took his hand. (I'm hatani, Sagot, you're not supposed to—) But he never told Sagot no. She led him by the hand to the door in the side of that room, and led him through it into a small room that left no illusions about meds in this room. It was a cramped small place, all machinery and a table. Sagot's hand held his. She was evidently not going to argue the matter. (She's afraid. What should *I* be?) But he stood there while meds came out and told him to take off his kilt and lie down.

"I'll be all right," he told Sagot; he did not want to undress with her there, not because he would shock her—(I have fourteen great-great-grandchildren, boy)—but precisely because it would not, she would look on him as a child, and child-Thorn was already too naked. But Sagot stayed, and Thorn turned his back and unfastened his kilt and got up on the table when the meds told him to. His head swam; his limbs felt distant from his brain; he drifted in a vast calm which itself alarmed him.

(It was a drug Sagot gave me. Does Duun know? Does he know where I am, what they're doing, did he order this?)

They pasted electrodes about his body. He felt this far distant from him. They spoke in whispers or his hearing had gone wrong. They adjusted a screen above his head. Something soft and rough settled over his naked body and he realized vaguely that someone had put a sheet over him; he was dimly grateful. (It's cold in here; they never realize how cold I get sometimes, they've got a coat and I don't and I'm sweating now—) Something tight went over his legs, once again over his chest. "*Talk* to him, for the gods' sake, he's not a piece of meat you're handling."

"Sagot-mingi, we have to ask you to be still, with respect, mingi Sagot."

Something weighed on his shoulder. Shook at him. "Keep your eyes open. Look up."

Thorn obeyed that voice. He heard the sound of his tapes over and over again.

"Blink. That's right. You can blink when you have to."

"He's following that, isn't he?"

The voice drifted out again. He heard another voice babbling at him; there were images, he was in the simulator; more voices, more images, there were people like him moving in the dark, there were faces that babbled at him, there were machines and more machines—

He tried to leave this.

Eyes stared at him, mirrorlike. More machines that spun in dark and arms that moved—

He fought. He evaded and escaped and fought.

"This is your heritage," a voice told him out of the dark. "Accept it, Haras-hatani. This is your heritage. Accept what you hear and see.

Stop resisting. Accept this. This is your heritage."

Chaos of images.

"Listen to the sounds. Learn this, Haras hatani. Remember these things."

"Wake up."

He was lying on the table. The sheet was over him. He was drenched in sweat. He wanted only to lie there and his eyes stung as if sweat were in them; it might be. Someone wiped his face and the cloth was neutral-feeling, wet and rough but neither cold nor hot. Someone lifted a weight off his chest and legs. "Are you sure you ought to? He's not awake yet." He was, but he preferred to keep that secret to himself, and stare at the stark steel of the machinery, ignoring the faces and the touches, the sudden nakedness of his body as they peeled electrodes away in small twitches he ought to have felt keenly and did not.

"His color isn't good."

(I'm cold, fool.)

Something stung his arm. It was not a great pain. In a moment he began to feel his heart thumping the way it did in nightmares.

(Go away. Let me alone. Don't touch me.)

"Hold him, don't let him move."

He blinked. Meds held his limbs in a hurtful grip. He lifted his head. "Let go. I'm awake. I want to sit up."

They looked foolish, with a dropping of their ears. After they had mulled it over they let him go and one at his side got a hand beneath his back and one and another helped him sit up, holding him.

"Are you through?" Thorn said.

"We're through," one said. They rarely spoke to him at all. "We'll put you to bed awhile."

"I'm going home." Thorn gave a sudden heave and landed with his feet on the floor. His feet were numb, but his knees held. The med reached and he stopped that reach with a backhand lift of his arm, slow-motion, gentle warning. The med took the warning when his stare followed the turn he made, and backed off.

"Sagot," someone said, "Sagot, get in here fast."

Thorn waited then, if Sagot was coming. He remembered he was naked. "I want my clothes." A med gave him his kilt, and he took it and worked with numb fingers and diminished balance to put it on.

A door opened. He looked up at Sagot. "Sagot," he said; he was very careful to be polite. Duun would hit him if he was rude to the meds, and he was desperate. He made his voice ever so calm and courteous, and stood as easily as he could. "Sagot, they think I ought to go to bed here and I'd much rather go to my own and sleep. Please get me home, Sagot."

Sagot looked at him with her thin mouth all taut. A long while she stood there. "All right," Sagot said. "Call his guard and call Duun and tell him we're coming back." Sagot came and took Thorn's arm, wound her thin, fragile forearm about his and locked both her hands on his, and he walked with her, out of that room.

"We'll wait here a moment," she said in the other room; and stood there with him, holding to his arm. In a moment the door opened and the guard was there who walked with him everywhere. Ogot was his name. He said little, but he was a pleasant man; he was Duun's, and if Ogot had taken him to this place and never told him, perhaps Ogot had not known half as much as Sagot had. Ogot looked worried to see him, and Thorn felt ashamed to be so helpless.

"It's all right," Sagot said, "they've just given him a little sedative; we'll walk slowly. The boy wants to go home now. Come on, Thorn."

He was not in his bed, he was lying on cushions on the riser that touched the main room wall, the windows showed branches lashing in the rain, glass spotted and distorted with water. The audio played thunder and rain-sound. Lightning flashed. The air-conditioning wafted moist, cool air and the smell of woods in rain. He lay against the cushions in the room he knew (but the walls always changed) and blinked. He knew those trees, the one that bent, the crooked limb, the rocks, the way one could climb—

"Here." Duun sat down on the riser and took a cup and poured him tea. "It's got aghos in it, don't spit it: you could use the calories."

He took it in one hand and sipped at it. The spice was sickly sweet, but it tasted better than his mouth did. He blinked at Duun. His neck was stiff; he had been sleeping wrong.

"That's good," Duun said. "I moved you in here."

"Carried me?" He remembered bed; remembered Duun rousing him once and making him drink.

"I still can."

"Duun, they—"

"Hush."

Thorn caught his breath. So he had been about to embarrass himself. (You have a need, Thorn.) He felt drained and placid now after the storm before. The illusory rain spattered the windows. "That's Sheon, isn't it?"

"I saved that image. I had it done about a year ago. I thought I'd use it someday."

(Some special day. Today? Is it a gift? To make up for the other thing?)

"More tea?" Come on. I want you to wake up now. We're going to have a round in the gym this afternoon."

"You'll kill me."

"I'll go easy, minnow." Duun's face staring at him, half good, half bad, with that forever mocking smile. "You'll manage."

(Is he happy with me now? Was it a test I passed?) "Duun, they had me—"

Duun lifted his right hand, the single finger. Silence, that meant. (I don't want you to talk.)

"They—"

"It didn't happen."

"Dammit, it—"

"It didn't happen. Hush."

Thorn's pulse picked up. He lay there staring at Duun's scarred face, at the unblinking stare. His heart thumped against his ribs. (What are you doing to me? What are you doing to me, Duun-hatani?)

"You're slow, Thorn. Slow. Speed!"

Thorn tried. He spun and lost his centering, dived backward to save himself as the capped knife crossed his belly: he felt the touch of it, spun away and brought his blade up in defense at what followed. Time, Duun called, and hunkered down. Thorn sat down and wiped his face.

"I'm off. I'll get it back."

"You'll go on practicing," Duun said.

"What—'go on'?" (Has something changed? What's wrong?) *Go on* had the sound of finality.

"Three mornings of a five you'll have your study. Every other day you'll go back to that room. It's another kind of study."

"Duun—"

"—which we won't talk about."

"Duun, I can't!"

"Can't?"

Thorn flinched. He clenched his arms about his knees. "Have you? Have you been through it?"

"We won't talk about it. Every other day you'll face that. You'll know you're going to face it; and you'll walk in on your own and be polite with the meds. This is the only time I'm going to tell you this. If you truly begin to suffer they'll put you down to once a five-day. But that's something the meds will decide for medical reasons, not your untutored whims."

"Forever? For the rest of my life?"

Duun hesitated. Duun rarely hesitated in answers, though he might stop to consider. In this, the pause was minute and Duun frowned. "It's a test, minnow. You're not going to fail it, hear? I'm not going to tell you how long it lasts. You're not going to bring the matter through that door. Next time you'll sleep it off in the medical section. When you can walk home on your own you'll do it; and you'll walk in at whatever hour and say Hello, Duun, I'm home, what are we going to do?—the way you do every day. Sagot was soft and let you do as you pleased, and I should have sent you back right then and not coddled you. Life's not likely to coddle you.''

"Neither are the meds, Duun! It *hurt*, it—I don't know how to handle it, Duun, give me some help, for the gods' sakes tell me how I ought to handle it!''

"Accept it. With dignity. Embrace it. With all the strength and cleverness you've got.''

"Did I fail today?''

"No,'' Duun said. "No, you did marvelously well. You can be proud of yourself. You've made a lot of people happy with you, people you've not met. But we won't talk about it anymore. You'll come home and you won't have to talk about it; we'll do everything we always do. I think you'll be glad of that.''

"You won't shout at me.''

A second time Duun looked taken aback, and that was rarer still. "No, minnow, I won't shout at you.''

XI "Good morning," Sagot said.

Thorn walked across the sand the length of the room to where Sagot sat, as she had sat the first time he saw her. Reprise. He walked to the riser facing hers and sat down on the edge, feet dangling, hands locked in his lap. Sagot's face was a stranger's face, withholding everything behind the eyes, an aged, white-dusted mask.

"How are you, Thorn?"

(As if we started over.) "I'm fine, Sagot. Duun says I have to go back there tomorrow. Is it going to be the same?"

"I can't discuss it, Thorn."

He sat there a moment. "I want to know, Sagot. What are they doing?"

"I can't discuss it. Can we get to our lessons?"

"Will you go with me tomorrow?" (Please, Sagot.)

A long silence. "I don't think I can really make much difference. They won't let me bring you home; they're going to insist you stay there; they think they woke you up too fast. They weren't happy at all about my taking you out of there; you were on your feet and you were being reasonable—" Sagot's mouth puckered in humor. "—but a drunk hatani's not to argue with. Tomorrow you'll know what to expect and you won't argue with the meds, all right?"

"I know. I'd still like for you to stay."

"Thorn—"

"Don't talk to Duun about it. I know he'd say no. Just do it, Sagot. I don't trust the meds. I've never liked them."

"I'll be there." Sagot smoothed the heavy fabric of her kilt and rested her hands on her ankles. "Let's talk about the weather—like atmosphere. Like the interaction of the oceans and air masses. When I was at the north pole, that was back in '87, I flew up there, but I went out on this exploration ship, *Uffu Non* was its name. Ask me about the hothonin some time—"

"'What are hothonin?"

"It's this kind of fish, about shonun size.

They catch birds. That's right. They have this white spot on their heads which looks like a small fast-swimming fish when they run just below the surface; a bird dives down, the hothun dives up—snap, no bird. See what assumptions do? Anyway, we put out of Eor port and headed out to sea—"

"He's still sane," Duun said. Ellud faced him, hands on knees, in the normal clutter of Ellud's desk. Duun sat opposite, in the accustomed place. "Let's not push it, Ellud."

"I'm not pushing it," Ellud said. "Council's pushing me. Betan's surfaced. She's alive."

Duun let his face relax in his surprise. "That's no good news. Where?"

"She's in seclusion. Shbit's got her, of course, in his house. That's the report that's gotten to me, via a councillor who talked to a councillor who talked with her. Don't go in there, Duun. For the gods' sake, don't try it at this point. Everything's going our way and Shbit's got nothing but a failed agent."

"The bureau agents must be in Shbit's bed if they're sure what he hasn't got. I don't like their complacency. Tell them that."

"Stay out of it, Duun, Gods, you go after Shbit and you could blow this whole thing into the public eye again, and gods know we've been there too often as it is. The council's rid-ing even just now. The appropriations keep coming."

"I know when Shbit will move. Shbit doesn't know it yet." Duun decided on the tea and poured himself a cup. "One has to suppose he restrains Betan; but I'd rather not suppose at all. What's the report from Gatog? Any details?"

"They've got the problem solved. It turned out to be a software glitch. They took each other out."

Duun frowned. "I figured. False alarm, then. Dammit, Ellud. Those ears go down again and we'll have councillors in the trees."

"It could be worse."

"Believe me, I never quite forgot that." Duun picked up the cup with two fingers of his right hand and turned it with his left, feeling the incised design, natural clay, the costly happenstance of obu art, which was like Ellud, both clever and lacking plan. The paradoxes of the man confounded him lifelong. "I want to see the reports on Shbit. I want to know when he breathes in and how long he holds it. To the second, Ellud, tell your agents that."

". . . in 1582 the first reactor went on line in toghon province—"

". . . in 1582 the Dsonan League established the international council. The immediate motivation was the drought which occurs in cycles

204

in Thogan and which in that year had created considerable hardship on the seventeen million who inhabited the region stretching from—"

". . . in 1593 the first satellite was launched from the Dardimuur coast—"

(Satellite?)

". . . in 1698 Botan no Gelad became the first shonun into space."

"Sagot." Thorn's heart beat very fast. He looked up from his monitor at a placid, aged face. "Sagot, we're in space."

"I was a little girl when Nagin walked on the moon. I remember my oldest brother coming and bringing me to the television and telling me that was the moon and shonun were walking on it. Nagin and Ghotisin and Sar. I went outside in the dark—it was spring and it was a clear night; I looked up at the moon and tried to see where they were, but of course I couldn't. I stared and stared and my brother came out and stood beside me. 'I'll go up there someday,' he said. He did. He flew all the way to Dothog and he walked on another world. He sent me a picture of him standing there in front of a sea of red dunes, you can't tell it's him, of course, the suit's big and cumbersome, and the sunvisor's down, but I know it's him. I still have it."

(Machines in the dark. Things spinning.)

("The world's wide, minnow, wider than you know.")

"Can I see it? Can I meet your brother?"

"He's dead. He died, oh, forty years ago. He had an equipment failure, out on the Yuon desert, on Dothog. Air ran out. I've got the picture, though. I'll bring it."

"I'm sorry, Sagot."

"Child, you grieve and you get over things. I just remember my brother now, not the end of him, just the living. You know the shuttleport, just outside Dsonan? You can feel the ships take off. You can hear them when they come in, like thunder, even through the walls—"

"Is that that sound?" ("Duun, what's that?" "I don't know, buildings have a lot of sounds. Mind on your business, minnow.")

"—about every five-day. They carry cargo up to the station, pick up what the station makes, medicines and such, and bring it back down. There's still the Dothog base, it's quite a little town now, all domes and connecting tunnels. All scientists. About once a year you can get a tour out from the station, but it's horrendously expensive, the kind of thing only the rich can afford and too rough to please most of that sort, but they still have a few visitors. I've dreamed about it, I'd like to go, but it takes a year each way; and something always comes up. I don't know—" Sagot looked at her hands and looked up. "I think, I think deep down I'm superstitious about it, I think my brother's still there, still climbing about over the dunes and enjoying himself, but if I went there it'd be just a place, I'd see the town all grown up and the damn tourists and I'd go out in the desert and he wouldn't be there. Then he'd be dead for me, really dead—oh, gods. I'm sorry, boy, the old woman talks on and on. You wanted to ask me about space."

"Have you been there?"

"I've been up to the station. It's a barren kind of place, all tubes and tunnels—"

(Tunnels. Metal tunnels. Going on and on, bending up when you walk them—)

"—and one part of it looks a lot like all the other parts. And strangely enough you don't really get to see the stars much. You can see them from the shuttle if you get up front—they let you do that. It's beautiful. The world's beautiful. Haven't you seen it in pictures?"

(The dark globe with the fire coming over it, the spinning place—)

"No, of course you haven't. I've got this marvelous window-tape. I bought it on the station. It's the earth from space. I think I can find a copy for you. You get to watch the sun come up over and over again round the curve of the world; you get to see all the seas and the clouds all swirled—"

* * *

"He's coming round—he's coming round. Hold the injection. He's coming out of it."

"That jolted him. *Something* happened."

"Quiet. He can hear. Let's get him out of here."

"Do you hear us, Thorn? Move your hand if you hear us."

"*Aaaaaaaaiiiiii!*"

It was his voice. Thorn was the one screaming. He came fighting up out of the dark, and dark was about him, stars aglow in giddy distance.

Light blazed, white and awful; he flung himself out of bed blind and hit the wall with his back before he saw Duun in the doorway, against the dark of the hall, Duun naked from his sleep and staring at him. "Are you all right, Thorn?"

Thorn leaned against the cold surface at his back. His limbs began to shake in aborted reaction. "I'm sorry, Duun."

Duun kept on staring at him. Duun's ears were back. Thorn peeled himself off the wall. The windows were sunrise now, sun coming up over grasslands. Duun had disrupted the timer. The air-conditioner wafted grass-scent, dewy and cold. Thorn shivered again, feeling the draft on his skin. Bedclothes made a trail over the side of the bed and onto the sand, the route his flight had taken.

"It was a nightmare," Thorn said. "I dreamed. . . ." (Faces. Sounds.) He began to shake again. "Faces like mine, Duun—they didn't make me up!"

Duun said nothing. His face had that masklike look that it had when he was not going to say anything.

"Did they?" Thorn persisted.

"Who said they didn't make the tapes up?"

"Don't do this to me, Duun!"

"You don't sound sleepy. You want a cup of tea, a bit to eat?"

Thorn surrendered. Duun was being kind. Duun was leading him off again. Thorn knew the tricks. He ripped the sandy bedclothes loose and threw them down on the floor. The bed wanted turning and thumping anyway, and the blankets could use washing. Duun had left the door and left it open. Thorn pulled the bin open in the side of the riser and took out yesterday's clothes, but it was before baths and he had to dress again before class.

Duun was in the kitchen when he came in, setting the teapot on the riser. "Sobasi?"

"It's all right." The microwave was busy. It went off and Thorn pulled the plates out and set them on the table. (Faces. Faces. The station. Ships coming and going. Dots and sym-

209

bols. Chemistry. The value of pi. Numbers.)
Thorn sat down and swung his legs about,
crossed; Duun did the same and poured tea for
himself. "I drink too much of this stuff," Duun
said, "it ruins my sleep."

"So do I. Duun, can we talk about it—once?"
Duun's ears went flat.

"Dammit, please!"

Duun held out the teapot to him with a bland
look on his face. "One question. I'll listen to it.
Only one, Haras-hatani. You don't have to ask
it now if you want to think about it. Snap
judgment's never good."

Thorn took the teapot, composed his face
and poured. (I hate him. I hate him. He hasn't
got a nerve in his body.) "I'll tell you when I
ask it: I don't want you taking the first question
I ask and claiming that lets you off. Have you
got a lover?"

(Got him.) Duun's ears flicked; the eyes dilated and contracted. "Was that the nightmare?"

"No. I'm just curious."

"None now. A companion for a while. I sent
her off." Duun filled his mouth and swallowed.

"Why?"

(Another strike. I hadn't thought that.) "She
would have wanted marriage eventually. I
didn't."

"How old are you?"

"Minnow, when you started this, we were talking about one question. Is this all pertinent?"

"You were onto me yesterday because I always take the defensive; attack sometimes, you said. I realize I do that even outside the gym. So I'm attacking. Do you think you're old?"

Duun grinned. "You'll go too far pretty soon, Haras-hatani, and I'll call this game. Do you think I'm old?"

"What was your solution for the government?"

"To make you hatani. Which I've done."

"Why didn't you want me to learn about the world the way it is?"

"You have now, haven't you?" Duun shrugged. (Gods, not a flicker.) "It never came up; too much of Sheon and too little of the world. When we came here—two years early, and not quite my planning, I might remind you—" (Counterattack and hit.) "You were pretty badly shaken, if you'll recall, and you knew too damn much you were unusual." (Hit again. Gods! he's got no mercy.) "What was I going to do? Throw the world at you in a day? Listen, minnow, I had a problem on my hands, I had a boy to bring up without newscasts, without pictures of cities, without any hint what went on outside Sheon's woods, because any photograph with people in it was going to show a smart young lad that people all look a lot like me and none of them like you. I had to educate you without educating you, if you see the problem, because I didn't want you to suffer with your difference. I wanted to give you a childhood, and I gave you the best one I knew: I gave you mine."

(He's working on me. He's telling the truth. What *was* the experiment? They're not done with it. It's still going on.) Thorn felt sweat gather in the folds of his knees and beneath his arms.

"You have to admit," Duun said, "the last two years there's been a lot poured into your head. A lot of facts. You've come from the past to the present. I'll tell you: when I started I didn't know what your mental capacity might be, whether it was normal, you understand. I didn't know whether I *could* do what I planned. I had to know that before I let anyone else set hands on you . . . whether you could be hatani. Remember Ehonin's daughter."

"Why is it important—to have me be hatani?"

"Is that your question?"

"I told you I would say when it was my question."

"Well, I'll tell you that one someday."

"This is my question: Why do the things they make me see have the station in them and why is the station full of people like me?"

"That's two questions."

"It's one. A hatani ought to see the unity."

"Well, I'll treat it as one. The station isn't, it's full of ordinary people, and I told you the truth, you're unique. Probably the tests are making you dream in strange ways; it's got psychological implications I'm sure the meds are interested in."

"The experiment's still going on, isn't it?" (Gods, he's twisted me up again. Everything. Everything's an illusion, like the windows.) "Isn't it, Duun?"

"That's still another question. I'm not going to answer that. I told you I didn't want to bring the matter through the door; I'd think you'd be glad of a place where people didn't take your mind apart and play games with what you know."

"Gods, tell me where that *is!*"

Duun smiled; or maybe it was the scar. "Eat. You woke me up. You can damn well eat the breakfast you made me cook."

"It's a language, Sagot. Why don't they just tell me that?"

"Hush. I can't talk about it."

"*What are they doing to me?*"

"Thorn, there's no way I can discuss it. Please."

"I ache when I get out of there. I feel like someone's taken me and twisted me inside out. I see things in my sleep. I've had the windows changed. It was stars. I'd wake up and not know where I was and I felt like I was falling, like the sleep-falling, only worse. It's woods now, and sometimes Sheon's woods in the rain, I can't sleep without that. I wish they'd change that awful desert picture in the lab."

"It's meant to be restful."

"There's too much sky in it. It's dead. I dream of a place like that and I don't like it."

"I'll ask them to change it. I'm sure they will. They really try to be good to you, you know that."

"They hate me."

"Boy, they're professionals. They have to be cold. Their minds are busy thinking what to do and they're like all professionals, they get to handling people just like they push their buttons and expect things to work. They forget there's a person attached to that leg and that arm because they're looking down into their minds seeing on a different level, like how the veins and nerves run. On that level your body's just a map with pathways going here and there, and I'm afraid they're on those tracks without much thinking that somewhere up that network there's a skull with a brain in it and a very anxious young man living there and watching and listening to what they're saying to each other."

(Sagot, you're redirecting. I know that trick.

I'm a boy between two crafty adults and they keep me off my balance all the time. I get tired of fighting the storm. I just want to sink down and quit sometimes.)

"I'm thinking about killing myself."

Panic. Sagot looked at him in shock. Thorn grinned and ached inside.

"I was joking. You're very good at getting me off the subject. I thought I'd do it too."

"Don't joke about a thing like that, boy. I had a husband do that on me. I don't think it's funny at all."

"Don't tell me about your husband! You're doing it to me again! I won't listen to you!" He flung himself off the riser and stalked across the sand, headed out. Sagot was silent behind him. He got as far as the outside door, in the room with the vase and branch; and the door was locked. He hit the switch. Hammered on the door. "Open it up! I want out of here!"

There was no escape. Eventually he had to go back (as Sagot planned) into the room. But he sat down on the last riser and folded up his legs and studied the veins on his hands and ankles, which were distended in anger. Maps. Pathways. Sagot's husband had probably killed himself, she was not making it up. She was sitting up there with an ungratefully rude boy sulking in front of her and he had struck at her in a hatani way. He had hit Cloen. He had hit

Sagot. Both times he had perverted what he knew.

He got up finally, and walked up and sat down in front of Sagot. "You can shout at me, Sagot. Please."

"I don't need to."

(Hit. Deft and killing as Duun's wit when he was crossed.) Thorn flinched inside. "Forgive me, Sagot. Sagot, don't hate me."

"Wicked boy. By guile and redirection. I can tell you're Duun's handiwork. Back to the meds, are we?"

"Just don't tell me they don't. I can read bodies; I can read eyes, Sagot. They hate me and they're afraid of me and they made me what I am. Is that reasonable of them?"

"Maybe it's the hatani they're afraid of. Did you think of that? People don't like being read. A hatani stops at your door, you give that hatani food, a place to sleep, and you start thinking over every move you make because you know you're being read, constantly, every tiny move. It would take a very stupid person or a very innocent one to relax with a hatani under his roof."

"A hatani doesn't judge if he's not asked to. Sometimes not even then. Why should they worry?"

"Guilt. Everyone's guilty of something. A hatani makes you know what you're guilty of."

"Even hatani are guilty, Sagot."

"But they cover it. They know how not to be read, don't they? If they really try. Sometimes they don't." Sagot got up and came and sat down next to him, put her arm around him. "Sometimes they don't want to, do they? Come on, lean on me, I won't tell anyone."

"Tell me about the test, Sagot."

"Wicked lad." Her hand pressed his shoulder, close to his neck, and made him nervous. He shrugged and she slipped it to the middle of his back. "You have a hatani mind, all right. You're growing up."

"I hear words, Sagot, sounds run in my head and I hear words in them."

"What do they say, these words?"

"They tell me hello, they want something, I can't tell what, they talk about the sun and the earth, they talk about math and chemistry, oxygen, they say, and carbon, over and over, and they talk nonsense, the elements, the reactions inside the sun, the lifecycle of stars—"

Sagot's arm had gone tense. He turned and looked at her at close range, saw her eyes dilate and contract. "Did I just scare you?" Thorn asked.

"Go on talking."

"I'm not supposed to talk to you about it. You keep telling me that."

"You can tell me about this. Go on."

"There isn't anything more. I can't remember anything else. I see that desert place and a place like a space station, I see the earth in space with the sun coming up, and faces—faces like mine, I see the space station full of them, I see people like me coming and going and talking to each other—sometimes they're mad, and I can read them if I can't figure out what they're saying, one wants something and she's a woman—Duun says I imagine it, but I'd never imagine a thing like that, her mouth is all red and her hair is long and her eyes are all painted round the edges: she wants something very bad and she's angry with a man but he's sorry and they go on meeting in this place, these places where people eat and have clothes, clothes for people with no hair, and she's shaped like—" He shaped the image of fullness of his chest. (White all white, and large and strange-looking.) "And finally—there are a lot of people that come and go—she goes off with this other man and they go into his bedroom and they love each other, but it isn't love, she doesn't even like him, and he's mad about that, maybe about something else; then she leaves and she goes and finds the first man but he's about to go somewhere and he doesn't want to talk to her. Her eyes run. He goes away. She goes to this place where people eat and she's very unhappy. Then he walks through the door and he comes over to sit with her, but not on ordinary furniture, on these legged things, all the furniture's like that. She's pretending she's not glad to see him, she keeps eating. He knows she's pretending and he says something and they look at each other and say something about going somewhere, and then it stops and I don't know where they went."

Sagot took his face between her hands and he was so lost he let her. She pulled his face down to her level and washed his eyes with her tongue, which made him feel strange and loved, even as old as Sagot was.

"Is that what I'm supposed to see?"

She let him go. "Go home. I'll call Ogot."

"What am I supposed to see? Is it over? Am I through with that?"

"I don't know. Go home."

XII

Ellud paced the floor and flung his arms out: "I can't cover this!"

"You don't have to." Duun stayed seated. "I'm taking him this afternoon. I'll want the copter on the roof, I'll want the plane at Trusa, no slip-ups; take one off the line. I'll take it myself."

"Gods, your license is expired. I won't have it. You don't fly these damn things nowadays, the damn computers do. I'll get you a pilot." Ellud threw that out and lost his case.

"Do that. One hour. I'm headed out." Duun went for the door.

"They'll have my post, they'll move the minute you're clear of the roof, I'll have councillors at this door."

"Watch Shbit, that's all. I'll get him back for you."

"The Guild won't take him!"

"Is that hope they will or hope they won't?"

Ellud stood there with his mouth open. Duun left.

Thorn hurried; he had a bundle under his arm that was a change of clothes, his and Duun's and Duun's gray cloak, wrapped around things they needed from the bath and tied with a cord; he had new winter-clothes on, quilted coat, baggy trousers, quilted boots: so did Duun, striding along beside him to the elevator.

"Where are we going, Duun?" Half protest and half question, third time posed. (Have I broken some rule, have I made Duun mad?) But he could not read Duun now, except that there were secrets and Duun was in a great hurry to get him out—(Outside?) He had not worn pants and coat since Sheon, in the coldest weather. Had never worn boots. It was only the beginning of fall.)

(He knows what I told Sagot. I've done something wrong! We're running again, like we ran from Sheon—men with guns, people are hunting us— But that's crazy. They wouldn't. I haven't talked to anyone I shouldn't, I haven't done anything—)

(Have I?)

The elevator door opened. Duun went through last and used a card to operate it. The elevator shot up and up, past all the floors between them and the roof.

The door whisked open in the cupola. Beyond the windows was true sky, gray cloud, a copter with its blades turning. Guards were waiting there to open the door for them and the wind skirled in with bitter chill. "Head down!" Duun yelled at him and ran, ducking low when he got near the copter. Thorn remembered that, ran, with the wind of the blades burning his face. He kept low until he reached the copter, and clambered in like Duun did, as fast as he could, flung himself into the seat and started fastening straps. (Like the simulator. But this isn't. This is real.) The copter upped power and surged upward with a vengeance. The tops of Dsonan's tall buildings spun dizzily into view, the deep chasms of rail-courses and maintenance-ways, the distant port with the gray light shining off the water beneath a smear of clouds.

"We're going to the airport," Duun told him, shouting in his ear. "We've got a plane waiting for us."

Thorn looked at Duun with question available to be read. Pleading.

"We're going up to Avenen," Duun shouted at him. "The Guild headquarters. You'd better settle your mind on this trip, minnow. As many hatani as they can muster are going to be coming in there and you're going to have to do it this time or not at all. There won't be a second chance."

"For *what?*"

"To get you Guild protection, that's what."

They ran from the copter to a building and shed their quilted winter gear for suits that hugged the body. Attendants impersonal as the meds worked at fastenings, jerking at them, two at a time, rough in their frantic haste: masks next, that dangled about their necks, and helmets with a microphone inside. "Run," Duun said then, bending to snatch up the baggage, and they ran, out the door attendants held open for them, into a thunderous noisy building open at either end, where a plane sat with its fans at idle, a dip-nosed machine with stubby backswept wings. "This thing uses a runway," Duun yelled over the noise. "We're going to roll out from here—go round behind the wing, there's a ladder."

There was, pushed up against the plane. The canopy was up. Duun tossed the baggage to a guard, scrambled up the ladder and Thorn hit the treads behind him, hampered by the suit that restrained his limbs, panting when he reached the wing surface and crawled over the side close on Duun's tail. There was a pilot and co-pilot and two more seats in back in a cockpit that hardly looked big enough for the seats up front: Duun trod on one seat and dropped into place in the second, grabbed complicated belts and fastened them, and Thorn slid into the one beside him—belts like the simulator. Plug-ins for the mask hoses between their legs: Duun showed him and rammed it home. "Communications switch," Duun's voice came over the speaker over his ear, and Duun turned a face unrecognizable in an insect-like mask to show him the three way sliding switch and button on the side. The canopy was sliding forward with a whine of hydraulics. The pilot turned his head and made some signal with an uplifted hand to Duun and Duun made one back. The pilot turned around but the co-pilot was handling things: the fans picked up and the plane began to roll out of the building, faster and faster under open, overcast sky, the tires bumping on uneven pavings, the Dsonan skyline to their left unreal as a city window-view.

Faster still. They swung out onto a long expanse of concrete and the engine whine increased. The force slammed them back as the plane made its run and thundered out over the river, pulled a sharp bank and showed river for a long dizzy moment until the pilot decided to fly rightwise up again.

"Gods," Thorn said. His heart raced as clouds shredded past and still the climb kept up. (Why this fast? Why this sudden? What's Duun up to?) "How fast can this plane go?"

"Mach two plus if it has to. It's a courier plane—armed, in case you should wonder. And in case you should wonder again, yes, there's a reason. It's problems on the ground I'm worried about. I don't expect trouble, but there's that remote chance. There's a remote chance of trouble even up here. There's a ghota unit over in Hoguni province that's got one of these and I'm worried where its orders come from."

"Ghota? Aren't they guards?"

"Hired. Warrior guild. One of two. The kosan and the ghota. Our friends up front are kosanin. They take one service for life. Ghotanin rent themselves out; you don't trust them until you know how long their contract's for and whether you're the only one paying them. Like one-year wives. They're always hunting for their next advantage. Kosanin won't serve with them. That's why they're in separate units."

"Duun-hatani, I might not know enough!"

"Whatever you do don't lie and don't flinch. No one ever knows enough. That's all I can tell you now. Two rules. A third. Remember Sheon.

Remember the knife on your pillow. Remember the pebble-game. But always be polite."

They came screaming in at a runway that jutted out into the sea, braked in a straining effort, and turned sharper than seemed likely toward another collection of buildings and aircraft of all sizes, most small.

And none sleek as their own. "Well," Duun said, "no one's beat us here except the locals and the happen-bys."

Thorn looked, searching. There were insignia on most of the craft. Some were striped and most were white. A copter waited, rotors turning. "Is that ours?"

"We'll hope it is." Duun's hand gripped his, painfully hard. "Hear me. From here on there will be no mistakes, Haras-hatani."

A massive building spread across the land beyond the airport. They had it in sight as they came in, a flat sprawl unlike other buildings Thorn knew. Gray stone. Hatani gray. The guild-hall.

Avenen.

The plane stopped. Engine-sound dwindled. A vehicle whisked up and towed a ladder into place. The canopy slid back, admitting chill wind.

Duun pitched their baggage out into an attendant's hands, climbed out and Thorn followed in haste. (Think, think, watch these attendants, watch everything.)

(Is it all some test? Did Duun lie? Are there really ghotanin after us and would they come here?)

Duun recovered the bundle of their belongings and headed for the copter. Thorn ran at his heels, mask flapping and the suit impairing his movements. (Watch these people. Watch all of them, watch their hands.)

Up the short couple of steps into the copter, the pilot in his place. (Duun's nose is better. He'd smell fear if that man meant trouble, even through all this oil stink.) Thorn fell into his seat beside Duun and belted in as the copter lifted, turned, heaved itself off in its tilted fashion and ground flew along in surreal intimacy after the courier-plane's sun-dazzled altitude. There was only the illusion of speed. It took long minutes to come gliding over the gray walls, over buildings that looked like a dozen architects had quarreled and each changed the plan.

A landing circle came up on a rooftop. There were men standing near it, gray-cloaked, looking up at them as the copter settled.

"They're all right," Duun said. "One thing you can believe: no ghota would wear that color here." The rotors slowed and Duun handed Thorn the baggage and climbed out.

Thorn dropped off the step and followed Duun out from under the blades. The copter roared off again, pelting them with dust, fluttering the gray cloaks.

Duun took his helmet off and walked with it under his arm. Thorn managed the bundle enough to get his off and the wind caught his hair, cold and unforgiving. He looked at the five standing there to meet them, handsome men, one he thought was a woman, all in their gray cloaks and black kilts; and he and Duun were disheveled and dangling masks and hoses like two animate machines lately disconnected. They gazed at Duun and at him—for the first time, at him who had no like, at blowing hair and his smooth face in all its strangeness, and he could not read what they thought. That before anything else convinced him where he was. No one but Duun could go so unreadable to him until now.

But these could. These great sprawling buildings were full of those who could, every one.

"He's more imposing than the pictures would indicate," Tangan said, a wisp of a man, so old his cheeks were gaunt and even his crest had whitened. The hands clasped in his lap were gaunt and crossed with knife scars, gotten in a youth so long ago it stretched into myth in the Guild, among novices. Duun sat on the white sand which novices had raked into artistic patterns among the five huge rocks which adorned this ancient room. The lights here were electric but that was the only change from the fifth century. Generations of hatani hands had worn these great boulders dark, smoothing them as surely as the river had from which they were taken. Generations of irreverent novices had sat on them and perched there to do their raking, springing from one to the other and (sometimes, novices being the same in every generation) making it a game, leaping and jumping and thrusting at one another with rake handles.

Tangan had caught a certain rebel and oft-warned novice in that game, among others. And Duun had rued it. Four ten-days of cleaning the sand by hand. It shocked him, how much this man had aged.

"I've gotten used to his looks," Duun said.

"Have you?"

Duun met Tangan's guarded stare. "I've had near twenty years."

"Twenty years of power beyond any precedent."

"Sixteen hiding on a mountain, in a woods. Five performing unmentionable tasks which teach any man humility. So does dealing with Dsonan."

"Ah. How is the capital?"

"Carrying news to you is like bringing water to the well."

"How is the capital?"

"There are more ways to cheat on an agreement than they teach here, Tangan-hatani."

"Paradoxically prosperous times. Money. Is that what you see?"

"A lot of new money—paid out in the least educated provinces, to elect fools who'll take orders, who can only see ways to entrench themselves and make sure contracts go to the right companies. Some of these fools are evident, and shrewd country-folk keep voting them in because the powers in their districts might buy one ten times worse and far more subtle. I tell you we should send one of the novices walking in Elsnuunan and Yoth. Some herder might be passionate enough on some given day to pose us a question. But some of these fools have passed for astute councillors, and protect themselves so well they make and break young politicians on their own."

"Shbit no Lgoth?"

"He will want to challenge."

"He has. His agent is on the way."

Duun smiled softly. "This will be a ghota, I suspect."

"You know this person?"

"Likely we've met."

"You're managing Shbit, then. How well?"

"I could do better. My hours have been occupied. So this man is a danger. I would have removed him arbitrarily but I was crippled by too much power. I could have done too much. So I could do nothing."

"I predicted this."

"I predicted Shbit but I didn't know what his name would be. There was too much money being made. And I was in Sheon wiping noses. Master, you know an answer, maybe: was there another way?"

Long silence. Tangan laced his hands and studied them and looked up. "I saw where you might put us. I thought back over all my years and all the years of the Guild and wondered where the crux was. I think it was when walls were raised. Everything led to this. You put us in a hard place; if we deny him protection we light the fire that will destroy us; if we take him we loose a firestorm. I don't want to contemplate this choice. I'm being frank with you: I ask myself at night how I taught my student that you find yourself capable of this. A hatani ought to have a flaw. A hatani ought to doubt himself enough to have a little guilt of his own. You have none. You burn with too much light, Duun-hatani. You blind me. I can't see whether you're right or wrong. Perhaps it will stop mattering. Perhaps the dark comes next. I confess to trusting you in one thing; I confess to cowardice in this. I didn't believe you'd come here, even when I knew you were training him. Free-hatani would have been my solution."

Duun contemplated a long while. "Master, you say in one breath you predicted my power-lessness; in the next you say you couldn't pre-dict my coming here at the last."

"To infect us with your powerlessness?"

Duun looked up. "Tangan-hatani, in many re-spects he's a boy like other boys. Remember that."

"Is that your wisdom?"

"Tangan-hatani, if I'm a fire I'm the safer for having had a hearth to burn in."

"Do we make a lamp out of this one and set him on a shelf?"

"You might, but I'd hope it's a damn steady one."

"Keep him here?"

"Set him where you choose. The guild itself is a principal in this solution. So am I. I let you judge."

"We have another choice."

"The guild won't abdicate this."

"Do you predict what the Guild will do?"

"Is that anger, master Tangan?"

"Of course not. It's overweening pride. My student has set us all in a trap. Angmen must have felt pride like that when Chena pulled the guild gates down."

Duun folded his hands in his lap. "You'll handle it."

"Do the scars ache, Duun-hatani? You were such an agile student."

(Strike and draw.) "I have my ways of compensating, Tangan-hatani. You taught me patience, after all."

Thorn searched the room they gave him: it was a confortable one, all bare wood and aged stone. A fire of real wood burned in the hearth: he had not had that comfort since Sheon, and it might have lured him at once to warm himself there. They gave him water with the assurance it was safe; they gave his meat and cheese with a confection of preserved beanberries. They gave him a bed of furs, and the sand on the floor was white and fine and deep, newly baked and arranged in meticulous spirals. In the next room a hot bath was waiting, milky with aromatics and soothing oils. They smiled at him, hatani smiles, neither false nor true.

And he searched the place, hunting pebbles. There were none. He was thirsty after the long flight and the running. His limbs were chafed and sweaty from the flight suit. He had set their baggage on the wooden riser that was also the bureau. "Is that gray cloak yours?" a hatani had asked, watching while he unfolded these things. "No," Thorn had said with a clear-eyed stare, knowing that they knew whose it was. "It must be Duun's," that hatani said. "It is," Thorn said back. "Give me his belongings," the hatani said then; "I'll put them in his room."

Thorn had smiled then, as certainly as he could. "I'd be a fool to disobey him; forgive me, hatani: when he blames you, tell him it was my fault. In my inexperience I couldn't tell what to do, so I followed his orders."

Another hatani had come up beside him then and reached out his hand. "Please, visitor: let me at least put these things away for you."

"No," Thorn had said, turning the hand with a slow move of his own. "No, hatani. Forgive me."

That hatani drew back. "No one will trouble you till morning, visitor," the other said. They closed the door behind them.

(It can't be that easy. There's another trick.)

Thorn searched for it. He stripped off the suit, down to his small-kilt. He investigated the food, breaking up the cheese and tearing the meat apart. He drained the tub. He turned out the bed. He searched the closet and pulled out the bureau drawer to look at the space behind it. He racked his brain then. (Even the furniture could hide something.) So he probed the boards of the closet, he investigated the toilet and the bathtub riser, and the sink.

The faucet was dry. That was one thing amiss.

He felt into it and found nothing. (Damn. *Something's* wrong there. Maybe it's to prevent my drinking that and not the pitcher.) He tried to move even the tub and the bed and the big riser near it. He investigated the walls.

And finally, he knelt down in the corner near the door and began to move the deep sand.

He found the small panel in the stone beneath when he had shifted half the sand in the room. He was panting by then. He wiped at his face with a dry and dusty arm. (No.) He remembered Sagot's fish and the bird. Duun laying his pebble on the table beside the teapot. (Trust nothing.)

He got his dress kilt and pried up the panel with his thumbnail through the cloth. He laid it back. There was a pebble in a small recess. He went to the bureau, got his razor from his kit and a square of tissue. And with that he raked the pebble out and wrapped it in tissue, replaced the lid and contemplated the long wave of sand which wanted redistributing.

("Be polite.") Perhaps it extended to leaving the room in order.

And then another thought came creeping into his mind. ("Snap. No bird. See what assumptions do?")

(Fish and bird. Pebble and pot.)

(Is there any assurance there's no second stone?)

Half the room remained. (And—gods—how much time? It might be in the sand. I can't move it except by hand.)

He put the one stone securely in his belt and started scooping the rest of the sand away.

The other secret well was in the far corner. There was no third. He stared at a great mound of sand over by the door and went and cleared the plate of the mangled food, and with the plate scooped and scattered sand as quickly as he could. His back and arms ached; his knees were raw, for all that he had tried to pad them with his spare clothing in his crawling about. His hands were abraded of their calluses, all the protection he acquired on them. He was thirsty and thanked the gods he had had breakfast at least, for he would not touch the food. (There might be a pebble in the source vessel, not even in this room. How could I trust it? And the sink. Something's wrong. Do I fail if I don't use the safe things? I'm sweaty. I smell awful. I can't go to any interview smelling like this. I look like this and now I have to offend their noses too. And I've used the only change of clothes I had.)

(Use Duun's? Gods, no.)

(What time is it?)

Thorn threw sand and spread it, waded into it and kicked it as level as he could with his feet and tried to think. He stood panting, returned to the bath and worked at the sink plumbing until his hands bled. Nothing budged it, and he sat on the cold tiles with his legs going numb. (It's not going to give. It's just the pitcher they want me to use, that's all.) And his mouth was dry, his throat raw with dust and exertion. (I've won. There were two pebbles. I've got them both. I won't drink the water, I won't eat the food; I won't sleep in the bed.)

(The mattress. Is there a rule about not breaking things?)

(In Duun's game we never did.)

(His rules. He'd have taught me. He'd have done it right.)

He heaved himself up off the tiles, limped in to the warm sand in front of the fire and sank down there, gritty and sweaty and chilled. (Gods, at least I can use the razor and the lotion I brought. That smells good. Maybe it will cover some of my stink.)

(I daren't sleep. They promised no one would bother me. I daren't believe that either.)

He felt after the pebbles in his belt and took out his prizes, never touching them with his fingers. They lay in the tissue, each unique, one with a white vein, the other white with a black. (Would someone ever cheat?)

(Fool!)

He looked at the fire, the abundant embers in the grate.

He went to the table and got the pitcher and poured it out on the coals. A great hissing of steam rose up and there was still a vivid glow in the coals.

(Oh, damn, damn, *damn!* The bath I drained. The water that won't run.)

He took the pitcher to the bath and tried the taps again, got down on his knees and dipped out all the water in the toilet with his hands: it filled the pitcher once.

The coals had livened again when he got back. He poured the water on and got the platter and poured sand on, waited a while and scooped some of it out with the plattter. There was still heat. There had been a metal grate beneath the logs. The coals lay at a forearm's depth in sand.

(How much time? O gods, I daren't wait for this.)

He cast the top sand away. He got down to the coals and used his razor again to rake them onto the platter, to turn them and examine them. Bit by bit the collection in the bathroom grew; and he got down to the deeper coals and into the heat. There was a metal grate. He got that out using his flight helmet for a hook. He moved more coals, and heat cracked the plate in two. He used the larger piece and raked more gingerly. His hands blistered now. The pain was a new encounter every time he reached in; everything he held was hot. The shard broke again and one by one the pieces he used broke to smaller and smaller shards. He abandoned his taking the coals to the bath, he only slid them out onto the sand and examined them and reached back for more. He set his knee on a hot ember and tears blurred his eyes, ran on his face and dried.

From far down in the coals, he scooped out a small black ember which was too regular and too smooth. He rolled it in the sand to cool it and scratched it with his razor. It was a pebble.

He wrapped it with the rest and never flinched at the heat. (Should I stop hunting?)

He kept going, to the last. Off to the side of the hearth, beneath old ash, he found a metal trap, and pried that open with his razor. He burned himself again getting out the small stone at the bottom. But he rolled it into the tissue too, and gingerly searched what little ash was left until he was sure there were no more.

He sat down then, slumped with his arms on his knees until he had rested. And then he began to pick the grate and the dead coals up and restore them to the fireplace.

The door opened when he was in the middle of this task. The hatani who had put him into the room were back. They looked about the room.

One walked into the bath and came back again, and Thorn got to his feet.

"Come with us," the first hatani said.

Thorn took his sooty kilt and wrapped it about himself, then started gathering up all the rest of his and Duun's belongings, every one.

"Visitor," the other said. "it's clear you're not leaving, from the condition of this room. There's no need to pack."

"Please." Thorn wrapped Duun's cloak and change of clothing in his flight suit, which, with the cloak, was the only thing left unsoiled. He gathered his razor off the floor and put it in the helmet along with the lotion bottles.

"Oh, don't be a fool!" the other said. "They'll laugh at you in the hall. You're going to meet master Tangan, with all the hatani in the house! You can't drag all that stuff in!"

"I never got to give Duun his cloak. I don't know. I might lose these things. I'll let him tell me what to do."

"Come on, then, fool. But I warn you they'll laugh. Gods—you're filthy. Do you want a change of clothes? I can lend you some."

"Thank you. I'll ask Duun when I see him."

The other gestured at the open door.

* * *

The corridor gave way to an open hall, a pit sided with many steps; and gray-cloaked hatani sat on those steps, hundreds of them. The floor was sanded and swirled with raking. There were great boulders on the sand. On each of them a hatani sat.

At the bottom of the steps in front of him stood Duun, the only one without a cloak. Duun lifted his chin slightly and Thorn walked down the steps, his escort behind him.

"You brought my cloak," Duun said. "Have they touched it at all?"

"No, Duun-hatani."

Duun held out his hand and took it and put it on. Duun extended his hand toward the farthest of the rocks. "The last is master Tangen."

Thorn walked down and across the sand, along the narrow path the hatani on the boulders had walked, like the form of a tree. He heard others walk behind him. He stopped in front of the farthest. His belongings were still in his arms.

"You may set those things down." master Tangan said, and lifted his hand in that way Duun had which meant a thing could be trusted. "You will stand." Duun came and stood near him. The two who had brought him stood on the other side. Thorn set his belongings on the ground in front of him.

"You are untidy, young man," Tangan said. "Is this a way to come to this hall?"

"Forgive me, master Tangan."

"Was there something amiss with the room?"

Thorn hesitated. It seemed the right question. He reached into his belt and drew out the tissue. He unfolded it and showed the pebbles. His burns hurt and his sooty hands bled onto the tissue, shaking in spite of all he could do. (Were they all? Did I miss one?)

"Did he drink the water?"

"The pitcher was empty," one of his escorts said.

"Did he eat the food?"

"The food was crumbled," the other said.

"There was a pebble in the pitcher from which that pitcher was poured. There was a pebble in the plate from which that plate was served. Did you drink or eat?"

"No, master Tangan. I poured the water on the fire. I didn't eat. I didn't touch my hand to my mouth after touching the food."

"How can I know this is the truth?"

At first it seemed an accusation. Then it occurred to him it was another question. "You're hatani, master Tangan. If I couldn't find a trick like that you could read me too."

A moment of silence, all about the room. "Did you bathe?"

"No, master Tangan."

"That seems evident."

He was too weary. He only stared up at Tangan, still holding the pebbles.

"What did you do with the water?"

"I let it out, master Tangan, hunting for pebbles."

"Was there one?"

"Not in that tub."

"Lay the pebbles that you found on the sand one by one."

Thorn bent and slipped them from the tissue one at a time. At the third there was a stirring in the seats; at the fourth a greater stirring. He straightened and looked up at the old, old man.

"Four is unusual," master Tangan said simply. "Two beyond the food and water would have passed you. That's the first test. The second is myself. Tell me the worst thing you ever did."

Almost Thorn let his face react. And stopped himself. He thought a moment. (Losing Sheon? But that wasn't from knowledge. That was my ignorance. That blames Duun.) "I shouted at my teacher Sagot, master Tangan. Yesterday."

"Have you stolen?"

"Only from Duun."

There was another stirring in the seats.

"Have you lied?"

"Sometimes."

"Have you killed anyone?"

"No, master Tangan."

"Have you used your skill in a wrong way?"

He shut his eyes. And opened them It was easy to count. "Three times, master Tangan. When I shouted at Sagot and when I hit another student and when I threatened him."

"You're very fast on that answer. Aren't there more?"

Thorn thought again. "I've quarreled with Duun."

"So have I, visitor." A mild ripple of laughter went about the hall. Beside him Duun ducked his head. The master's face never changed. "We have a case in the guild. One member claims a knife another claims. How will you resolve it?"

Thorn bit his lip. Panic rushed through him. (It's a wrong question. There's no answer. Dare I say that?) He found himself shivering in the chill. "Master Tangan, there aren't any such hatani in the guild, who would quarrel over property."

"We have another case. Two sisters marry a man for a one-year each in succession. But no sooner has the first marriage been consummated than the man divorces that wife and marries a third for a three-year. How will you judge?"

"Master Tangan, how do they make the question?"

"The first sister says: Judge between me and my sister and that woman."

(Not the man.)

"That's not a hatani matter, master Tangan. They ought to go to the magistrate."

"They persist. They make the same request."

"Where is their property?"

"They have a house and shop from their father and mother. The man is living and working with the new wife in a property he owns. The new wife is tanun-guild."

"Let them go live in their own house and find a new husband."

"Explain."

"The women want this man more than he wants them and they hate the new wife. They could never share with her."

Master Tangan lifted a hand. Beckoned to someone. Thorn resisted the impulse to turn, but he heard someone walking up. More than one.

"One more case," Master Tangan said. "Look at this woman."

Thorn turned and his heart jolted.

It was Betan. Betan, in a pale blue kilt, a dark blue cloak, with her hands folding before her and her ears laid flat. Her scent reached him on a waft of wind. It was still flowers.

(O Betan.) Exhaustion battered at him. (Hatani after all?)

Her face betrayed nothing.

"Look at me," Master Tangan said. "This

woman accuses you of assaulting her. Of using your persuasion to seduce her and when she saw you naked and knew your physical difference would harm her, she tried to get away, and you used your skill to restrain her until Duun no Lughn intervened. She asks a hatani judgment of me."

(*Was* that what she thought? Was that what I did?)

"What do you say?"

"I—was in a room alone with her. Everything she says could be true."

"Duun-hatani, you were a witness."

"I came in and this woman ran out," Duun said. "I ordered her to leave. I witnessed an embrace in which the woman struggled and broke free."

"As you came in."

"Yes, master Tangan."

"What else did you observe?"

"Anger on my student's part, toward me. He said: 'I wish you had come later.' The woman said nothing. Later my student said. 'I wanted to love her.' I explained the differences would have harmed her."

"He had no knowledge of this?"

"It's possible he didn't understand."

"Did you?"

"No. Yes." Thorn struggled for his composure.

"I pushed her back, master Tangan. She smelled afraid and I pushed her back."

"Away from you."

"He's lying," Betan said. "He's hatani and he's lying with a straight face."

"What do you ask for him?"

"Send him back to Dsonan. Don't let him in the guild."

"What do you ask for her, visitor?"

"I think it's a trap," Thorn said. "I think this is another test and she's hatani."

"Why do you say that?"

"She moves like one."

"You're wrong, young man. She's not hatani, free or guilded."

"She's ghota," Duun said. "Or I'm blind. And she's a fool to come here."

Betan stood there. (Ghota?) Thorn stared at her. He had expected men with guns. (Betan? Ghota?)

"This is my judgment," Tangan said. "Leave this house. I'll not begin a guild war. You have half an hour to reach the airport. Take my warning seriously."

Betan turned on her heel and walked, carefully, up the track past the hatani on the boulders, up the steps at the end of the hall. Thorn trembled, but it was cold; it was the burns. Where Betan had been, where part of his youth had been, was cold inside.

"One more question," Tangan said.

"Master?" Thorn turned and looked up at the old man on the rock.

"What have you done today that you take the most pride in?"

Thorn blinked. It betrayed him and he was chagrined, but his eyes stung and his knees wobbled under him. "Getting Duun's cloak here."

There was laughter, all round the room, stinging laughter, hoarse and harsh.

"It's a novice's trick," master Tangan said. His face relaxed and kindness came through. "Novices who grow up in the guild house never get caught by that, except the first day they arrive. But you weren't told. And you honor your teacher. They laugh because you found four pebbles besides the water and the food. That's very rare. I do fault you on letting the water out. But you made it up the hard way. Those burns will scar, young man. I think you should get them treated before we send you back."

(I've lost, then.)

"You're apprenticed to Duun no Lughn for as long as Duun sees fit. Beyond that point you'll do as you see fit. You have the wisdom to refrain from judgment where you have no knowledge. That's very important. Be gentle. Be merciful. Give true judgments. All other rules of the guild flow from these. A free-hatani judges and the guild will not involve itself. When you judge, the guild will shed blood to back you. Always remember that, Haras-hatani."

"Yes, master Tangan." And for a moment the master's face let him see past another barrier. (This is a worried man. The hatani up there see it now. They were startled into laughter. There is anger in this room.) He slid his glance toward Duun and saw the other half of that expression. (They know something. No. Duun knows and master Tangan discovers it.)

"Take him and get those burns looked to, Duun-hatani."

XIII

"Take care of him," Duun said in leaving him. These were hatani meds, who took Thorn's clothes and made him stand on a plastic grating and rest his hands on tables on either side for them to work on. Two more meds with soap and a small clear water hose started with his hair and washed him on down with sponges: gray water spattered down and swirled away into the white plastic grate, smoke and sand, and the knee stung and throbbed, but their touch was quick and gentle. The meds washed his hands too, but in a different way, with greater care. "This will be cold," one said: something smelled pungent and likely to hurt; it hit his burned right hand with a shock that seemed for a moment to go to the bone, as the med sprayed a clear liquid on. But numbness followed, or the cessation of pain. It was so great a change Thorn knew then how much pain he had been in. The washing went on, and they did the other hand. The right they immersed in something gelatinous; and immersed again in something else, and that hardened to a shiny plasticity while one dried his hair and another saw to his knee and bandaged it. Their touch was kind. So was their manner. "Please, could I have a drink?" Thorn said, meaning from the hose when they could spare a moment. He had wet his lips while they rinsed his hair and face, but was thirsty again. The one drying his hair left off and brought him a cup of water, holding it for him to drink because they were working on his hands. Thorn looked into this man's eyes and saw nothing but kindness.

"You ought to go to bed," the med said who worked on his right hand, "but we understand otherwise. That's finished now. Carry the elbows bent as much as you can, don't close the hands or lift anything, hear, till the gel peels."

But the one working on his left hand finished and drew him by the elbow over to ordinary ground. Another brought a flight suit and a helmet, his own, Thorn thought dizzily, because he had scarred one earpiece. They took it up and began to put it on him with as much efficiency as they had used on his wounds.

(So we're going back.) The meds in Dsonan would take him then and lay him on a table and mutter dark things while they poked and pried into what these meds had done, and they would hurt.

There would be the tapes again. Nothing would have changed. Thorn shivered while they were seeing to the fastenings, and one stopped and felt of the pulse in his neck. "Go straight to bed when you get to Dsonan," the man said.

"We can't give him anything," another said, and looked worried, not the way the meds at home looked, but gentle. "We don't dare. Hope to the gods he doesn't react to the gel." A pat on Thorn's shoulder. "Are you sick at your stomach?"

"No, not very."

They went on with their pulling and tugging. The suit grew tighter. "Damn. He can't manage the helmet."

(Why this haste? What's wrong? Why were they worried? Ghotanin? They let Betan go. Did she get to the airport? Did she go?) The thought of Betan dying afflicted him with pain. (Even if she's my enemy. She was brave to come here.)

"There." A last tug. "That's right. Hold the helmet in your arm, don't use your hands. Call Duun, someone."

"He's outside."

"Thank you," Thorn said, looking at them. He meant it. And one of them opened the door and called Duun in. Duun was in his flightsuit again and had a gray cloth bag with black straps slung over his shoulder, and his helmet in that arm.

"He'll manage, will he?" Duun asked.

"Take care of him," a med said. And to Thorn: "Keep the arms bent. All right? Good-bye."

That was all, then, Duun waited by the door, threw one look past him at the meds as if to thank them, and let Thorn out into the hall. Hatani came and went, none in their gray cloaks now. Most looked to have business on their minds and some looked to be in haste. Many looked at him and Duun as they passed.

(They don't hate me.) Thorn was used to that special look people had when he walked in on them. Even Elanhen. Even Sphitti. Especially Cloen and especially the meds. And Betan in the hall just now. (Their faces don't show it, maybe.)

(But they're hatani. They know me. They know me, inside, past the skin and the eyes and the way I look, that I'm like them. True judgment, master Tangan called it. Hatani judgment.) Thorn felt his throat swell and his eyes sting. (I want to know these people. I want to stay here—just a day or two, just that, I want to talk to them and be with them, and live here all my life.)

There was one hall after another, and at last a stairs leading up to the roof. Duun stopped here and took him by the arms to make him look at him.

"Betan made the port. She took off and they're tracking her. The radar net shows another pair of ghota aircraft just left the ground at Moghtan. The kosan guild is putting planes up from Dsonan."

Thorn blinked, trying to take this in. (For me. For my being here. That's impossible.) He felt numb. "What's Betan up to?"

"She won't get through to the guild. Missiles ring this place. Hatani are headed for Ellud and Sagot this moment, to protect them. And others whose lives might be in question."

Colder and colder. The numbness reached Thorn's heart. "We've got to get there!"

"Others are doing that job. We've got another one." Duun let go Thorn's left arm and pulled him up the stairs in haste. "The first part of it is getting you out of here."

It was no easy matter getting into the plane. Duun shoved up from behind the way they had gotten into the copter and Thorn clambered over the rim and into the cockpit. The skin on his knee tore as he tumbled into the seat, wriggled in and groped as best he could for straps; Duun fell in beside him and snatched the buckle from him, jammed it together, took his connections and rammed those into the sockets before he saw to himself. The engines were roaring, pushing them into motion, and the canopy was sliding forward overhead. Pilot and copilot were ambiguous creatures of plastic and metal, moving thin arms to flip switches in the interval of the seats. The plane picked up speed, swung out onto the runway and straightened itself into a run that slammed them back into the seats.

Wisps of clouds poured past; the sun chased reflections across the cockpit and the plane came about and kept on with the sun on its right wing.

"We're going to pick up our escort in a few minutes," a thin voice came over the speaker in the helmet. The pilot or copilot was talking on their channel. "They'll meet us at Delga."

Duun acknowledged that. The voice came again. "We've just got word. We've got ghota craft headed our way. Our escort's going to intercept. Planes are in the air at Homaan. Council's going into session now."

Thorn leaned his head against the cushioned

seat and stared ahead of him at the milky glare of light, the black, surreal figures of the pilots. There was no world but this, no past or future. He hung motionless above the earth while the sky rushed faster and faster at them and small voices from the ground spoke to the pilots (who themselves could do nothing) and told them that the world was in chaos. Duun spoke of missiles. Of intercepts. Of aircraft which would be lifting from one city and another around the world, across seas and continents. People down there were looking up in fear at planes they could not see, expecting missiles to fall on them. Children standing on that brown rock at Sheon, next the bent tree, would look up and wave at white trails in the sky. ("See us, here we are! Hello!") —while dreadful missiles roared off in fire and smoke.

(This can't be happening.)

(There is no *can't*, minnow.)

"Someone's on intercept with us." The pilot's voice again. "Bearing 45 low."

"From the sea," Duun said. "That's Betan. I figured. Hang on, minnow."

The plane turned in flight. Pressure dragged at them, pulled at jaws and eyes and bowels and Thorn's nose ran; there was a pounding in his ears. The plane rocked. They went into a steep bank. (We're going to crash. We were hit.) Thorn rolled his head against the seat as his heart went wild and the sun spun up again and over the right wing.

"That's a miss on their side, a hit on ours. It's down."

(What are they talking about? The other plane? Betan?)

The milky light surrounded them again, implacable. On a screen a tiny point of light went out and Betan no longer existed, a plane scattered itself in shards and fragments, lives went out— ("That's a miss on their side, a hit on ours.") Their own plane had fired. That had been that shaking. And Betan was dead in a moment, with all her courage and her skill. ("It's down.")

"Betan," Duun said. "headed out over the sea and came back again. Points to her. She might have won it right then."

"She's dead."

There was a silence for a moment. The sky was incredibly smooth. Surreal again.

"There's a man named Shbit," Duun said. "A councillor. You know Dallen Oil? You remember your companies?"

"Yes."

"Well, they're not only oil, they're a lot of things. Energy, trade, manufacture. They've got a lot of power in council. They saw it slipping. They got Shbit elected: one of their own. Shbit wanted you transferred out of Ellud's wing and

into one where things are more accessible—
where you'd be more—public. Where politics
could benefit by controversy. Where I could be
weakened. They can't overthrow a hatani judgment. But they can undermine it. They can
come at you from so many sides you can't track
them all. Shbit tried that. He had a few ghotanin
in his employ. Personal guards. They're ordinary as rain in private service. He had a few
free-hatani he knew where to reach back home.
A few kosanin, gods help them. And the fool
got Betan past a fool of a personnel supervisor,
the security chief, the division chief, Ellud—
gods, five years ago; while we were still at
Sheon. Brightest young security officer Ellud
had. She ought to have been.''

"Elanhen and Sphitti and Cloen—"

"Security as well. Sphitti's a free-citizen, son
of a woman I know. Elanhen and Cloen from
the station: kosanin. Damn good kids. Betan;
free-citizen, career security. So they said. They
left out pertinent details in her case.''

The smoothness continued. The milky light
never varied. To one side and the other cold
terms like *intercept* flew on radios; ("It's down.
. . .") Lives ended. Beyond illusion-forests in
city windows missile silos opened like flowers to the sun.

". . . Betan knew we were succeeding. That
was what tipped the balance. She had help,

gods know; all of Shbit's resources, forged records. She made a foul-up of it even so—a free-ghota might be that careless. But she wasn't working for Shbit. She meant to foul things up. Kill you if she could. Doublecross Shbit. I know it was a possibility. I took my time settling that affair and it was damn near too much time, while I was working on those tapes."

"You—"

"While you were out. Daily. Constantly. Never mind that. I'd spread myself too far; I'd hastened things, and my time was occupied; and I was held to law. I traced Betan as far as Shbit. When I learned she'd surfaced again in Shbit's keeping and stayed alive—then I knew either Shbit himself was ghota or Shbit was being worked by one. I saw the pattern."

Thorn turned his face from the sun a second time and looked at Duun, at a face rendered faceless by the mask, sun reflecting on plastic eyeshields.

"Betan," Duun said, distant through the speaker, "may have been aimed all her life for what she did. Guild-service. A special kind of ghota. Gods know what the ghotanin had been feeding Shbit for information out of the department. Shbit was up against the ghota guild and totally outmatched ... playing their moves against me and thinking they were his. Even Dallen Company. I can't say I didn't expect guild trouble. But there was law, again—I was trying to keep from destroying the council's autonomy. Dammit, they gave me too much. I let Shbit live because I knew he was a trigger I could pull, one the ghota would respond to. There's a spy in Ellud's office I've let stay. Sagot's mine."

(Something's still faithful in this world. O Sagot, one bit of truth.)

". . . And you did what we'd been waiting for."

"What did I do? That *tape?* That damned stupid *tape?* The numbers and the pictures?"

"You survived it. You survived it, minnow, and you read it. And the meds would know what you knew in one more day—and the instant they knew, that unstopped leak would send the news straight to our enemies; while Ellud wouldn't want to let you leave the building—I could overrule him, but he could have fought me on it and fouled things up beyond recovery. He's a good man; and honest; and he always wants more time than the opposition gives him. Some things I couldn't even tell Tangan himself. Like guild war. Like the fact I'd pulled the trigger."

"This Shbit sent Betan when he knew we'd left the city."

"You're catching onto it. He gave a ghota a courier plane and never suspected she'd been hired by her own guild to be hired by him. He had to give her a ghota crew: no kosan would fly her to us."

"Why come here for the gods' sake?"

"She couldn't overtake us. For Shbit—she was supposed to go in and wail and howl and put on a good act. Disgrace you. Keep you out of the guild. Create scandal. For the ghota—she was to walk in there just the way she did and deliver a message from her guild. You read Tangan. He wouldn't bend. That's clear to you and me—but ghotanin have a guiding belief that everything can be bought if you set the terms up right; she walked in there and saw she hadn't the right coin . . . by her way of looking at it. It was clear when she said keep you out the way she did she wasn't talking for Shbit. Tangan knew it then. Read what she was and knew what I'd done to him and knew why. And forgave us both." Duun was silent for a long while.

And men and women died for them, would be dying, now, in planes which darted and fired missiles no one saw except on screens.

(Damn you, Duun. Is even this a maneuver?)

"I liked him," Thorn said at last. "I liked Tangan, Duun."

"I didn't betray him. I gave him the power he needed. I set him free. Do you understand?"

"To stop the ghota?"

"To back what I do. Don't you understand it

yet, minnow? You will." Static sputtered, Duun's hand at the side of his mask clicking the other channel in. "How are we doing?"

"Dsonan's screen's going to drop in a minute to let us through," the pilot's voice came to them. "It's hot up ahead. Two missile strikes got to the base. The 3rd Wing's going to throw everything they've got at them while we get in, sey Duun."

"Gods save them," Duun muttered. "Gods save us all. Do it right, Manan."

"Damn sure trying."

Thorn eased over to look out the canopy as best he could. There was no sight of anything beyond their wings, beyond the pitiless sun and the endless sky.

Static snapped again. "Not to make you nervous, minnow," Duun said. "but what that means is Dsonan's keying its missile defenses down to give us a window to get in, and don't ask me what happens if something glitches. Kosanin are moving to be sure nothing gets through that gap for the five critical minutes it's going to take us to get through that screen. Then it goes up behind us. When we get on the ground we get over that side and off that wing: and it's going to be hotter than hell. You go down that wing edge and jump once I'm down. I'll steady you in landing. Don't think about anything, just run for that shuttle pad and go."

"Shuttle?"

"Tallest thing you'll see in front of you."

"I know what it looks like! Where are we going?"

"Station."

Static snapped. The nose of the plane dipped in a dive. Altitude traded for speed.

("Mach two plus if it has to.")

Thorn trembled. There was pain, pain from his burns, from warmth; he gasped at the sluggish thin feed of the mask and his nose and throat and eyes were raw. Sweat ran on him. There was a high strange sound, a sense that quivered through his bones and bowels like elemental fear. (I'm scared, Duun; Duun, I don't want to die like this—)

There was a blur ahead of them, the first substance there had been, a shadow in front of them, a blaze of light.

(That's ground coming up, that's the river—O gods, that's ground, the city—)

Pressure began, a constriction of his limbs, the pain again—the world tilted violently and became half earth and sky split vertically, flipped straight again as Thorn felt the straining of the straps. (They'll break, I'll go up and into the canopy, I can't hold on—)

Then another force slammed in, and they were losing speed. One ear failed to pop, reached a painful point and pressure went on and on in acute agony that made one fabric with other things.

Smoke on the horizon. Smoke palling the city in the one direction, a gray blur to either side.

A runway ribboned out of the forward perspective, a straight pale line ahead. The plane came in knife-straight, sank on its haunches in a long jarring rush before the thunder of the reversing engines made headway against their speed. More speed down. More. Tires squealed and the jets roared again as a gantry loomed up, a shuttle poised like a white tower against the smoke-stained sky. On the horizon a red sun burst and swelled and faded. Another, burning bright.

Closer and closer. The plane jolted and thumped and rocked over uneven pavement; there was a truck coming toward them. The plane's canopy retracted and metal stank, pinging and popping with heat. Duun reached and yanked connections as the engines whined down; popped Thorn's belt and his own, stood up and vaulted the side. Thorn scrambled up on the seat, flinched at heat and saw Duun spring from the wing's back edge to the truckbed and go to one knee as he landed; Thorn rolled over the side and hit the wing as Duun got up, strode once on a yielding surface and leapt for the truckbed and Duun's arms.

Duun and he both went down, rolled, and the truck lurched into motion, leaving the plane dwindling behind. On the horizon more suns burst, and one flowered in the sky and faded in a smudge of smoke.

Duun held onto him. Thorn trembled, felt Duun unfasten his mask for him and let him fill his lungs with cold gasps of air. Duun clenched him the tighter as the truck whined and jolted and the gantry towered into view, white girders against the smoke-ravaged sky. It braked. "Out," Duun said, and helped him balance as he got up, vaulted the rear of the truck to the ground and was there to steady him when his feet hit the pavement.

"Come on. Run!" Duun dragged him for the gantry, for the white wall that was a shuttle fin. There was an elevator, its door open, and a woman who motioned at them hurry, hurry, in a violence like an oath. They made it in: the woman shut the door and moved a bar-switch that set them moving up. The whole elevator reeked of their suits and sweat and fear, and Thorn staggered as it lifted. Duun's hand met his chest. "Hold on, dammit, Thorn! Hold on!"

Thorn locked his knees, leaned on the wall with his forearm. Girders whipped past the window in a blur; then the woman jammed down the switch and the car slammed to a stop. The door opened, showing them a thick-walled open hatch.

"Come on," Duun said, and shoved Thorn into it and followed. Thorn looked back in distress as explosions came like distant thunder.

Still outside, the woman swung the hatch shut, disappearing in a diminishing crescent of the murky sunlight. Thump. (What about her?) The world seemed an unsafe place, no place to leave alone. But Duun spun him about and all but threw him into a seat in this cubbyhole of a place, one of three seats built flat on this dimly lighted floor.

"Belt in," Duun said, and Thorn groped for belts as Duun fell into his seat and got them, fastened them for him and got his own helmet off. Duun hugged it to his breast and pushed a button on the arm of the seat. "We're set, we're set back here."

"Understand you clear."

Thorn stripped his helmet off with his wrists; Duun helped him, bent and stowed it in a bin in the floor beside his seat. The lid latched and echoed hollowly. Thorn lay there breathing in great gasps while Duun secured his own belts. "They're waiting on the attendant to get down the escape route," Duun said, his own head back, his eyes shut. "Driver of that truck's got to get out too."

"What about the plane?"

"Maran and Koga—they're headed out and over to Drenn. Refuel and up again.It's their wing that's taking the beating out there. They'll have a window—ours: they've got to take that missile screen down again for us to clear this port."

(People are dying. Everywhere those shells go off. All those people—)

A thunder began to grow. (They're hitting close to us.) Sweat flooded Thorn's body in a sickly sense of doom; then the sound went to his bones and the force came down on him, dizzying and all-encompassing. Another thunder began, pieces of the ship rattling, as if it was all coming apart. (We won't make it, we won't make it—some missile will stop us.)

The weight grew, pressing him down into the couch.

They were leaving the world. Everything. There was void ahead, incomprehensible and without end.

(I looked up at the moon and tried to see where they were, but of course I couldn't.)

(The world's wide, minnow, wider than you know.)

(The world's beautiful. Haven't you seen it in pictures?)

XIV There was peace, eerie peace and stillness, in which moving cost little and breathing cost far less. A gentle air touched Thorn's face and a breeze stirred against his cheek.

Duun floated above him, balanced crazily on one arm that gripped the back of the seat. Thorn blinked, and Duun freed him of the restraints. A little move of Thorn's arm against the seat freed him from the cushion.

"We're up," Thorn murmured. "We're up."

"Where the worlds spin, yes. You can be easy awhile, minnow. It's a great ocean you've come to. It's easy to move and easy to move too far." Duun grinned at him. (Can he smile after all that? Can he be happy? Can anyone ever, after that?)

Duun pulled gently at his wrist— "Keep your arm stiff. Never mind, don't try to hold." The fastenings of the flightsuit gave way. Duun's own suit drifted in pieces, loosed at chest and wrists and ankles. Duun worked him free: torque set them spinning and they drifted together while the cabin revolved slowly about them.

Freedom, then, Thorn drifted, shut his eyes in exhaustion, half-slitted them to watch Duun come and go through a hole he had not seen before. A hatch had opened above them. In the lazy spin Thorn caught sight of white light, of shonun bodies that drifted to and fro about some business. Duun went up to that place and sailed down again like some graceful diver. Duun's ears were up; his eyes were lively and bright.

(He knows this, he knows all of it, he's been this way more than once.)

"Where are we going, Duun?"

"Hush. Rest. People are busy."

"What's happened to the world?"

"It's still there. Fighting's centered mostly now around the shuttleports and Avenen and Suunviden. but it's dying down now—now that we're away and there's not a damn thing they can do about it."

"Why did we do it? Where are we going?"

"Why, why, and why? There's a shower on board. I'm going to use it. When I have I'm going to tape some plastic around those hands of yours and make you pleasanter company." Duun drifted off from him. Thorn twisted in midair and saw him disappear down yet another hole. Thorn tried to maneuver himself, spun and brought up against the cushions, remembering only at the last moment not to use his hands; he rebounded helplessly and drifted, waiting.

A vacuum went on in the shower and Thorn watched the water droplets run in clinging trails until they were gone and the lamp dried him. He elbowed the latch and drifted out again, turned once in midair in slow revolution before Duun snagged him and wrapped a plain blue kilt about him, tugged the self-belt about his waist with a touch familiar years ago, exactly the snugness, exactly the way Duun had done it then—Thorn looked into Duun's face from a grownup angle, met him eye-to-eye when Duun finished with the small pat on the side he had given him when he was small. Time went backward and forward, spun like the room.

"Follow me," Duun said, trod on the cabinet wall and drifted upward with unerring grace through the narrow hatch.

Thorn kicked off, angled his body with what grace he could manage and sailed through in Duun's wake, followed him again, up into a light, into the mind and heart of the shuttle where crew came and went.

They stared—(they shocked; they want to be polite; they don't know whether to stare or not, whether staring's honest or only rude.) Duun drifted on and stopped and Thorn imitated his move, ignoring the stares— (The world in flames. They ought to hate me. I don't blame them. I was born for it.) And he floated strangely free, taking all their blame, ignoring their eyes on his smooth pale skin, suffering Duun's grip on his arm that drew him toward the window.

The bright blue world—was there. Its fires were invisible. The perspective denied everything—the fires became one more illusion beyond a window; his life shrank to invisible scale, lived out on a mountain and in a city whose burning could not even stain the clouds.

He stared and stared, and the tears beaded in his eyes until his blinking drove them. He wiped his eyes and a droplet floated free from his fingertip, perfect, a wobbling orb like the world in space.

"Do you love it?" Duun asked. "Do you love it, minnow?"

"Yes," Thorn said when he could say anything at all. He wiped his eyes again. "It's still there."

"So long as you aren't on it," Duun said, and it was truth; he had seen it. Thorn's chest ached. He put out a hand and touched the window and the world.

The ship left the world, while they belted in below. The engines kicked them hard and long.

Thorn shut his eyes. I can't sleep, I can never sleep, he told himself, but the strength ebbed out of him and he felt the pain reminding him of what he was and what it cost, constantly, like the beats of his heart. "Drink," Duun said, and fed him something through a straw that he wanted no more of after the first sip. "Drink it." Again, in that voice that had drilled him all his life, and it left no choice. Thorn drank, and slept; and when he woke Duun slept by his side—his unscarred side toward him, that side that gave its own illusions, of what Duun had been before.

Thorn shut his eyes again. (Is Sagot alive? Did Manan and the other pilot live? The guild— did the missiles defend it?)

(Children standing on the rock at Sheon;

seeing red suns bloom on their horizons. Smoke palls the sky. Thunder shakes the ground.)

(In the halls at Dsonen people run in confusion, not knowing where to go.)

The sun whirls past the canopy and men like great insects manage the controls. The plane hangs in the sky and time stops. The war goes on in a moment frozen forever, all war, all time.

Sagot sits in her lonely hall. There is thunder. She sits frail and imposing at the end of that room, waiting in front of all the empty desks.

A shuttle flies in place and the universe rushes past it, sweeping the world out of its reach.

There were mundane things. There had to be: there were bodily needs, and Thorn cared stubbornly for himself, once Duun had shown him how things worked; there was a breakfast of sorts, and Thorn found his hands a little less painful. Crew came drifting through their compartment in the urge of like necessities and coming back again. There was still the surreal about it, like the drifting course they took, a leisurely pace, a slowness like a dream.

"Where are we going, Duun?"

"Gatog."

"Is that the station?" Thorn had never heard it called that.

"It's one of them." Duun said.

(Is there more than one?) Sagot's teaching developed cracks, fractured in doubts. (Is no truth entire?)

"We had a report," Duun said, "the ghotanin have sent a messenger to Tangan offering to talk. The kosan guild refused at first, but they're going to relent."

"Is that part of your solution?" Thorn asked. His mind worked again. Duun looked at him with that closed hatani stare to match what Thorn gave him.

"Balance is," Duun said. "It was never my intention to destroy the ghota."

"They call you sey Duun."

'It's a courtesy these days."

"You led kosanin?"

"Once."

No more than that. Duun would not be led.

More of sleep and meals and bodies. The gel on his hands began to peel. The crew grew familiar: Ghindi, Spart, Mogannen, Weig. Half-names. Pet-names. But it was enough. Duun knew them and talked with them in quiet tones, and talked sometimes with voices on the radio from one end or the other of their journey.

None of it concerned Thorn. And everything did. He eavesdropped in mortal dread and caught nothing but city names and Gatog's name and jargon after that.

Intercept, Thorn heard once, and his heart

delayed a beat. He looked Duun's way and kept looking Duun's way when Duun stopped the conversation.

"Minnow," Duun said to him, drifting toward Thorn. And nodded to him that he ought to follow.

Duun drifted down into the place they slept in and came to a graceful stop. Thorn reached with his foot and a half-healed hand and did almost as well. "Are there ghotanin here?" Thorn asked.

"Maybe there are," Duun said. "They're not our job to fight."

"Is it a game?" Thorn asked in anger. "Am I supposed to discover what we're going to? Where I am? Isn't it over, Duun?"

Duun looked at him in a strange, distant way. "It's only beginning. It's not the right question, Haras-hatani. None of those is the right question."

Thorn grew very still inside.

"Think on it." Duun said. "Tell me when you know."

The void that had sped past him, about him, shrank to a single familiar dimension.

("Again," Duun said, standing over him on the sand. "Again.")

Thorn sucked in a breath and stared at Duun as Duun pushed off and soared up through the lighted hatchway like some sleek gray man-sized fish.

(He's been waiting for me. Where have I been? Where has my mind been? It was pity he felt for me.)

(He belongs here. This is his element, like Sheon; and the city-tower and the guild-hall never were.)

Thorn pushed off and extended his body the way Duun had, with the same grace, conscious of it. He came up into the light of the crew-compartment, found his touch-point with one sure motion and drifted to the counter-hold he sought, there where he could see Duun and the others.

They were receiving and sending messages again. Duun listened and answered in that jargon again which made little sense. "Is it custom," Thorn asked when there was a lull, "to talk like that; or have we enemies up here?"

"Is that your question?" Duun asked.

"I'll tell you when I ask it." Thorn held to the counter and felt the sensitivity of his burns. "If this is an ocean, this minnow had better learn to swim. He should have learned days ago."

Duun looked at him and slanted his ears back in an expression Thorn had seen a thousand times. "There are enemies. The same as we met on earth. The companies who maintain

factories and mines up here use ghotanin for
guards. And some of them have ships. Not like
the shuttle. The shuttle's not built for what
we're doing. Ships are moving, some friendly,
some not. We've burned all the fuel we have
getting out of earth's pull. It wasn't a sched-
uled launch. It was the reserve shuttle we used.
One's always kept launch-ready: the companies like their schedules kept. And getting it
powered up without letting Shbit and the
ghotanin trace that order to me—that took some
work."

(You knew it all in advance, then. Dammit,
Duun—)

Duun might have smiled; on the ruined side
such motions were ambiguous and made him
deceptive to read. It might have been a grimace. "Right now," Duun said, "we're on course
for Gatog. It lies some distance out. We're not
capable of stopping, of course. But that's not a
great problem. A miner's already moving into
line to be on that course a few weeks hence, a
simple salvage job. If nothing intervenes. We're
moving very slowly. Our enemies are closing at
ten times our speed. We have no weapons.
Those ships do. Fortunately so do our friends.
It's a very touchy business, minnow, hour by
hour. A ship spends fuel; the other side does;
each move changes the intercept point and the
schedule. We're the only fixed quantity because
we can't maneuver, no more than a world or a

moon. We just sail on. And hour by hour those ships out there burn a little, figure, discover what the enemy's doing, refigure, maneuver and do another burn. Faster and faster. It depends on how willing crews are to die, and at what point they commit themselves. For the nearest of our friends the earth is close to the infinity point: they were never built to land, and if they overspend on fuel they'll not have the capacity to do the necessary vector change and get back again: the gravity well is just that, a treacherous slope, and a ship that spends everything can find itself going downhill. For our enemies, the infinity point *is* infinity—or some star a hundred years away. And someone could eventually fetch them back. They don't need to be as brave. Or as careful."

"What will our friends do?"

"Some of them are hatani."

"They'll do what they have to, then." The guild house. The laughter which no longer sounded cruel, but innocent and brave. (They didn't know then they were in such close danger. Even hatani failed to read it. They saw the ghota; they knew trouble had come in, but they couldn't know it all.) "Are they armed?"

"Yes."

Thorn looked about him, at the crew who worked so unceasingly, who talked calmly over the radio and sometimes joked with each other or did whimsical things, like sailing a morsel of food toward a fellow crew member for that one to catch. "These are brave people," Thorn said, as if he stood at the foot of some great mountain. It was that kind of awe, making him quiet inside. He thought of Manan and his co-pilot, the plane runnning ahead of the maelstrom the shuttle would kick up. The woman at the shuttle hatchway, sealing them in, staying in the shattered world.

Sagot kissing him good-bye.

Tangan accepting an old student's betrayal of him and giving kindness to one more incoming boy.

Tears filled his eyes and he wiped at them and found Duun looking at him. "I'm sorry, Duun. I don't know why I do that."

"Don't you know by now I can't?" Duun asked him.

Thorn stared at him with the streaks drying on his face.

"Duun," Weig said. And Duun went to see what Weig wanted.

"We're down to twenty hours," Weig said.

There was suit drill. "If we get hit, at least there's some chance." Duun said, and opened that long locker which hugged one side of the bridge, where spacesuits nestled one behind the other like embryos in a womb. Duun pulled one out and shoved it at him, fastenings all undone. "Try it."

Thorn tucked up and got his foot inserted, struggling with the rest. Duun showed him once how to do the fastenings, then made him do it over and over again until his hands hurt. Duun showed him how the backpacks fit against the rear of the seats, and how an automation on the seat back would bring the helmet down and release it in his grip. "So you don't have to sit in that damn rig for hours," Duun said, and showed him the air connectors to the shuttle's own emergency supply, and how to disconnect and use the backpack. "Helmet first, then disconnect and you've got air enough in the suit to get to the pack and get it started." Duun made him work it all again and again until he was exhausted.

"Sleep awhile," Duun said then. "You'll need it."

It amazed Thorn that Duun could do that so readily, anchored to his couch down in their own compartment; and most of all that up above in the activity and bright light of the bridge, Ghindi and Spart tethered themselves in a corner by the closets and went to an honest and quick sleep, while Weig and Mogannen kept computing changes. Thorn tethered himself beside Duun and tried, succeeded at least in resting; but the plane got into his half-dreams; so did the flight; and Betan.

Then he unclipped and sailed up to the bridge to discover Ghindi and Spart at work and the other two asleep. The computer ticked away. Thorn came gingerly closer off the overhead, hanging upside down over Ghindi's post and a little back so that he could see the screen.

Ghindi turned her chair around and looked up. She had that look people had when they came face-to-face with him; and then she banished it for one he could not well read. Exhaustion. Sadness. Was it love? It made no sense. He tumbled over and righted himself with a move of his hand that helped him turn. Perhaps the look made more sense right-side up.

"I'm sorry," Thorn said, meaning for bothering her in her work. He wanted to go and hide himself below before Duun found out.

She started at him, bewildered. They were both tired and a little crazed. They could not make sense to each other. "We'll get you there," she said.

(To Gatog?) Thorn was dismayed. He showed it like a child. Less seemed dishonest toward Ghindi. "Are you kosan?" he asked. He remembered the pilots.

"Tanun," Ghindi named her guild. Tanun, seafarers. It seemed appropriate to him.

C.J. Cherryh

"Ghindi," Spart said from his computers. "We've got another burn from *Kandurn*."

Ghindi turned as if Thorn had fallen suddenly from her world. "We're getting short, aren't we?"

"We're getting short. I think we'd better get Weig and Mogannen up."

Thorn began to turn, found purchase with his foot and dived for the downward hatch, sailed through into that dim light and tumbled to hit a wall and stop. "Duun. They're calling the crew up. It sounds like we're short of time."

Duun moved in his drifting and looked at him. "How short?"

"I don't know. I don't know how to tell, except there's some good bit less time than we had, forty minutes one time and now they've had another burn."

Duun touched bottom and shot up like a swimmer for the light. Thorn touched and followed.

Mogannen and Weig were getting into spacesuits. There were three spare seats at one counter that could be powered back from it and locked. Duun did that with the two of them that were assigned to them when they were on the bridge. "When matters get to it," Duun said. "Suit up now."

All very calm. The routine of the bridge went on, except the suiting. Spart and Ghindi took their turn and got back into their seats. Duun drifted loose, suited, helmetless. The waiting became tedium. Thorn's heart once beating in panic could not sustain it. Panic ebbed down to long vexation. He wanted a drink of water. If he did that he might regret it. In such small indignities the worst moments proceeded. Thoughts of itches inaccessible. His own sweat inside the suit, gathered and undispersed. He hung in midair, watching the viewpoint for want of other distraction in this slow creeping of time and the beep of incoming messages droning methodically about the insane business of ghotanin who wished to kill them. Ships had begun to overcommit. Calm voices reported the facts and called it things like zero-return and no-turnaround.

(Strangely enough you don't get to see the stars much. You can see from the shuttle if you get up front. . . . It's beautiful.)

A star brightened while he watched, brightened and brightened, and his heart slammed into rapid beats. "Duun! Weig!" It began to be a sphere.

"Get to that seat!" Duun yelled, and shot that way himself. Thorn dived, caught the back of one and hauled himself into it by the armrest, reached for the furled restraints and started fastening them. He looked up, ahead of them where the star had vanished. "Where is it?"

They had not turned, could not have turned: the shuttle had nothing left.

"Helmet," Duun said. Thorn pushed the button on the armrest, pulled up the connnecting hose and communications plug and inserted them as the helmet came down. He locked it in place, selected the third communications channel. One was unified and two was crew-only, three was non-crew. Himself and Duun. He could hear his breathing, could hear Duun's, and it was steadier than his own.

(O gods, how do people get used to this?)

There was another star. All in silence. Only the breathing sounds, the faraway noises of the shuttle's operations that were everywhere ambient, but dimmed by the helmets.

He switched channels, heard the crew talking and the messages coming in. The sweat gathered on his body and his arm was going to sleep until he shifted it. ("Damn suits never fit," Duun had said.) It was better than the flightsuit. Looser.

(Another star. Are those missiles or are those ships? Are those ships dying?)

The crew-talk made no sense to him, full of codes. He cut third channel in. "Duun, what's happening?"

"They're within range of each other. And of us, with far less accuracy. The hatani have headed them off. Outmaneuvered them, if they

284

don't let one get past. If they do they'll never get a second chance and we can't stop it."

The flashes went on. Thorn shut his eyes and opened them again, wishing he dared take the helmet off. The air was cold and stung his throat and nose and eyes.

"That's *Ganngein*," Weig's voice broke in on third channel. "They got them all. We've got debris on intersect. That's all."

"How's *Ganngein*?" Duun asked.

A pause. "Zero-return. So's *Nonnent*. *Ganngein* wishes us well and says they'll stay in contact. They're trying to determine their numbers now; they've been skewed."

"Can't the station send something out?" Thorn asked. "Couldn't earth?"

"Station's in ghota hands," Duun said. "Unfortunately. Hatani there were too few. But there's no ship at the station now—Hatani got that, thank the gods, or ghotanin'd have overhauled us from behind. It was the ghota outliers that hit us up ahead. Station's got one shuttle left; earth has a few. But a shuttle can't stop *Ganngein*. Not a question of slowing down that mass, which they couldn't in the first place. Just of catching them in a docking maneuver. They can't match those speeds even to get the crew off."

(Sphitti's voice: "Here's an application now.

If you were drifting in mid-air—no friction and no gravity—)

("You can't.")

("Say that you could.")

(Angles and lines on a schoolroom screen—)

There was a long time that the crew and the doomed ships talked, business only.

"That's it," Thorn heard one say. "We're going to hit the well—looks like three days on. It could be worse. Like four."

"We hear you," Weig said. There was sorrow in his voice. Thorn listened and stared at the points of light. His arm and his leg were numb. No one moved to take off the suits. *Debris on intersect.* He remembered that. The other two ships talked awhile. There was no better news.

(This is more dreadful than the planes. This silence. This inevitability of ships that meet that fast, with distances that take days. For Betan it was quick. These men and women will have time to talk and eat and sleep and wake three times before they hit the ground. Before they skim through the well and get caught and dragged in.)

". . . we think," *Nonnent* said, "we think we may have the angle to transit. We don't know yet."

"We'll miss your company then," *Ganngein* said.

A long pause. "Yes, we hear that." Quickly, from *Nonnent*.

"Don't be embarrassed about it. This isn't a trip we want to share."

Hatani. Or tanun guild.

There was long silence. Eventually there began to be a hole in space, small at first, that grew and ate the stars. "Something's out there, Duun. Isn't it?"

"Dust," Duun said. "Particles. We won't use the lights. We're conserving all the power we've got and we can't dodge it anyway."

(How long can it take us? What if a mostly whole ship were in our path?)

(Fool's question, Thorn.)

Wait and wait and wait. All the stars were gone. The ships talked now and again. They talked about the cloud.

Static began. Transmission broke up. A noise penetrated the helmet, a distant hammer blow. Another. The sounds accelerated to a battering. It stopped.

"We're still in it." Weig said. "This is going—uhh!"

The shock rang through the structure and up through the deck. Thorn clenched his gloved hands on the armrests and forgot the pain. Silence a time.

"Clipped the left wing," Mogannen said. "We've got a little spin now. Don't—"

Another shock. Shock after shock. Silence then. An occasional strike, none large.

(Pieces of the ghotanin. Or of one of our own. We're flying through dead ships. Dead. Bodies. Or bits of them. Blood out there would freeze like snow.)

The stars came back. "Hey!" Weig shouted. We're through!"

(For me. For me and Duun, the dead back on earth. *Ganngein* and *Nonnent*. Ghota and hatani ships.)

"There's a ship out there," Spart said, and Thorn's heart stopped. "It's *Deva*. It's going to serve as pickup. It's about nine hours down."

"Thank the gods," Mogannen said.

"We go out to it," Duun explained. "They can't stop our spin to pick us up. We're easier to manage in suits."

Deva shone a light for them. The shuttle turned slowly, wedge-shaped shadow against the sun. Debris trailed from one wing edge, and from the tail. A touch came at his leg and Duun snagged him, maneuvered and got him by the hand. Near them three became a chain. One of them was still loose but in no danger. *Deva*'s beacon brightened among the stars, a white and blinding sun.

Deva was not so fine inside as the shuttle— was all bare metal and plastics; but it had shonu-nin in it. It had welcome.

"Duun-hatani," the captain said.

"You're a good sight, Ivogi-tanun," said Duun.

Thorn held his helmet in his hands. He saw the others' looks, the crew who stood gazing at him. As they might look at some strange fish they had hauled up in their nets.

"This is Haras," Duun said. "Hatani guild."

"We heard," Ivogi-tanun said.

There was silence from *Gann-gein* now. For four days. Static obscured *Nonnent*'s voice. Earth spoke in code, and *Deva* had no facilities. Gatog spoke back, constantly; and that was coded too, even when it was *Deva*'s code. Machines read it out. There was seldom a voice, until the last, when Gatog began to shine in *Deva*'s viewport like a scatter of jewels.

(It seemed sinister till we saw it. It's like an ornament. Why is it out here?)

"Duun, what is this place?"

Duun was silent. Thorn trembled, looking at it from the place on the bridge where Ivogi-tanun called them. It was foolish. Perhaps it was all the other shocks. But there seemed no other destination. Earth and Gatog spoke in some hieratic tongue past them, sharing secrets; and earth had drunk down *Ganngein*—"Gods," the last transmission had been, or it had sounded like that. Then static from *Nonnent* too. "They're behind the earth," Duun said. They expected transmission to pick up again. But they never found it, though *Deva* asked Gatog. "We've lost it too," Gatog said, one of the few uncoded transmissions they had gotten from this secretive place.

(Can silence be worth so much here, so far from earth?)

The lights shone against the stars, white and gold, a cluster here and removed from it, another.

"Five minutes to braking," Ivogi said; and: "Go aft," Duun said. *Deva* had no spare seats for six passengers. They had to brace themselves in a narrow place where *Deva* had provision for passengers during maneuvering: there was no viewport there, and nothing more than padding. Thorn went with them. Duun did not.

But Duun came for him after the hard burn. "We're going to suit up to cross," Duun said.

It was a cold place, *Deva*, gray and smelling of chilled metal and electrics and their own bodies and their own food. But *Deva* was a known place, and Thorn looked over it while he fastened up his suit. He did these things for himself and looked at *Deva* and thought of Sheon's woods, and the hearthside. His mind leapt from one to the other. From that to the glittering lights.

(Duun, I'm afraid. I want the world again, Duun, I want to go home. I knew things there; but I go from one thing to the other, and you change, Duun, you go away from me, you talk with Weig, you talk with Ivogi, you talk a language I don't understand and you've lost interest in me. You go farther away.)

(Don't look at me like that. Don't think about leaving me. I can read you, Duun, and it scares me.)

"Good-bye," Ivogi said, and *Deva*'s hatch spat them out as impersonally as it had taken them in.

Thorn's hand froze on the maneuvering gun in all that unforgiving dark. He drifted. His eyes jerked wildly from light to light to light—a great dish suspended, building-wide, or close to them; his eyes refused perspective. A web of metal stretching to insane thinness in the distance, dotted with brilliant lights. "Gatog," Duun said, a voice gone strange with the speaker. "That's the great ear, that dish. It listens. So does another, considerably across the solar system. Out in Dothog orbit."

(What does it listen to?) But Thorn could not

ask any question. His soul was numb, battered with too many answers. Duun dragged at him and turned him, and aimed him at another down with such a shift in perspective his sense of balance sent terror through him.

A great pit yawned, all lit in green: it went down a vast rotating shaft to a core; and his peripheral vision formed it as the hub of a vast wheel.

Yet another turn, and Weig and the others were there, their backs to them, their faces toward a great lighted scaffolding prisoning something from which the lights could not utterly remove the darkness—it looked older than the shining girders which embraced it: a cylinder of metal no longer bright.

"That's a ship," Duun said. "The ship."

Thorn said nothing. He hung there, lost, held only by Duun's hand. He had no more wish to be inside, wherever inside was, than to hang here forever in the blaze of these lights. (Is this the place? Is this what cost so much? Do I go beyond this place or is this the stopping-point for us? Duun, Duun, is this your Solution?)

Duun held him by the hand and dived down (or up) into the well, which was green as Sheon's leaves. The walls spun and turned about them.

In the heart of the well in the hub, was a hatch that flowered with gold light. They came into it, and Weig and the others did.

Then it closed and delivered them to another chamber with several metal poles in it and a sign that told them where down was. Duun grabbed a pole holding onto Thorn; Mogannen and Chindi did; Spart and Weig took the other; there came a great shock that made them sway and then rise.

"Hang on," Duun said when Thorn grabbed the pole for himself. "It does it one more time. We're bound for the rim."

It was like a ship moving; down began to feel alarmingly sideways, and the cylinder seemed slowly to change its pitch before it jolted into contact and the door opened.

There were attendants, men and women wearing ordinary kilts, all white; Duun pulled his helmet off and Thorn did so with the rest.

(Look your fill. Stare at me.) Thorn kept his eyes from them and handed the helmet to a woman he never looked at. "Sey Duun," a man said, "they'd like to see you in the office."

"They'll have to come to me," Duun said. He peeled his suit off, sat down and removed the boots. One attendant started to touch the baggage and Thorn moved and stepped on the strap. The attendant changed his mind. And Duun smiled with the twisted side. It was right. After drifting so long Thorn knew something, if only so small a thing. They did not touch him and they did not touch Duun and they kept their hands off the baggage.

Weig and his crew took their leave. "Duun-hatani," Weig said, nothing else. He seemed moved. "Weig-tanun," Duun said. "Appeal to me if things don't go right." And Duun gave a twisted smile: "Not all my solutions are so cursed difficult."

"I'll remember," Weig said, and took his crew away; but Ghindi looked back once, and Thorn paused.

"Come on," Duun said, standing up. Theirs was another door, that opened narrowly.

(Tubes. The spinning place. Tubes and people like me—)

But there were no such people. Thorn picked up the baggage and followed Duun, along the deserted corridor which bent upward and brought them to another room.

Hatani waited for them there, three of them; Thorn saw the gray cloaks and felt profound relief. "Tagot, Desuuran, Egin," Duun said. "Haras."

There were courtesies. Thorn bowed, looked up into careful hatani faces which did not intrude their passions into anyone's view. He held the baggage with hands to which the last shreds of the gel still clung, and it was as if he had stood in a battering gale of others' feelings, others' fears; others' needs—and found a sudden calm.

"We'll rest," Duun said.

"Duun-hatani. Haras." Tagot's hand indicated the way, and he walked with them, the others at their backs, and that order was all settled with the slightest of signs that left no doubt Duun would let them at his back. Thorn slung the carry strap to his shoulder and walked a little at Duun's heel, rumpled and with his knee abraded raw again, with the red scars of burns on his hands, his hair loose and tending to fall into his eyes; but so was Duun scarred; but so was Duun's silver hide stained dark with sweat at his shoulders and the small of his back.

(Have we found a place, finally? Hatani live here. Is this a place we won't be driven from?)

They passed doors; they rode down two levels in an elevator; they walked down a bowed hallway that might have been the city tower in some distorted mirror.

They opened one door; a hatani waited there in a short hall and opened yet another for them, on a large bare-floored room to which they had to step, as if it were all one riser on which other risers were built. The walls were barren and white. An elder hatani waited here. "Your rooms are safe," that hatani said, and walked out, quietly, economically, with everything said that needed saying.

"Food, bath, bed," Duun said. Thorn set the baggage down and Duun opened it and took out his cloak. It wrapped another one. "This is yours." Duun laid it on the riser. "When you need it."

Thorn looked at it and looked at Duun. And Duun walked away, himself in search of those things he had named.

It was not, ultimately, safe: Duun knew this. There were always, where shonunin existed, ways to corrupt and ways to strike at a target. The ghotanin had thought at Gatog One they had chosen the most vulnerable target in the shuttle; at Gatog Two the fight was likely to be closer to the station itself, but ghotanin might change their minds and divert their attention here. Dallen Company was not funding them anymore. There was a likelihood they would try to hold the earth station now, and stalemate Tangen, who with kosan and tanun allies held the shuttleports and the earth-based controls of satellite defense. No great number would get into space in those few shuttles. Space was out of reach for most of earth now, perhaps for years and years, and the earth-station would be deprived of ships, if ghotanin risked the few they had left still outside the zone of the conflict.

Duun padded into the darkened bedroom, taking no great care for quiet; and exhausted as Thorn was the boy likely waked. "It's Duun," Duun said. "Go on sleeping. "I've business to take care of. Hatani are at every entrance to this place and I know them. Go on sleeping."

Thorn stirred in the bed, turned on his back and looked up at him in the twilight. Thorn smelled mostly of soap now. He had scrubbed and shaved. "You'll be back."

"Oh, yes." (So he perceives something.) "Deep sleep, Thorn: you can do that here. With them outside. Relax."

Duun left and closed the door this time.

Duun was back and there were visitors. "Who?" Thorn asked Duun at breakfast. "People who want to see you," Duun said, looking at him across the unfamiliar table in a guarded, critical way. "Finish your breakfast and make yourself presentable. I don't want to be ashamed."

Thorn laid down his plate in front of his ankles and put the spoon in it. "No, finish," Duun said. "You have time. You've lost weight."

"I never liked this." It was the green mince that was on his plate every day at home. It tasted like the fish oil that was in his pills when as a child he had bitten down on one. "My stomach's queasy as it is."

"Do people worry you?"

(Do you have a need, minnow?)

"Their faces shout at me," Thorn said. It was the best way he could explain it.

Duun looked at him, still as a pond in winter. "Too many needs coming at you, is it, Haras-hatani?"

"Duun, how is earth? Have you heard?"

(He doesn't want that question. He doesn't want it at all.)

"Sagot wishes you well," Duun said.

(He's lying, surely he's lying, his face is so good at it.) But it looked like truth. (Sagot in her room, Sagot waiting for me—O gods, I want to go home, Duun!)

"I'm glad," Thorn said. "Tell her that from me."

"I'll relay that. Eat your breakfast."

Thorn turned on the riser and put his feet off, missing the teapot.

"Thorn."

Thorn stopped; it was reflex.

"Wear your cloak," Duun said.

They were mostly old, the visitors, two very old, with the pale mask of age on them: one was hatani and another kosan guild. There were a scattering of shonunin of middle years, one with the dark crest of the Bigon; one with the silver-tip of the icy isle of Soghai: Thorn had heard of such people and never seen one. It was a woman, a hatani, and she was the most beautiful woman he had ever seen. Sogasi, Duun named her, and Thorn stored away that name the way he stored the names of the others, in their sequence and their guilds, which were hatani and tanun and kosan. The tanun gazed at him with that frankness he had seen in Ghindi and Weig and the others; the kosan with something of dread and longing. The hatani shielded him from such things and he was grateful.

The visitors never spoke to him. Few even looked him directly in the eyes, but the hatani did. (Thank you, Thorn sent to them in a little relaxing of his face, and got that message in return, the mere flicker of the muscle above an eye.) "We'll talk later," the old kosan said to Duun. "Tell him we're glad to have seen him," a tanun said, and Thorn was even gladder of the hatani cloak that gave him some protection, that lent him something to be besides smooth-skinned and different in their eyes. "Thank you," Thorn said softly for himself, without a hint of pain. "It was a long trip, Voegi-tanun. I wish others could have made it here."

He shocked them somehow; he intruded himself with politenesses he thought were right and at least were true, and refused to care whether

they spat on him or thanked him. He had
missed saying that to Ghindi and Weig; to the
woman at the hatch; to the pilots and to Sagot.
He frightened Voegi. (That man was not supposed to talk to me, and now he thinks he did
something his guild will disapprove.) Tanunin
shouted everything in their movements, the little step back, Voegi's drawing near his senior
with a worried backslant of his ears. The other
tanunin moved and made vague bows and
showed every sign of leaving; the kosanin were
more definite. The eldest hatani looked at Duun
and got his dismissal. So the hatani turned and
showed the others out.

"What was that about?" Thorn asked.

"Take a walk with me," Duun said.

They passed through a huge room, after many
halls, where a handful of workers in white,
body-covering garments labored over terminals
in their laps. It was all computers, row upon
row of mostly empty risers. The few workers
that were there turned in curiosity and stared
in shock, and one by one began to get up. "Stay
seated," Duun said. His quiet voice went to the
walls of that vast place, stopping all such movement. And more quietly still: "This is the control center. Nothing's coming in now: this is all
housekeeping."

"What do they do here?" Thorn asked, since questions seemed invited.

"They monitor the equipment." Duun brought him to the nearest corner of the room and used a card to open an elevator door: it was the sort they had ridden into the wheel. Thorn seized on the nearest support pole as the door shut; and they both held on.

"Where are we going?" Thorn asked. Duun's reticences maddened him. (But what would I know if he told me? He can't tell me. He can only pose me riddles and let me get there as best I can.)

"To the future," Duun said. (Truth and untruth.) The elevator shifted and the strongest force was the grip of their hands on the pole, while other forces seemed more and more ambiguous. "You've seen the earth, from its simplest to its most complex. Its past, its present; you're in Gatog, do you see no paradox?"

"I'm helpless, Duun. Am I supposed to see?"

"Change is your world. Flux and shift."

"Will we go home again?"

"Is that your question?"

The car shifted yet again, a violent sway, and seemed to have changed direction. Thorn clenched the pole and looked at the control panel and back to Duun. "We passed the core," Duun said. "Now we're going out again."

"Why did they make me, Duun?"

Duun met his eyes belatedly. There was dreadful amusement on Duun's face. The scarred mouth tautened on that side. "Is that the question? I'm answering it."

"In this place?" Thorn's heart sped. Panic afflicted him. "Is this where I come from? This?"

"I'll show you something. We're almost there."

(I don't want to see. Stop it, Duun. Duun, *tell* me, don't show me anything!)

The car slowed again, turned, slammed home. The door opened on another room much like the last, but all the risers were vacant, their in-built monitors dark. Thorn walked out into it in Duun's wake. The floors were bare and cold as all floors in this place. Like a ship. Like a laboratory. No foot left traces. There was no record of passage, no hint of time or change: it afflicted him. There were windows. Duun touched a wall-switch and they came alive clear across the far wall, showing the lights, the girders, the strange shapes that were Gatog.

"Quite a sight, isn't it?" Duun said. "Don't you see discrepancies?" Duun walked to a counter and pushed a button.

Sounds began, static-filled, a sputtering crackle. " . . . stop . . . " a voice said; it *was* a voice. " . . . you . . . world . . . "

(Gods. Gods. The tapes.)

Duun pushed another button. (One beep. A word. Two. Word. . . .) Thorn came as far as the console and leaned on it beside Duun. His heart slammed against his ribs. "It comes from here."

Duun cut all the sound. The silence was numbing. Duun walked away, up the aisle toward the illusion of the windows and Thorn followed, on the trackless floor and stopped when the windows were all the view. Duun lifted his arm and pointed. "That's what the ear picks up. It listens, minnow, it's turned beyond this solar system. What does it say to us?"

"Numbers." Thorn looked and lost all sense of up and down. The vision reeled among lights and Gatog's shape and the occasional bright stars, and Duun a gray-cloaked shadow against that bottomless void. "It talks about the stars, the elements— Stop playing games, Duun! What's sending it?"

"People." Duun turned toward him. "People like you, minnow."

The room was very still. There had never been such a voice. There was nowhere such a voice. The windows were illusion and the world was.

"No, Duun."

"Do you know differently?"

'Dammit, Duun—don't do this to me!"

"You wanted your answer. There's one more question. Do you want to ask it?"

"What am I?"

"Ah." Duun walked to the window rim, eclipsing a light. "You're a genetic code. So am I. Yours is different."

"I'm not shonun?"

"Oh, gods, minnow, you've known that for years." Duun faced him, twilight shadow against the glare, gray against the void. "You just didn't know what else you could be. The world held all your possibilities. I created you. A code into an egg, not the first trial; there were thousands of tries till the meds got the right of it. A technology had to be built: we had the most of it, our own doing; but you were a special problem. And you—were the success. They brought you to me: they didn't want to. They'd labored so hard to have you. Do you believe me, minnow? Am I telling the truth?"

"I don't know, Duun." Thorn wanted to sit down. He wanted to go somewhere. There was no refuge, on this floor, beneath these windows.

"It is the truth," Duun said. "The ear picks up those messages. Perhaps there's something in the pathways of the brain; perhaps it's knowing one's own face; perhaps both these things. You duplicate the sounds on the tapes perfectly; no shonun can manage all those consonants—no shonun could read the faces on that tape—except maybe myself; except Sagot sometimes. You taught me. You taught me your reflexes and your inmost feelings; and when we gave you the vocabulary we've been able to guess for ourselves—perhaps it's pathways, gods know—you began to handle it. That's what you were made for."

"To live here? To work with *this*?"

"It doesn't appeal to you?"

"Duun—take me home. O gods, take me home again."

"Haras. Don't break down on me. You haven't come this far to beg me like a child."

Thorn came over to the window and turned his back to it. It took the sight away. It put light on Duun's face and hid his own. "Don't play me tricks. I can't—" (*Can't*, minnow?") There was silence.

"The transmissions come at regular intervals," Duun said in a calm, still voice. "They repeat, mostly. What do they say?"

"I told you what they said."

"You encourage me."

"To what?" Thorn looked up at the window; perspective destroyed the illusion, made it only glare and dark, meaningless. He flinched from it and looked back. "Is that why they're afraid of me?"

"I took an alien, I held it, fed it, warmed it—it was small, but it would grow. I took it up on a mountain and lived with it alone. I slept under one roof with it, I made it angry, I encouraged it and pushed it and I had nightmares, minnow, I dreamed that it might turn on me. There were times I held it that my flesh crawled; I did these things."

(Duun—o gods, Duun—) It was beyond hurt. " . . . I was more than fair with it. I gave it everything I had to give; I went from step to step. I made it shonun. I taught it; argued with it; discovered its mind and step by step I gave it everything I knew how to teach. Every chance. You grew up shonun. No one knew what to expect. When I told Ellud I would make you hatani he was appalled. When the world knew—there was near panic. No matter. It never reached you. When I told Ellud I would bring you to the guild—well, hatani was bad enough: their judgments were limited. But to put you in the guild— That was earthquake. And you won it. You won Tangen. You did it all, minnow."

"Do you love me, Duun?"

(Thrust and evade.) Duun's scarred ear twitched and he smiled. There was sorrow in it and satisfaction. "That's a hatani question."

"I was taught by the best."

(Second attack.) Duun's mouth tautened on the scarred side. "Let me tell you a story, minnow."

"Is it a good one?"

"It's how I lost the fingers. You've always wondered, haven't you? —I thought you had.

No one asks the questions of their relatives that they really want to know—after they grow up. And they never discover the good questions until it's far too personal to ask."

"Was it my fault?"

"Ah. I got through your guard."

"Tell me the story, Duun."

"We were rank beginners—I'm sure Sagot told you most of this: tanun guild took us into space, just the merest foothold. The moon. A station. The companies moved in. We had scientific bases here and there. Hatani guild, ghota, tanun—kosan here and there; not many. A lot of ordinary folk, doing what ordinary folk do—making money, mostly; or learning things. The world fared pretty well in those days. Then a ship turned up." Duun's face lifted slightly, a gesture toward the window, toward the lights. "The one out there."

"Not shonun," Thorn said.

"Not shonun. It was pretty badly battered when I first saw it. It's not clear what happened at first: it scared hell out of the Dothog mission and someone started shooting, it's not clear which side. They were ghotanin, of course. There wasn't much left to question to fix responsibility. But the ship didn't leave the solar system then—too heavily damaged. It moved off, faster than anyone wanted to believe; ghotanin and kosanin chased that thing where they could—we could at least tell each other where it was heading. And for the next two years we chased that ship and battered at it. We. Tangen sent me up. I wasn't chief of the mission then, but I survived longer. We battered away at it; we lost ships. Its maneuvers got slower. We knew it was transmitting. We knew it was transmitting to someone outside the solar system, and we finally silenced that. We chewed away at it and finally we got it at a speed we could match. We boarded. There was one of them still alive. We tried to take him that way. That was my mistake." Duun lifted the maimed hand, palm outward. "He got all the rest of us. One blast. I got through it and got to him. I killed him. We found out later the ship was rigged in a way that might have destroyed it. But he never did that. We found four others frozen in vacuum. And this one. Maybe he was crazy by then. Maybe he thought he could live a little longer. Maybe he was afraid to use that last trick. But I got back; we hauled that ship in with all it contained.

"It changed the world, Thorn. Until that time we thought we were alone. And this thing was a nightmare. Two years. Two years of throwing everything we had at it and it was five of these people. Just five. They nearly wrecked the world. They cost us—O gods. Nothing was the same. And there was panic. They came to me, the council did. I was very famous then. It was those first days: we'd stopped it damn close to the earth. That was why we fought like that, and why it cost so much. The council asked me to do something: Tangan had refused them. Hatani judgment? I asked them. Is that what you want? We'll give you anything, they said, any help. All our backing. I told them they were fools. They had all the provinces hammering at their doors demanding action, they had the companies, they had the guilds all pulling in different directions, and kosan and ghota at odds. You've been out there, they said; give us a solution. And I took them up on it." Duun motioned to the window. "I knew there were transmissions that went out from that ship while we hunted it. I thought there might be answers we couldn't hear. I called in scientists. I ordered Gatog built. I ordered that ship studied. I ordered it duplicated if we could. I ordered you—created. You're him, Thorn; you're the man on the ship. Born from his blood, his cells. You are my enemy. I made you over again. You are my war, my way to fight a war we didn't know how to fight. You're my answer. I knew what you would look like—what you will look like, in another ten-year. I knew what you'd grow into—physically. But now I know what I killed. What he might have been. If he were my son."

Thorn shut his eyes. There were tears. ("Don't you know by now I can't?") They ran when he blinked and shattered Duun's image when he looked at Duun again. 'You're maneuvering me."

"I'm hatani. Of course. I always have been. I told you that."

"The way you maneuvered Tangan. Gods— why? What do you want?"

"You're the world's long nightmare. A bad dream. Everything earth has went to build Gatog, to build that other ship— You understand what it is to jump that far that fast in industry? New materials, new processes, new physics—new fears and new money and all that goes with it. Politics. Companies. A world that had just reached out into space—and all of a sudden— discoveries that shatter it. Energies that, gods help us—we're still unraveling, technologies with potentials we're not ready to cope with, with all that means. We didn't know, when that ship transmitted, how long we had before an answer might come. We know now that ship came from a star nine light-years out. That's when the first message came—nine years after that ship first transmitted. We don't know how fast the ship traveled. We're beginning to understand that. It's fast. It's very fast. Translight. I was naïve at first. I imagined we had years— half of a century—to get here. Duplicate the ship. Teach them a lesson. Send the kosan guild to deal with them and hatani to settle matters. We know a lot more now—what the cost of a ship like that is when you have to develop each part and joint as a new technology; the social cost of changes. It's made us rich. It's made us capable of blowing ourselves to hell. The tapes, minnow, the tapes—we salvaged off the ship. The machine that runs them, the drug that we found with them. A whole new category of drugs; a new vice. Gods, I had to be so careful with you. Every substance, every damn plant you touched—drove the meds crazy. Livhl you could take; sjuuna and mara; dsuikin, never—"

("Try this, minnow, try it on your tongue, never swallow first-off—")

"—you tolerate most things; we tolerate most of yours. Thank the gods that's so, or you'd have lived in virtual isolation."

(Sheon, the leaves moving in the summer wind, green and fragrant—)

(The stinging smell of lugh-flowers on the long road down from home to exile—)

"Am I the only one, am I all, Duun?"

"Yes. There was argument on that point. A lot of it. All they could see was the tapes; read the tapes; if he doesn't live, if he should meet with accident. ... But there was only one of me, minnow; and I had to teach you, my way; learn from you, my way. If you'd been in isolation, I would have been too. We were bound together. To make you what you are took me, and it took those tapes, minnow— Some of them, gods know, maybe simple entertainment for the crew—the one that was the key. There are others. The audio you heard—that's from Gatog. The messages come regularly. You know what I imagine they say? 'Here we are. You killed our messenger.' But I don't know what they say after that. I don't know how long they'll wait. They know we've got a ship. They know whatever that pilot told them. 'They're killing me. I can't leave. They're poor primitives. They're not worth much. But look out for them.' "

"You think they're going to attack."

"I planned to be capable of coming to them— whatever they're doing. But the way that ship works—the way they think it works— We guess wrong and we might lose Gatog. We might lose everything. The irony is, minnow, we can push it out to some safe distance and try—but we'd be flying that ship with no knowledge how to do it. Even if it works. And we can't start that kind of engine near anything else. And not from a standing start, they tell me. The awful truth is we don't know the last things. We don't know how to fly it. If we did we could have saved *Ganngein* and *Nonnent*. It's that fast— even inside a solar system. Outside—gods help us, we don't know."

"Am I supposed to do something about this?" Thorn trembled, a brief convulsion. "Am I what the ghota want to stop?"

"There are three kinds of people I've found: those who think the universe is good, those who believe it's corrupt, and those who don't want to think about it any more than they can help. I prefer the first two. The last can be hired by anybody. Dallen Company wants you stopped because they're scared of you: so do others; the ghota are just damn scared of your being hatani and not theirs, and of more and more knowledge in hatani hands and not theirs. They're dying and they know it. The world can't afford them anymore. It can't afford ignorance. The tanun, the kosan guilds—you're their hope."

"To do what? *Fly* that ship?"

"I don't know. Maybe. Someday. What would you do?"

"O gods."

"*Now* you know what you're for."

"Don't ask me this! Duun—"

"Haras-hatani, what will you do?"

Thorn walked off across the floor, raised his hands to his head, dropped them. There were no thoughts. Nothing but a tumbling of images. (The boulders in the sand, each with a hatani.

Tangan's aged mask and Sagot's blurred. Manan's impersonal voice: "That's a miss on their side, a hit on ours. It's down." *Ganngein's:* "This isn't a trip we want to share.")

He looked back at Duun. At a quiet shadow against the vast illusion of the windows.

"Well?" Duun asked.

"I'm not even eighteen years old!"

"I didn't say it was all in your lap. You're not responsible for the ghota. You're not to blame for the world's foolishness; but it's burning, Haras-hatani. And maybe that eighteen years is all the world is going to have. What will you do to stop it?"

(Go back to earth? How could I stop it? Who would hear me? Hatani. Tanun guild; kosanin would hear Duun.)

(A room with a bed, a bath, a fire, and hidden tricks. What is my room? This place. This world. How do I put out the fire but with my bare hands? Am I twice a fool?)

(*Now* you know what you're for.)

Thorn looked about him, the windows, the glittering sprawl of Gatog; the computer banks. (The ghotanin are afraid of something. This. Of its use.)

(The tapes. The voices.)

"I see," Thorn said. "You already know what you want me to do. You think you know. You wonder what I think. Pathways? Is that It?"

"Maybe just the hope of something better. Tell me your solution."

"The ship transmitted. Did the message go out translight?"

"No. Lightspeed."

"The pilot knew they wouldn't be in time then. He wasn't asking them to save him."

"No. There was no hope of that. So what did he want, hatani?"

"How can I know? You taught me."

"Perhaps you can't. A great deal of you is shonun."

"But the messages started nine years later. They say, 'hello; here we are.' And they go on saying it. And he said: 'I'm dying; they're killing me and they have such little ships.' They know we can't come to them. Don't they?"

"They've known at least since that message got to them, seven years, nine years after he was dead. And nine years after that attack on their ship their first messages came to us. And still come."

"How long have you been getting them now? Five years?"

"Near seven."

Thorn shut his eyes a moment. Opened them. "People should have been relieved."

"Some were. Some were simply reminded. Others said the ship wasn't really translight, that nothing could do that, that the message was a trick and timed to take us off our guard: that ships would be arriving sublight. And soon. And they hired the ghota, who saw only money and a chance to stop the hatani guild from getting control of the war they believed would come. The war they've already started."

"To see who meets those ships."

"That, yes."

"Is it so simple, then? The ship out there could transmit."

"Even simpler. Gatog can."

"They wouldn't hear me for nine years!"

"But then earth would know there's no stopping it. No undoing the messages once we've started sending. And we can hold here at Gatog indefinitely. We can stand off the ghotanin, and it won't take much more than that nine years for ships from the other side to get here if they hear us: some think so, at least. One year, two, at the rate that ship might go. They might have been here years ago—if we're right about that speed. They might come tomorrow. They may be waiting for their answer. We had no way to read them—until now. When they come, whatever they intend, you'll be here. Safe. A voice like theirs. Perhaps they'll remember their pilot when they see you. Perhaps they'll wonder. Maybe they'll begin thinking and hesitate at whatever they plan. Gods know, in ten years maybe we'll have learned to fly that ship."

"Does the earth have to bleed that long?"

"Maybe it does. Or maybe when earth knows what your solution is a lot of people will stop and think about it. Remember you're hatani. Of the guild. That's something the world understands. That's part of my solution too. When the panic dies, shonunin will remember the guild passed you. They'll know it's a true judgment."

"No one likes a hatani under his roof. Sagot told me so."

"Yes, and you've been near eighteen years under theirs. It's true. People begin searching themselves for guilt. They imagine judgment on their sins. They know you read them. They see your face and they know you read them. Even I, minnow. I killed you once, remember. Conscience is dreadful company."

"Duun." Thorn walked back to him, slowly, on the trackless floor; Thorn reached out his hand, slowly, slowly, and touched Duun's face, the scarred side. "So you know I could," Thorn said. And took his hand away.

There was quiet in the room. Technicians stood about the walls, hatani, tanunin and kosanin. "Sit by me," Thorn said, and Duun settled down in the seat beside him. Thorn hesitated over the keys, checked this and that. He spoke, quietly, steadily into the microphone and it went out, starting the long journey messages would take each day. Minutes to the earth and hours to Gatog Two and Dothog; nine years to another star. Duun's skin tightened. He had heard that voice, speaking that language, for two years before they silenced it the first time; doubtless others had the same reaction. It would create new panic on earth, in the station. Perhaps *Nonnent* would hear it in their lonely journey, if they had waited to hear it, and know that they had won.

There was a translation. Thorn read that out, which was only for their solar system. ("I'll have to keep working with the tapes," Thorn had said, for there were the originals at Gatog: there were written documents. They had a vast library of them here; and other tapes. Thorn dreaded it; Duun knew how much. Thorn had heard that voice too, twin of his own, in its rage and agony. But the computers built more and more complex fields. They had certainty on some words. They had broken the alphabet. They worked out the phonics and that study branched and multiplied, on a strange story of strange people a hatani had learned to read.)

"The message is," Thorn said: *"I am Haras. One. Two. Three. I am Haras. Star G. Oxygen. Carbon. I am Haras. I hear you. The world is the earth. The star is the sun. I am a man. Hello."*

PRESENTING C. J. CHERRYH

Two Hugos so far—and more sure to come!

The Morgaine Novels
- [ ] GATE OF IVREL — (#UE1956—$2.50)
- [ ] WELL OF SHIUAN — (#UE1986—$2.95)
- [ ] FIRES OF AZEROTH — (#UE1925—$2.50)

The Faded Sun Novels
- [ ] THE FADED SUN: KESRITH — (#UE1960—$3.50)
- [ ] THE FADED SUN: SHON'JIR — (#UE1889—$2.95)
- [ ] THE FADED SUN: KUTATH — (#UE1856—$2.75)

- [ ] CUCKOO'S EGG — (#UE2083—$2.95)
- [ ] THE PRIDE OF CHANUR — (#UE1694—$2.95)
- [ ] CHANUR'S VENTURE — (#UE1989—$2.95)
- [ ] DOWNBELOW STATION — (#UE1987—$3.50)
- [ ] MERCHANTER'S LUCK — (#UE1745—$2.95)
- [ ] PORT ETERNITY — (#UE1957—$2.50)
- [ ] WAVE WITHOUT A SHORE — (#UE2101—$2.95)
- [ ] SUNFALL — (#UE1881—$2.50)
- [ ] BROTHERS OF EARTH — (#UE1869—$2.95)
- [ ] THE PRIDE OF CHANUR — (#UE1694—$2.95)
- [ ] SERPENT'S REACH — (#UE2088—$3.50)
- [ ] HUNTER OF WORLDS — (#UE1872—$2.95)
- [ ] VOYAGER IN NIGHT — (#UE1920—$2.95)
- [ ] THE DREAMSTONE — (#UE2013—$2.95)
- [ ] THE TREE OF SWORDS AND JEWELS — (#UE1850—$2.95)
- [ ] FORTY THOUSAND IN GEHENNA — (#UE1952—$3.50)
- [ ] HESTIA — (#UE2102—$2.75)

NEW AMERICAN LIBRARY
P.O. Box 999, Bergenfield, New Jersey 07621

Please send me the DAW BOOKS I have checked above. I am enclosing
$_____ (check or money order—no currency or C.O.D.'s).
Please include the list price plus $1.00 per order to cover handling
costs.

Name _____

Address _____

City _____ State _____ Zip Code _____
Please allow at least 4 weeks for delivery